RAVAGED WOLF

I0695078

THE FIVE PACKS
BOOK SIX

CATE C. WELLS

This book is a work of fiction. Names, characters, places, and incidents are the product of the author's imagination or are used fictitiously. Any resemblance to actual events, locales, or persons, living or dead, is coincidental.

Copyright 2025 by Cate C. Wells. All rights reserved.

Cover art and design by Fay Lane
Developmental edits by Jean McConnell of The Word Forager
Copy edits by Ishita Gupta
Proofreading by Danica Sorber
Interior art by Serendipity Formatting and Graphics

Special thanks to Megan R., Jen L., Grace C., Kara M., Sara F., Elizabeth L., Michelle B., Bree Y., Sarah S., Olivia D., Brooke T., and Tracey R.

The uploading, scanning, and distribution of this book in any form or by any means—including but not limited to electronic, mechanical, photocopying, recording, or otherwise—without the permission of the copyright holder is illegal and punishable by law.

Without in any way limiting the author's exclusive rights under copyright, any use of this publication to "train" generative artificial intelligence (AI) technologies to generate text is expressly prohibited. The author reserves all rights to license uses of this work for generative AI training and development of machine learning language models.

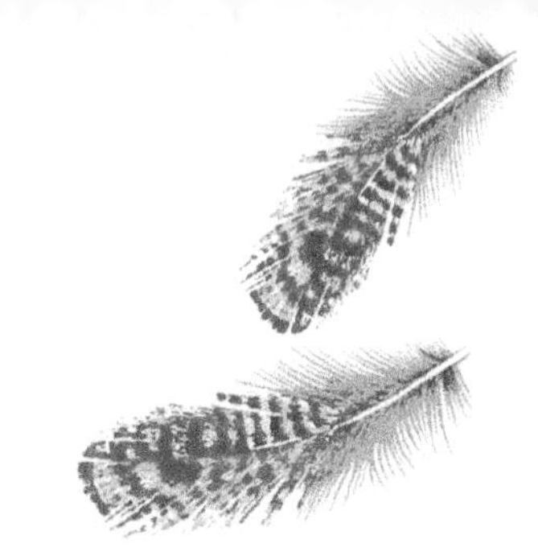

AUTHOR'S NOTE

This story contains scenes that may be difficult for some readers, including a detailed, on-page description of the male main character sexually assaulting the female main character when in rut. The attack happens in chapter three and there are brief flashbacks in other chapters. The male main character also considers suicide.

A full list of content warnings can be found at www. catecwells.com/content-warnings.

1

IZZY, FIVE YEARS AGO

"That low ranker is staring at you again," Brynn says the same way she'd say that she just stepped in a wad of chewed gum.

My heart lurches as I whisper, "Where?"

"Over by his truck."

I dart a glance over to the far end of the parking lot where the low ranks park, but I'm not quick enough. Our gazes catch, and my stomach swoops like I'm going to throw up. It's been like this since last week when I looked up at the salad bar in the dining hall, and he was on the other side of the lettuce, and I knew instantly. Trevor Floyd is my mate.

His eyes are stormy blue, almost gray, and his eyebrows are so thick that even when his rowdy friends get him to smile, he looks serious.

His friends are nowhere to be seen now, and he's not smiling. He's watching me expectantly, leaning against his fender like he's got all the time in the world, his idle hands shoved in the pockets of his canvas work pants. Doesn't he need to be at his work placement?

There's a breeze whipping off the lake, and his curly hair

tangles, the wheat blonde streaks catching in the noon sun. He wouldn't be allowed to wear it past his ears if he was interning at the High Rise like me, but he's apprenticing with facility maintenance, and they're much more relaxed about regulations.

I hike my chin and turn my back so that Brynn, Teagan, and I form a tight circle.

"It's so creepy," I say and instantly my skin prickles with guilt. I'm such a phony coward. My friends noticed him hanging around at a distance a few days ago, and Brynn called him a perverted, rank-grubbing stalker. I was too embarrassed to know what to say, and then somehow, it was too late to say anything.

"Do you want me to get Cadoc to kick his ass?" Brynn asks.

"No. He's only looking." I roll my eyes like it's nothing.

I'm not so sure that Cadoc would beat someone up just because Brynn asked, but he'd definitely take Trevor aside and have a word with him. Then Trevor would spill the beans, and since no one can keep a secret in this pack, and Cadoc is never alone, by the end of the day, everyone would know.

I'm not ready.

Dad is going to lose his ever-loving mind. Mom will try to calm him down while simultaneously freaking out herself, and she'll end up making it a hundred times worse. Then they'll call Uncle Howell and Aunt Catrin to come down, and I'll have to sit on the sofa like a misbehaved pup while they melt down because my mate lives on a low floor of the Tower.

My whole life, my parents' dream has been to move from the teens to the twenties. If I mate a male from all the way down on the fifth floor, Mom will go moon mad. Dad very well might disinherit me and send me to live in the bog with the scavengers. He's threatened to do it for less.

I sneak a peek over my shoulder. Trevor is still there. The corners of his mouth curve tentatively as he tracks me under his smoky, sweeping lashes. My belly fizzles. It's never fizzled before.

He's really pretty, prettier than me. I have a plain face, brown hair, brown eyes—nothing remarkable. He looks like a Renaissance sculpture. He seems sweet, though, not arrogant like most of the hot guys around here. His body is cut, but he doesn't hold himself like a high-ranking male, like he needs to take up as much space as possible. He has an air like he doesn't care if people are looking at him or not.

I wrap my goose-bumped arms around my waist and pretend I don't see him. I can't deal with this right now. My internship with accounting begins today, and after the underwhelming debut I made during my rotation in Corporate Communications, Dad is expecting me to make an impression. I have no idea how to do that. I'm good at math—better than I am at communications, that's for sure—but neither my wolf nor I are dominant or outgoing.

Honestly, my greatest ambition for today is to not screw up big enough that someone notices, and it doesn't help that my body is going haywire. My stomach's doing its weird fizzy thing, my boobs ache so much that I can hardly stand the sports bra I'm wearing, and I'm burning up.

Without thinking, I tug at my collar and huff the strands that've come loose from my professional updo away from my forehead. A bead of sweat trickles down my temple.

Brynn's eyes narrow with sly suspicion. "Are you sick, Izzy? Your face is bright red."

I shrug, and my cheeks blaze even hotter. "It's warm."

"Is it?" Brynn scans the clear sky and the Academy's

majestic oaks swaying in the gentle breeze. "I'd say the weather's very mild today."

She knows. I can hear it in her voice. My wolf leaves off her panting and lumbers to her feet as she becomes aware of the threat.

Even though Brynn's a year younger than me, we don't have a chance against her if she turns on us, and if I mate a male from the fifth floor, it won't matter that we're cousins. She won't just drop me—she'll dropkick me. I've watched her with the scavengers since we were pups. She's not content to ignore females who rank lower than her. She gets off on making them show neck.

"I guess I'm just nervous about the new rotation," I offer, praying she'll show pity and let it go for now. I need to report to the High Rise, and she and Teagan need to get to third mod. We don't have time for this.

"Really?" Brynn's eyes light up. Oh, crap. "Hey, Seth!" she calls. "Come over here a minute."

"Why?" He's tossing his messenger bag into the back seat of his SUV. "I've got to pull around and pick up Cadoc."

"It'll just take a second. Come on," Brynn wheedles and pops a hip, trying to look cute, but from the scowl on Seth's face as he jogs over, he's not impressed. Cadoc favors Brynn, though, so that means she ranks. Unless Seth's got a good reason to tell her no, he's going to humor her, even though he's the future pack beta, and his folks live only two floors down from the penthouse.

"What?" he grunts when he gets over to us, but before he even speaks, a foul stench smacks me in the face. I yank my shirt up over my nose like we used to do in primary school when a scavenger farted in class. He reeks worse than gas, worse than the port-a-potties over by the site where they're building the new Research and Technology Center. What's wrong with him?

This can't be what they talk about when they say that when you recognize your mate, other males start smelling a little musky until you seal the bond. There is nothing little about this musk. But then why are Brynn and Teagan gawking at me and not the source of the world's muskiest musk that ever musked?

They can't smell it. Because they're not going into heat.

Shit.

Teagan slowly drops her jaw, chomps her gum twice for emphasis, and says, "No. Freaking. Way."

She glances from me over to Trevor and back again. I wish the asphalt would crack open and swallow me. I can't do this right now.

Seth scowls, confused. "What do you want?"

"That's all we needed." Brynn waves him away. He doesn't waste time figuring out what's going on. With an irritated shake of his head, he continues with his business. As soon as he's gone, I can breathe through my nose again.

"Oh, Izzy, I am *so sorry,*" Brynn says. She doesn't sound sorry.

"Your mate is Trevor *Floyd*?" Teagan says Floyd like it's a bad word.

"Don't tell anyone," I hiss, as much good as it'll do. As soon as Brynn gets on her phone, everyone is going to know, starting with her mother.

I can't let my mom find out from Aunt Catrin. Mom stewed for a week straight when Aunt Catrin found out what my first rotation was going to be before we got the official letter. If Mom hears about my mating from Aunt Catrin, she'll never get over it. She's never going to get over it anyway, but I don't need it to be worse.

"I've got to get to my internship," I say, and even though I know it won't do any good, I stare them both down and try to instill some wolf in my voice. "Keep this between us, okay? Please?"

They both nod, but butter wouldn't melt in their mouths. They walk toward campus, and before they get ten feet away, they've already got their heads together, whispering.

I make my way to my car, a few rows back from where Cadoc's inner circle parks, and misery bears down on me like a lead weight. I'm eighteen, but I still have to do my rotations in Marketing and Product Development. I can't have a pup yet.

I thought I was going to be one of the lucky females who finishes her entire post-grad program before going into her first heat. I know most females balance their internships with pregnancy and newborns, but I also have no idea on earth how they do it.

You have to look your best at the High Rise every day, and even if I shower in the evening, it takes me an hour to do my hair and makeup in the morning, and if I have to get a pup ready for the on-site nursery, I'd have to get up at, what, five in the morning?

I can't do that.

I touch my belly. I can't grow a pup in there. I've got organs. Where would they even go? All of a sudden, my mind cannot fathom the physiology.

I'm standing by my car door, key in my hand, staring bug-eyed at the lock in a blind panic, when a scent like brown gravy, peppery and rich with sage and thyme, fills my nose. I'm not hungry—I lost my appetite last week at the salad bar—and it's a weird smell in the middle of a parking lot, but it's nice. Warm and homey. My wolf sits straight up. She loves it. The knot in my chest loosens.

"Do you want a ride to work?" Trevor asks. His voice is low, but also smooth and rich. Like his gravy scent.

I whirl, and he's right there, maybe three feet away. He's not crowding me, but I still retreat, shrinking back against the car door.

"W-What?" I say at the exact second my keys slip from my numb fingers. "Oh."

Before I can act, he ducks forward, plucks them from the asphalt, backs away immediately, and holds them out to me, dangling them from the picture keychain of my parents and me in front of the statue of the Great Alpha Broderick Moore on undergrad commencement day.

My arm shakes as I hold out my hand. He drops my keys into my palm and takes another step back.

My lungs inflate again. Brown gravy. My wolf licks her chops.

"I guess you've got a ride," he says, the corner of his mouth quirking. He shoves his hands back in his pockets and slumps his shoulders like he's trying not to loom over me. I'm average height, but he's at least a foot taller.

"This is my car." I put my hand on it, an excuse to steady myself. My knees are wobbling.

"It's nice."

I blink over my shoulder at it. It's a mid-size luxury sedan, the latest model year. My dad brags to his buddies about how he got the top-of-the-line trim level for less than asking price, and he didn't even have to flash his fangs at the human salesman, so I guess it must be nice. I don't know much about cars.

"Thank you," I say quietly.

For a long second, we're both silent. I stare at the

ground. I can see his feet. He's wearing tan work boots. There's a streak of grease across the toe of the right one.

Are people watching us? Are they texting about this? Are their moms calling my mom already?

"Izzy—" he says. His voice is firm, but gentle. Respectful.

My cheeks are burning. They must look like when I was little and got into my mom's makeup, and I thought blush went on in perfect circles. "Apples of the cheeks" means you paint your cheeks to look like apples, right?

I'm such an idiot.

"You know—" he begins, falters, takes a breath, and then continues. "You know what we are. Right?"

I nod and force myself to look up. It's not his fault that this is the worst thing ever.

He pushes a loose curl out of his eye. He doesn't seem any more confident about this whole situation than me. For some reason, that gives me a shot of courage.

"We're mates," I say.

He smiles shyly, not much more than a slight lifting of the corners of his soft, generous mouth, but it makes my stomach muscles tense, and all of a sudden, I'm aware of my entire body in a way I never have been before. My small breasts weigh heavy. Blood pulses between my legs.

I don't know what to do with my hands. I wish I could shove them in my pockets, but I'm borrowing my mom's work slacks, and they don't have real pockets, more like little slits where you can tuck a few quarters for the snack machine.

What is my brain doing? My thoughts are rolling all over the place like spilled marbles.

"If you don't need a ride, maybe I can come by your place tonight after work? We can go for a walk or something?" His soft smile rises a notch higher, encouraging and hopeful.

"No." The word comes out so much more emphatically than I intend, and his smile falls. His shoulders tense.

I hold up a hand between us, and I mean it like 'wait a second,' but his jaw tightens, and he takes a step back.

"I can't tonight," I say quickly. I don't want to explain—and I sure don't want to sound like a pup who has to pass everything by her daddy—but now I feel awful that I made him feel bad, so I force myself to say, "I have to talk to my parents first. About what's going on."

His eyes darken until they're more like a rainy, gray November sky than a clear, blue June.

"I get it." His mouth twists, and there's a bitterness that wasn't in his voice before.

I want to argue—or lie—and say it's no big deal. I just want them to hear the big news from me; they'll be happy to meet him. But I can tell from his expression that he *does* get it. Everyone at Moon Lake is rank-conscious. He knows that everyone is going to think that he got lucky, and that my parents are going to think the opposite.

"Maybe tomorrow?" I offer.

"Yeah. Okay." He exhales, blowing out his cheeks. "I guess I better—" He jerks his chin over his shoulder in the direction of his truck.

I nod and stand there numb, my brain buzzing, as he carefully takes my keys, opens my car door, and holds it open like the valet that greets the alpha when he pulls up in front of the Tower.

I blush. At least there's no way he can tell since I'm already bright pink from the heat my body's cranking like a busted boiler.

Once I'm settled in the driver's seat, he hands me my keys. "If you need me, I'm in 521," he says.

"I know." I gasp, horrified that I let on that I know where he lives, and then doubly-horrified that I gasped.

Trevor's eyes brighten, almost twinkle. "So you know where to find me, then," he says without the slightest hint of teasing in his voice.

I nod, bite my bottom lip, and stare desperately ahead. I'm wildly grateful when he gently shuts the door and backs up so I can drive away. I sneak a peek in the rearview, and he stands there in the middle of the aisle until I turn out of the Academy parking lot. His shoulders aren't slumped now. He's straightened to his full height, arms loose at his sides, his jaw set with calm determination.

My belly sizzles like a skyrocket. No matter how gentle and patient he was with me, he's a full-grown shifter male. He'll wait for now, but he's not going to wait forever. He can't. Neither of us can escape Fate. Even if we wanted to.

I'm going to mate with Trevor Floyd, and my parents are going to disinherit me.

If they don't kill me first.

2

IZZY

Except for the noxious smell and the crippling anxiety, my first day in accounting goes well. They stick all of us new interns in a windowless conference room for onboarding, and I'm lucky enough that my seat is under a vent, so whenever the air conditioning kicks on, I get a little respite from the heat and stench of the two males in our group.

I don't know why people don't make a bigger deal about the smell. Maybe because people tend to do the deed pretty quickly after they recognize their mate. When Steffan Dee recognized Morgan Lewis at the end of junior year, they snuck off that mod and did it in the art supply closet. It was a huge scandal when they came strolling out the next morning during homeroom. They'd gotten themselves locked in overnight.

I didn't notice the stink for the first couple of days after I saw Trevor at the salad bar, but now it's getting worse by the hour.

How much longer do I have?

What did they say in the shifter biology unit during

freshman year science? All I can remember is coloring diagrams and labeling fallopian tubes and the vas deferens and bulbus glandis, but I couldn't identify them now if you paid me.

My temperature can't get much higher. My skin is hot to the touch, and I'm not sweating so much anymore as maintaining a permanent sickly sheen. I've gone a pasty grayish white, and honestly, I'm sorry for the other interns because I don't smell very good either.

I've braced myself for the fact that Mom will know there's something wrong as soon as she sees me, but when I get home, it's still a jolt when I open the door and she's sitting with Dad on the sofa, stiff-backed and grim, waiting for me.

They know. Brynn told. I'm in trouble.

My throat swells shut, and my eyes burn. I want Mom to open her arms, and say, "Come here, baby," but she's not that kind of mother.

"Were you ever going to tell us?" she says instead, her sweet, prim voice as sharp as a papercut.

"I-I—"

"Sit down," my father interrupts. I sink into the chair across from them as my wolf springs to her feet, both of us on high alert. We scent danger, but it's crucial that we don't react. Dad's wolf reads defense as aggression.

I end up in this seat a lot—on report card days and after recitals and concerts and meets and games and science fairs. I can always benefit from feedback on my presence and delivery and follow through and tri-fold design. The process of continuous self-improvement cannot wait for a shower or a snack or a good cry.

I clasp my hands and wait. Pre-empting the lecture with

excuses will only make it last longer in the end, and it provokes Dad's wolf.

"Trevor Floyd?" my mother says. It's an accusation.

I drop my eyes to the beige carpet.

"Is he even in an internship?" my father asks, even though he must already know that he's not.

"He's in an apprenticeship." I force myself to enunciate so that I don't get yelled at to speak up. Dad gets mad if I mumble. His wolf gets mad if I raise my voice.

"An apprenticeship." Dad snorts and exchanges disgusted looks with my mother. "In facilities management?"

My shoulder lifts a quarter inch before I catch myself and splint my spine straight. Shoulder shrugs, stammering, fidgeting—the slightest motion can be a match to gasoline when Dad's committed to working himself up, and his wolf wants out.

"Well?" he demands.

"I don't know," I say, contorting my neck so that I can bend my head while maintaining eye contact. Dad has worked in human relations for his whole career, so he reacts to lowered eyes as disrespectful. At the same time, his wolf takes offense and rumbles, demanding a show of throat.

"Don't you think you should? Hasn't it occurred to you that that's the kind of information that might be material to your future? Izzy?" Dad's face flushes red as he waits for me to find my tongue.

"Yes." I don't know which question I'm answering or whether I'm responding the right way, but my damp shirt is sticking to my clammy back, and my pants stick to my skin everywhere my body touches the chair's cushions. I want to stick my head in the freezer and shove ice cubes in my underwear.

I can't think about my body now. I need to get out of this.

"I understand," I say. I don't, but that's what they want to hear. I understand, I'll comply, I won't make them repeat themselves.

"His father is an HVAC technician. Did you know that?" It's my mother's turn. "His mother doesn't even work. She's gone into heat *five times*." Mom clicks her cheek, and I think it's supposed to sound like pity, but it's clearly criticism.

"This is terrible timing, Izzy." My father jumps in. "You couldn't have waited until the end of the quarter? Two more weeks?" He blows his cheeks out and lifts his gaze to the ceiling, beseeching Fate for a better daughter. "That's all I need. Two damn weeks."

What happens in two weeks? It takes my slow brain a second to remember. End of quarter performance reviews. Dad's been hanging his hopes on this one. The male above him has been approved for a transfer, so there's a rare opening in his department. It would mean a raise, a new title, an office instead of a cubicle, and possibly, better housing. Up in the twenties floor. Maybe even the thirties.

My mouth drops open. How could I have forgotten the promotion? Dad's been talking about nothing else at dinner for months.

"I see you're finally thinking about someone other than yourself," my mom says. "Your timing could not be worse."

I didn't choose this. Everyone knows you don't pick your mate or when you go into heat.

"And you didn't even have the courtesy of telling us so that we could think about damage control. I had to find out from Aunt Catrin. At least Brynn talks to *her* mother." Mom swings her crossed leg and juts her chin forward so the tendons in her neck stretch taut so that I understand just how frustrated I've made her.

"I'm sorry."

"Sorry doesn't cut it," Dad says. I could have predicted his line in my sleep.

I say sorry.

Sorry doesn't cut it.

I say I won't do it again.

If you meant that, you wouldn't have done it in the first place.

"Do you understand what position this puts your father in? How hard he's worked to get this opportunity? And it's all in jeopardy now." Like always, Mom is Dad's mouthpiece, barking and snapping so he can sit there with his head high, his dominance not the least undermined by whatever's gone wrong under *his* roof.

I used to think that she did it because she loved him, and I wondered why she didn't defend me like that, whether that meant she didn't love me as much. I only figured out recently that she's defending herself, supporting him as a way to declare that she's on his side, she's not the enemy, she's not the one to blame.

She's as scared of his wolf as I am.

"Well, do you get it?" my father thunders, his red face splotching like it does right before the vein on his forehead pops. "Because that stupid look on your face doesn't assure me that you get *anything.*"

"Yes, I do."

"Really?" He stalks forward so he can tower over me and make my wolf cower and whimper in my chest. "I think you don't care about this family at all. I'm surprised you didn't go face down, ass up the first whiff you got of him. That's what I'd expect from you. No discipline. No consideration for anyone but yourself."

He paces back and forth, his wingtips leaving slight indentations in the carpet that disappear in seconds. I stare at the marks and try to scour the words *face down, ass up* out of my brain.

Mom crosses her arms, her bracelets clinking. "Have you even thought about how this will impact your father? Geralt Powell is going to have a field day, mark my words. He'll make all kinds of nasty insinuations about our bloodlines and whether your father's fit for leadership considering how low his offspring has sunk. Geralt's been angling for this role for *years*."

Geralt Powell has a bunch of kids with a scavenger female that he keeps down in the bogs while he lives in the Tower with a ranked female he treats like his mate. I wish I could say it's hard to imagine a male like him having the audacity to go after my dad about bloodlines, but that's how the High Rise works. That's how this whole pack works.

We act like skill sets and talent and merit and ethics matter, but it's all about who your grandfather was and who you can force to bend their neck, and it doesn't matter how you do it.

Sometimes I have nightmares that I'm skidding down a slippery slide, my fingers scrabbling for a handhold while gravity and my own paralyzed weight flushes me away into dark nothingness.

In a way, this all feels predetermined. Of course, I was going to mate a low-ranking male. Fate has been telling me every day in a hundred ways that I can't hack it, and it's only a matter of time before I get thrown onto the bottom of the heap. I'm supposed to be afraid, but in this moment, I'm just tired. If I was on that slide, I'd let go.

"There's nothing I can do about it," I mumble.

"Nothing you can do?" Dad barks. "Par for the course with you!"

He roars, letting his fangs descend and his fur sprout so

it tufts out of his cuffs and collar. A jolt of fear hits my veins, immobilizing me, crushing my elbows tight to my sides and rooting my wolf to the spot.

Like she always does, Mom hops up from the sofa to rub his shoulders, desperately trying to avert the inevitable, but I can see his wolf yellowing his eyes. I dart a glance at the front door. Can I get out before he catches me? Could I make it to the stairs?

521.

No. What am I thinking? Trevor is as big as Dad, but how big is his wolf? And can he fight? Would he fight for me? What if he lost? Dad's wolf is a beast, and Dad can spin anything. He'd say he was protecting me.

I can't run. I can only make myself small and bend my neck until it aches, but I'm so hot, and for some reason, my wolf isn't shrinking in her fur. She wants me to make a break for it. She's sure if we can get to Trevor, we'll be okay.

"You need to pull yourself together," Mom says to me as she strokes Dad's arm. "This mating cannot happen before quarter-end. Izzy? Are you hearing me?"

I am, but my thoughts are sludging through my brain, and my subconscious isn't serving me the usual script of apologies and promises designed to appease Dad and his wolf.

I blink, trying to focus, and I see Dad read my silence as defiance. Before I can open my mouth to make it right, his wolf snarls. Dad's sneer morphs into bared fangs, his long nose and chin lengthening into a muzzle.

I shove myself as far back in the chair as I can get and cower, bending my head until the tendon in my shoulder feels like it's going to tear, and right before I screw my eyes shut so I don't see the blow coming, Mom's phone rings.

Dad hesitates.

Mom holds up the screen. It reads *Howell*.

I don't move a muscle as Dad hisses around his teeth, "Well, answer it, Elen."

Mom taps a button. "Howell! You got my message."

Her bright voice is a glaring mismatch to the thick stench of fear and aggression in the room. My body shakes like it always does once the danger is over.

"Catrin told you? Yes, Izzy's here. She's fine." Mom rubs circles on Dad's back as she talks to Uncle Howell. "She didn't tell us, either. No. No." She cups the bottom of her phone and hisses at me, "When did you realize that boy was your mate?"

"A-At lunch the other day."

Dad's wolf growls.

"*What* day?" Mom hisses.

"Um. Uh." I can't think. "Last week."

Mom opens her mouth to ask which day last week, and I desperately try to remember while my thoughts grow slipperier the harder I try to grab them. She must see it on my face because she gives me an exasperated look and says, "She's not talking."

There's a long pause as Uncle Howell's muffled rumble pours out of Mom's phone. Uncle Howell is so dominant that Dad has to fight the instinct to bend his neck at the sound of his displeasure, and he can't help but tilt his head. He loves that he's related to the pack beta, but he can't stand submitting to his own brother. That's why Mom's always the one mediating between them.

"Yes, Howell. We'll come up. Give us five." Mom murmurs a few more times in agreement and ends the call.

"They want us to come up to thirty-nine." Even as mad as she is, you can hear the excitement in Mom's voice. Dad immediately sets about re-tucking his shirt. They live for being invited upstairs.

"Go wash your face and comb your hair," Dad snaps at me.

"Howell said to leave her here and let her get some rest."

I exhale. Thank goodness. I know they just want to plot behind my back, but it's still the first good thing that's happened today.

Mom bustles to the bathroom to freshen her makeup, and Dad gets a clean jacket from his room. When they come back, if not for the grim strain on their faces and the lingering reek of rage in the air, it could be one of their date nights.

I go stand by the door to see them off as I'm expected to do. Dad strides off down the hall, but Mom hangs back a moment and fusses with my hair like she did when I was little. She leaves off quickly, though, grimacing as she wipes her fingers on her slacks.

"Take a shower while we're gone." She spares me one last disapproving glance. "And then maybe help yourself to one of Mommy's pills. They're in the drawer of my night-stand." She pats my upper arm. "You'll look better once you've gotten some sleep."

And then she speeds off to catch up with Dad, and they disappear into an elevator, muttering urgently to each other under their breath.

What are they going to talk about with Uncle Howell? Mating isn't business. You can't call the team into the war room and come up with an action plan. Mating happens, and you deal with it. If you try to fight it, either the female loses control and presents—basically gets on her hands and knees and begs to be mounted—or the male goes into rut.

Nothing but a tranq can stop a male in rut. At least that's what they say.

I don't want to go face down and ass up.

Trevor Floyd's face floats up in my mind, his messy curls and warm eyes. His shy, wry smile. He'd probably die from embarrassment if I got down on all fours and flashed him my bare ass. I would die, too, obviously, but he might go first.

I look behind me at the empty apartment and the hallway to my bedroom. I do want an ice-cold shower. Desperately. I want to crawl naked in between cold cotton sheets with a fan blowing at high speed on my face. I want to be alone.

But I also don't.

My parents would flip if I left the apartment. I can hear my dad in my head. *Thoughtless. Ungrateful. Stupid.*

I can hear my mom, too. *How could you? What were you thinking?*

I'm supposed to do what I'm told, and if I do, then everything will be okay. But I always do what I'm asked, and nothing is ever okay. Of course, that's my fault because I never do things well enough.

A wild thought springs up from the fog in my brain.

If nothing's going to be okay anyway, why not do what I want?

My feet take the idea as permission, and without my say so, I'm stepping through the doorway, down the corridor, and past the elevators. The hallway stinks like garbage, I assume from unmated males who've recently passed by, but there's another scent, too, a faint trail, savory and warm and mouth-watering. As soon as my wolf catches it, she comes alive with anticipation.

Mate.

I follow my nose to the stairwell that no one uses except for fire drills. The space is glaringly well lit, and it's hard to track the scent of gravy over the stink of rubber stair treads and pine cleaner, but I know where I'm heading. Every flight I get closer to the fifth floor, the less awful I feel.

I'm not going to knock on Trevor's door or anything. We don't actually know each other. What would I even say?

I'm just going to get close to the smell and take a break. Collect myself. The stairwell isn't as stuffy as the apartment. I'm still warm, but the heat doesn't have the asphyxiating, in-your-face feel of getting into a hot car at three o'clock in the afternoon in the middle of August.

By the sixth-floor landing, I'm exhausted. I sink down to my butt, wrap my fingers around the balusters, and rest my cheek on the cool metal. It feels so good. My wolf is still on her feet, alert, fur bristling with excitement.

She's ready. She wants to come out, but she's not pushing. She seems content to wait for now. I kind of get it. That's how I used to feel on the morning of my birthday. I knew I had presents and cake coming, and hours beside the lake or on our boat when Mom and Dad would be all smiles for company. I would stay in bed as long as I could, luxuriating in that feeling of being on the verge of a wonderful day.

This isn't wonderful, though, is it?

If my mating Trevor causes Dad to lose out on the promotion, it'll be hell on earth. He'll make sure of it. Would he take it out on Trevor?

Dad's always talking about the cocky young pups in the office who try to show him up even though they don't know their ass from a hole in the ground. He loves forcing them into confrontations where his wolf can make them show neck. I bet he'd do the same to Trevor. Of course, he would.

My thumb sneaks into my mouth, and I suck on the tip.

Mom would be livid if she saw me. She thinks she broke me of the habit years ago, but at night in bed or when I'm alone, I still do it.

What am I going to do about Trevor?

Can I hold out for two weeks?

If I do, is Trevor going to want me afterward? Do I want him to want me?

Do I want to be mated for real? And what is Trevor even like?

He's cute. He doesn't seem aggressive.

He wouldn't have a chance standing up to Dad.

Without warning, hinges creak below. I startle, snatch my thumb out of my mouth, and shove both hands into my lap. The fire door opens, slowly, as if the person behind it wants to give fair warning, and when I'm about to jump out of my skin from the suspense, Trevor walks through.

He gazes up the stairs, solemn and unsurprised, like he expects to see me sitting here. My stomach leaps. He eases the door closed behind him.

Did he smell me here? What do I smell like? I hope *I* don't smell like gravy.

"Hi," he says softly and stays where he is with his back to the door. He's wearing cargo pants and a fitted gray T-shirt. His thigh muscles stretch the pants, and his biceps and pecs stretch his cotton T-shirt. Something deep in my lower belly flips like a fish.

"Hi." I straighten up, drawing my heels up to prop them on the edge of the landing and curling my arms around my knees.

"Can I come up?" he asks.

"Okay."

He climbs the stairs, no hurry, and lowers himself beside

me, leaving me as much space as he can without squishing himself against the wall.

"Oh. Shit. I forgot." He pats the pockets on either side of his cargo pants. "I brought you something."

He pulls out red cans of soda, one from each pocket, both beaded with condensation. All of a sudden, my throat is bone dry.

"You like this kind, right? You're not partial to the blue kind?"

"Yeah, this kind's good." Mom doesn't let me drink soda, but I've traded with humans at lunch before. I love everything sweet and bubbly.

He passes me a can and keeps the other for himself. I wrap my fingers around it. It's beautifully ice cold. I exhale and press the aluminum to my temple. I can't stop myself.

His lips curve. "I thought you might be thirsty."

I don't want to think about him knowing that I'm in heat. "How did you know I was here?" I ask, sliding the can down my cheek, bathing my burning skin with refrigerator droplets. It's heaven.

"This," he says. There's a sudden tug in my chest. I startle, my hand flying to press against my breastbone.

"What was that?" I squeak.

He flashes a quick smile. "The bond."

"Do it again."

I feel another gentle yank.

"Whoa." I tuck the can between my knees and press my palms over my heart. He yanks again. It's so weird, almost like the hard thump after a skipped beat, except the thud is coming from a place a little deeper and closer to the stomach.

"How did you know how to do that?" I pick the can back up and pop the top.

He shrugs a shoulder. "I just did."

"Do it one more time?"

He chuckles softly, and once more, there's a pulling sensation, like I've been hooked by an invisible line, but it doesn't hurt. It almost feels like that birthday morning excitement, only more physical. I reach out blindly to tug back, plunging into that neither-here-nor-there space where my wolf is watching, wide-eyed with her tail thumping, but there's nothing to hold on to and nothing to grab with.

"How do you do it?" A demanding note creeps into my voice, and immediately, my nerves blare a warning. I don't challenge males. Ever. But I'm also wildly curious.

"I had a leg up," he says. He doesn't react to my tone at all—no narrowing eyes or warning rumble from his wolf. "I was getting so much from you, I got a good sense of where it was coming from."

"What do you mean, you got stuff from me?" Again, before I can check myself, I speak with a sharpness that would get me either snapped at or smacked at home.

"Earlier. You were scared," he says, very quiet, but very clear. "I tracked the feeling upstairs. I was gonna bust the door down, but my dad, my cousin Art, and my two older brothers followed me, and they wouldn't let me do it. We had a whole showdown in the hallway. Then you seemed to chill out, so I let them drag me back home."

"You were at the door?"

He flashes another small, deprecating smile. "Before I got tackled, I was about to kick it down. It was going to be totally badass. You'd have been so impressed. You would have fallen in love with me—" He snaps his fingers. "Like that."

He's teasing. The situation is horrible and humiliating, and he knows it, but he's making fun, and he's not asking questions I don't want to answer. The gratitude lodges in my throat.

"I didn't hear anything."

"Y'all build the walls thick up in the teens."

"And your family held you back?" I can't even picture it.

A smudge of red appears high on his cheeks. "I hope to hell none of your neighbors checked their ring cams. We looked like a pack of idiots."

Did they smell my fear? They must not have if I didn't hear him. Still, shame roars in my ears at the thought of them knowing I was afraid.

To change the subject, I close my eyes and focus on the place in my chest where I felt the tug. There's something there. A haziness. I extend my mind, grab, and pull.

Trevor chuckles in surprise. "Whoa, there. Nice grip."

I lift my arm and make a muscle.

He grins. The corners of my mouth curl in response.

"Now you can call me in for dinner when I'm napping in my recliner in the den," he says.

"Is that what your mother does?"

"Nah. My dad's the one that cooks. My mom's the napper."

"Your dad cooks?"

"My mom's had five kids. After the third one, she told him he could have pups or homecooked meals. He had to pick."

"He picked pups?"

"Yeah. He wants his own little pack. He's an alpha at heart."

"Is he really?" I know it's supposed to be cute, but the idea of a dominant father-in-law sours my stomach. I've lived with it all my life, and it sucks.

My dad's fondest wish is that he had alpha blood. He

does everything Madog Collins does, wears the same clothes, golfs on the same days with the same brand of clubs, buys my mom the exact jewelry that Gwen Collins wears. His biggest disappointment is that my mom only went into heat once, and all he got was a submissive female.

"Nah. I'm joking." Trevor shakes his head, and his curls swing. I want to touch them. "He's a teddy bear."

"A teddy bear shifter?" A surreal picture pops into my head of the shabby brown bear that I've had since I was a baby morphing into a small man in green overalls held up with one buttoned strap. It makes me smile. Trevor can't know why, but he smiles right back.

"Hey, it's a big world, right?" he says. "Who's to say we're the only shifters in it?"

I don't know what to say, so I sip my soda. It's deliciously cold and sweet, but it tastes different than what I've had in the past. I look closer at the can. There is a cherry on it. "Cherry soda?"

Trevor nods, his smile widening. "Cherry cola."

I like it. The fizz tickles my nose. It doesn't taste like cherries, though.

Trevor cracks his open and drinks, too. We sit for a few minutes in silence. I set my can down between us and rest my hand on the landing. He sets his can down, too, and then leans back and braces himself on his palms so his pinky is centimeters away from mine.

I can feel every inch of my skin, just because his hand is close to mine. How weird is that?

I can't even tell if I'm cold or hot or comfortable or not, but I'm hyperaware of the parts of my body closest to him— the meaty part of my outer palm and the bump of my wrist bone and the underside of my forearm where blue veins run like tributaries. And my breasts. My breasts, especially. They feel so heavy.

Does he feel it, too? Is he doing it on purpose? He's so careful about keeping his distance, he must be aware that his closeness is affecting me.

Is this a move?

A male has never come on to me, but I thought it was supposed to be more obvious, like an arm around the shoulder or a hand on the small of my back. Those are human moves, though. I learned them from movies. What are shifter moves? How am I eighteen years old, and I don't know?

I don't know anything. Is Trevor into me? Is there a female he's talking to? Lots of males wait for mating, but a lot of them don't. What does he even do when he's not working? What does he do when he *is* working?

"I don't even know what you do." It takes me a second to realize that I've spoken one of my whirling thoughts aloud.

"You mean, like my apprenticeship?" He takes the random question in stride.

I nod.

"I guess I'm in repairs."

"You guess?"

One corner of his lips lift, like he's embarrassed. "I'm not exactly in the rotation."

"You're on suspension?" My stomach sinks. I've heard that happens when someone is more trouble than they're worth. They get sent home, and then they're reassigned to something like records where they shred documents all day.

"No, it's not like that." He lets out a soft chuckle. "During my first rotation, they, uh, kind of figured out that I have a knack for fixing stuff. So they gave me a workbench in a corner of the facilities building, and I just do repairs. Or sometimes I go onsite, if it's a big machine, like a boiler or something."

"You have your own office?" Even my dad doesn't have that.

"I mean, I don't have walls, and the windows are way up high, but the space is mine. No one touches my shit."

"Wow." Interns in the High Rise don't get cubicles. We get a desk in the department pool, but it's first come, first serve each day, so you can't leave your things, and if you sleep in, you get the desk closest to the supervisor, so you're running errands all day.

"Impressed?" His thick brow lifts, and his eyes twinkle.

"Yes!" The word flies out for some reason—maybe the stairwell acoustics— and it sounds painfully enthusiastic and uncool to my own ears. My face blazes.

He grins. "Wanna see something?"

"Okay." I'll agree to anything if he'll forget that 'yes!'

He stands, but he doesn't offer his hand. He jerks his chin, gesturing for me to head up the stairs.

"Where are we going?"

"You'll see."

I start climbing, slowing as we reach each floor, but over and over, he says, "Keep going."

My breath starts to come faster, but I don't want to pant, so I focus on inhaling and exhaling normally, which makes me lightheaded.

We pass the ninth, tenth, and eleventh floors. Finally, at the twelfth, he says, "Here." He opens the door, and I go through.

I've never hung out with anyone who lives in the low teens. My mom would never let me visit anyone who wasn't close to our floor or above. She said showing favor among the lower ranked causes envy and unnecessary conflict, but honestly, no one ever invited me, now that I come to think about it.

Trevor leads me down the hall, past doors hung with wildflower wreaths, wards against moon madness, and ring cameras. Except for the wreaths, it's identical to my floor. Superstition is frowned upon in the upper ranks. My mom's wreath hangs over the mirror in her walk-in closet.

When we get to an undecorated door with the number 1248, Trevor digs a key from his pocket and unlocks it. He opens it with a flourish. "After you," he says.

The apartment is dark, but from the light over the kitchen stove, I can see that the place is empty of furniture. The air smells like fresh paint and wood polish.

"Whose apartment is this?" I whisper, although there's obviously no one home.

"Ours," Trevor whispers, grinning. He shuts the door and flips on the overhead lights.

My jaw drops. "No. Way."

The floorplan is the same as ours, except this apartment is on the other side of the building, so everything is opposite. The open concept kitchen is to the left instead of the right. The hall closet is on my right, and the powder room is on the left.

"How did you get a two bedroom?" Males are assigned housing when they mate, but I had no idea it happened this quickly, or that they'd give two bedrooms to a newly mated pair.

His grin widens, shy and pleased. "I told you. I'm good at fixing shit."

"A lot of stuff must break."

He laughs. "You have no idea."

"This is yours?" It's still hard to believe. This unit must've been renovated more recently than my parents' because it has marble countertops and recessed lighting. And the carpets don't have that old doggy smell like the carpets do in units that haven't been rehabbed yet.

"Ours," he says again.

It does not compute. I stand in the entranceway, sweating, trying hopelessly to calm my breathing without letting on that I'm still struggling from the climb up the stairs. I spend a lot of time sitting at a desk these days.

"All of it?" I ask. It's a dumb question, but since my heat really kicked in, I'm not in total control of what comes out of my mouth.

"Well, you can have that half," Trevor says, bumping me with his elbow and nodding to the right. "I'll take that half."

He's teasing, and my heart warms again, even soppier. "But then you get the kitchen."

"Yeah, but you get both bedrooms."

"Seems unfair."

"Maybe we can do a deal." He's still smiling, watching me with those careful eyes, holding himself still and keeping a buffer between us, even though we're both standing in the narrow entry hall.

"What kind of deal?"

"I'll make you dinner every night, and you let me sleep in one of the bedrooms."

"As long as I don't have to give you a pack of pups." I snap my mouth shut. Did I really just say that? I stare intently across the apartment at the thermostat with something that feels like the world's biggest foot lodged in my throat.

From the corner of my eye, I see an intense, hungry look flash across his face, but as quickly as it appears, he blanks it out. "We can start with one and see how we like it." He crosses his arms and leans against the wall. "See if he matches the aesthetic, you know. If he enhances the place, or if he messes with the feng shui."

I look up, and he looks down. His expression is completely serious, but the blue in his eyes sparkles.

"I think you're talking about a sofa, not a pup," I say, letting my lips curve as I stroll into the living area.

He follows at my heels. "Nope. It's pups I'm thinking of. Rectangular, have four feet, upholstered. Definitely pups."

I giggle. He's being dumb, but it's about what my brain can handle right now. "Feng shui?"

I know about it because my mom is into human things, and she's always redecorating, but I'm kind of surprised Trevor has heard of it.

"The traditional Chinese practice of harmonizing people and their environments," he recites.

"I know what it is." I wander to the kitchen and run my fingers along the cold marble countertops. I want to plant my hot cheek flat on it.

"You want to know how a male like me has heard about it." He doesn't say it with reproach, but I still feel a twinge of embarrassment. I didn't mean it that way, but—I guess I did.

"I—" I chew my bottom lip and search for words.

"Books," he says, putting me out of my misery as he goes to the thermostat and fiddles with it, frowning. "Let's see how low you can go," he mutters and taps at a button.

A blast of cold air comes out of the vent above me, and it's the best thing I've ever felt in my life. I sigh so loud that I blush.

"Better?" he asks.

"Yeah." I swing myself up to sit on the counter and turn my face up to the vent. It's amazing. I've got my eyes closed so I sense rather than see Trevor come over and hop up next to me. He sits closer than he did on the stairs.

"In high school, the way shop was scheduled, I got stuck in study hall a lot. I read a lot of nonfiction, especially philosophy and paranormal phenomena."

I open my eyes. He's really close. I can smell the laundry detergent he uses under the gravy smell. The scents shouldn't complement each other, but they literally make my mouth water. I swallow and clear my throat. "You're into philosophy?"

He shakes his head and grins. "Nah. My assigned seat was by that shelf, and I was lazy."

I can't help but smile back at him. He's so pretty. Even though they're blue-gray, which is a more human color, his eyes still have a strong wolfish quality, but not in a predatory way. They're knowing. Calm. *Observant.*

I want to touch his hair. It looks soft.

For a second, he sways toward me, just the slightest bit, like my thoughts are drawing him in, but then he stiffens his spine, sniffs, and runs a nervous hand through his curls.

"Hope you're okay if I put my pool table there." He nods toward the middle of the living room.

"Fine by me as long as I can put up shelves for my antique doll collection along the wall."

"Which wall?"

"All the walls."

His thick brows pinch together. "You're pulling my leg."

I keep my face blank and slowly shake my head. "Not at all."

"All right, then." He slaps his thighs and blows out a breath. "I guess I'm making some shelves. How many dolls are we talking?"

"One...thousand."

His smile breaks like a sunburst. "Are you teasing me, Izzy Owens?"

He said my name. I want him to say it again, so I can listen closely and press it in my brain like a flower in a book. I want to tell him to repeat himself, but obviously, that'd be weird, so I shrug, sigh, and say, "I knew I should've said a hundred."

He nods. "You went too big."

It makes me think *go big or go home*, and that makes me say, "Are we really going to move in here together?"

The idea makes my heart thud faster, and I can't tell whether it's from excitement or fear or both.

"It's weird, eh?" he says gently.

"So weird." I peek up at him. He's examining the cabinets across from us.

"I don't know anything about pups," I admit quietly.

"I was lying about dinner. I can't cook," he says. "But I know pups. I've got two younger brothers."

"You've got all brothers? Two older and two younger?"

"Yeah. If we have a girl, just know my mom's gonna go nuts. Actually, she's already gone nuts. She's knitting you a sweater."

I can't even picture my mom knitting. She's not one to sit and relax. At night, she paces in the kitchen, making calls to her female friends. *Catching up on the day*, she calls it.

"Winter is months away," I say because I want to say "she is?" And I don't want to sound like no one's ever made me a sweater.

"She needs time to do the matching scarf and mittens."

"She knows about me." I guess so if his dad and brothers had to come and stop him from busting down my parents' door. My stomach churns, unsettled. I don't want to think about that.

"She's got a basket put together for you. Of, uh, blankets and stuff." Those dark slashes appear along his cheekbones.

It's tradition for the mothers and female relatives of a mated pair to give a female in heat the linens to make her nest. I've helped my mother put together elaborate baskets for her friend's daughters. She does them up with silk ribbons and posies of white roses and baby's breath. You always have to rush when you hear about a mating to get it together and delivered before it's too late.

Even though I've helped her make them, I can't quite picture my mom packing a basket for me, careful to pin the bow just so and arrange the folded quilts and blankets so they look like a flower. She makes the baskets to play up to the people she thinks are worth the time. I only get on her nerves.

Sadness creeps over me like a fog. I drum my heels against the cabinet below the island.

Trevor shifts so his hard bicep brushes against my upper arm. "Your folks are pretty pissed, eh?"

He doesn't even sound mad.

I shrug, and for a second, our arms press together. Shivers race across my skin. "Don't take it personally. It's not about you."

"Sure it is." He flashes his wry smile. "I'm not what they want for their smart, classy girl."

He is so wrong. He's not what they want for themselves. I'm not, either. I don't want to explain that, though. I don't want him to see me how they do—not worth the time or the effort.

"They'll come around," I lie. "Everyone knows that Fate decides."

He turns away from me to stare at the sink again, his shoulders tensing. "Yeah. We don't have a choice."

The fuzzy, warm feeling that had distracted me for a second when we were joking sinks away like water down a drain. All of a sudden, I'm shivering, hyperaware of my damp shirt clinging to my sweaty back, the painful points of my nipples, and the heavy ache in my breasts. I'm a mess. My hair is so wet with sweat, it's plastered to my neck.

I slide off the counter onto watery legs. "I want to go home."

He blinks, surprised, and hops down beside me. It isn't fair. I'm a wreck, and he seems even bigger and stronger than when I noticed him across the salad bar.

"I'm sorry," he says. "I didn't mean it like that."

I fuss with my shirt to give my hands something to do and my eyes a reason not to meet his. "It's just the truth."

"No." He crosses the space between us and grabs both of my clammy hands, drawing them to his sides, holding me there, not quite in his arms, but close. If I dropped the top of my head forward, I could tuck it under his chin. "That was my pride talking. Being defensive. What I meant to say was I'm glad. I'm glad Fate decided that you're for me."

There's a gruffness to his voice, an awkwardness that makes the smooth words terse and blunt and wonderful.

I let my forehead fall to his chest, and I can feel his heart slugging against my temple, fast but steady. My stomach hollows, and my blood buzzes through my veins.

He lifts my chin with a knuckle, gazing down, the blue and gray storming, and I finally understand what it means to be lost in someone's eyes. I forget what I was going to do, what I'm supposed to do, who I am.

"I'm going to kiss you," he whispers.

"Okay," I whisper back.

And he does. His lips are dry and soft and firm at the same time, and up close, he smells even better than gravy, and he tastes like toothpaste and soda and all the things I've ever craved and never gotten enough of—royal icing flowers and snow days and the pale, full moon and the woods at night.

He draws back, and I whimper. Somehow, my hands are framing his face, my fingers dug into his cheek, my thumbs pressing his hard jaw.

"Don't go home," he says. His fingers have plunged into my hair, and he's cradling my head.

"What?" I want to touch him, but I also don't want to let go of the grip I have, and he's talking about not going home, and I just want him to kiss me again.

"Stay here." His hands travel over my shoulders, down my back, tentatively wrapping around my waist, pulling me flush against his front. I can feel hardness poking my belly, and that's scary, but being held, being drawn close, that's new and strange and lovely. "Please."

I can't stay. My father would kill me. He'd kill *him*.

I don't want to bring that into this, though. I don't want any ugliness in this moment between him and me as we stand in an empty kitchen like we're slow dancing, but not moving, almost too scared to breathe in case we mess it up.

"There's no furniture," I say.

"I have sleeping bags. You can have the big bedroom with the bathroom attached."

"I can't."

"I'll leave you alone. I just don't want you to go back there." His voice is deadly serious.

I shuffle forward a half step until I'm standing between his tan work boots and give in to gravity, sliding my hands down to rest on his hard chest. It's so broad that I can splay my fingers and cover hardly any of him. His heart beats against the center of my palm.

I don't want to go back to my parents, either. I don't want to be anywhere but here.

"I don't want to pressure you or anything," he murmurs. "We can do things at your pace."

I just want him to kiss me. Why am I just standing here? He's my mate. I don't have to wait. I rise on my tiptoes and search for his mouth, my eyes closed so I miss and my lips brush his stubble-roughened jaw. His wolf growls, but I'm not scared, and neither is my wolf. She growls back, demanding, impatient.

He chuckles and takes my mouth, this time slipping his tongue past my lips, and I don't expect it, so I startle. He begins to pull away, but before he can take that tongue from me, I suck him back in, tangling mine with his as my whole body goes limp, and I cling to him by the neck like a dress on a hanger.

He holds me upright, his arms sure and strong, and my heart pounds, and my wolf feels like she's running so fast, she's flying.

And then the door flies open with a crash.

Instantly, Trevor spins, throwing me behind him. My hip bangs into the handle to the oven. The stench of fur and aggression swamps the room.

Trevor's wolf snarls.

"Whoa, son. Relax. Everything's fine," a deep, even voice calls from the entryway, but it's an obvious lie. Growls almost drown out the words. Three males. No four. I peek around Trevor's side.

My father is in the living room, fur sprouting from his unbuttoned collar and his rolled-up sleeves, his wolf twisting his face. Uncle Howell and my cousin Griff are poised to hold him back. The male who called Trevor "son" is my dad's age. He has the same curly hair as Trevor, but the honey streaks are gray, and his eyes are a worn gray, dark with worry. No, with fear.

My wolf growls, low and terrified.

"Get away from her," Dad spits, baring his descended fangs. Griff and Trevor's dad both flinch at the display, and they shrink, not much, but noticeably.

Trevor's chest swells. "She's my mate."

It's not a challenge, but there's no submission in his voice. I don't know how his head is still high. My dad outranks him by a lot, and Uncle Howell is backing him, and he's the alpha's second.

"Not yet, she's not," my dad barks. "Hand her over. *Now*."

I creep to the side. I don't want Trevor hurt.

Somehow, Trevor broadens his shoulders. "This is her home now."

Dad scoffs. "Pup, show neck before I rip it out."

Trevor's dad bristles, his wolf rumbling, and Uncle Howell and Griff grip Dad's arms. Dad's eyes gleam yellow. He likes that he's being held back, that Trevor's dad is too intimidated to do anything. Dad is enjoying himself, and the shame of it breaks through the heat radiating from my body. It's scalding.

I rest a hand on Trevor's arm. "It's okay. I want to go home now."

Trevor shakes off my hand and grabs my wrist. His muscles have grown impossibly tense, his throat closing on his wolf's snarl.

"She stays," he snarls like I didn't even say anything.

For a long moment, everyone is silent.

Trevor and Dad stare each other down. Trevor's dad, Uncle Howell, and Griff glance between the two males, assessing. I might as well be invisible.

No, I'm a bone. If Dad could come closer without fur flying, he'd grab my other wrist, and they'd play tug of war. I hate this. Everyone gets to decide but me.

Trevor doesn't even understand what he's risking. He probably thinks Dad won't go too far for my sake, and maybe he's right, but Dad's wolf thinks I'm so weak I should've been left out in the woods as a baby. Dad's wolf will tear Trevor limb from limb.

"I'm going home," I say and start forward, ignoring Trevor's iron grip. He can let go or break my wrist.

He lets go.

"Izzy—" His voice drops an octave. He sounds confused. My wolf whines.

My dad's lip curls back in a sharp-toothed smirk. "You can have her when it's time. Not before."

Uncle Howell and Griff surround me and hustle me toward the door.

"Be patient, pup," Dad tosses over his shoulder. Self-satisfaction and condescension ooze from every word. "You're getting much more than you deserve. You can wait."

Trevor's wolf howls and mine claws at the border between us, scrabbling to stay with her mate, but I let Uncle Howell guide me to the elevator, embarrassed and torn and scared.

"You didn't have a choice," Uncle Howell murmurs to me as the elevator door shuts. "You're outranked." I think he means it as a comfort.

But that night, after Mom presses a little white pill in my hand and watches until I swallow, the words circle in my brain until it knocks me out.

You didn't have a choice.

It's not a comfort. Not at all.

3

IZZY

The next morning, when I wake up fuzzy-brained and shaky with fever, Mom and Dad sit me down at the kitchen table, and Uncle Howell lays down the law.

Dad's promotion isn't just a big deal to him. Uncle Howell tries to explain, but it's hard to follow pack politics. I know some people want Alban Hughes to be the heir apparent instead of Cadoc Collins, and they think Madog is some kind of usurper, but I have no idea what that has to do with Dad's promotion.

Apparently, though, it's important that someone on Team Collins is in the role, and that would be Dad. The Council decides who gets the job, the vote is close, and there are enough rank supremacists among the elders that the news about me and Trevor might push the undecideds to go for Geralt Powell because he's shown everyone his distaste for "diluting the blood" by abandoning his own pups by a scavenger female.

The whole thing makes my brain spin, but Uncle Howell makes the bottom-line crystal clear. He's the head of our family, and he says I can't mate with Trevor until Dad gets confirmed by the Council. I'm not allowed to go to school or my internship, and they're going to tell everyone that I'm sick. This is about supporting the alpha, so I will comply. No arguments. Period.

Uncle Howell finishes up by clasping my shoulder and saying, "You've always been a good girl, Izzy. It's only thirteen days."

It doesn't feel like thirteen days. Alone in the apartment except for Mom—who's been posted to keep an eye on me—every minute feels like an hour. If anyone saw me, they'd have no trouble believing I'm sick. My skin is rubbery and gray, and I can't seem to catch my breath.

I move from cold water baths to my bed, back and forth, and since I can't bear the feel of fabric on my skin, on the walk to the bathroom, I drape a cotton flat sheet over my shoulders like a cape.

My bed is all wrong. I tear the linens off and pile them in the corner between my bureau and my desk, but I can't get it right. I fuss and fuss, but my sad little nest is lumpy and too hot, and I don't have enough blankets, so I can smell the carpet, and it smells like a chemical approximation of lavender, which somehow reminds me of a decomposing raccoon I stumbled on once during a hike on the far side of the lake.

Mom won't let me take anything else from the linen closet. She tells me to resist the heat. How do you do that? You can't resist a fever. Or your period. And that's what this feels like, the world's worst period stacked on top of food poisoning, minus the barfing.

This is supposed to be sexy? My brain is as foggy as the bogs. I can't focus on books, and Mom took my phone, so I "wouldn't be tempted." I can only stare at the wall, and think about Trevor and his curls and his eyes and how his lips feel and his tongue tastes, and then my stomach cramps and my nipples pucker, and I start thinking dirty, dirty thoughts until Mom bangs a cabinet in the kitchen and embarrassment crawls across my skin like ants.

Then, Dad comes home. The scent of dinner filters in under my bedroom door, but those are wrong, too. Mom knocks, but she doesn't hassle me when I say I'm not hungry.

Night passes. I sleep. I must because hours tick by, and I don't move, don't think, but still, I feel like I've somehow been aware the entire time.

My wolf huddles, sweat drenched and whimpering. She's confused. She expects Trevor, and he doesn't come, and every few hours, she realizes he isn't here yet, and he should be, and she reads this as terrible danger. He's been attacked. She wants us to hide in the back of the closet, but I haven't done that since I was a pup, and I won't. Not ever again, no matter what. She doesn't understand, though, so she cries and quivers in a ball.

The sun rises. I drag myself to the tub, but it's no comfort. My body heats the cold water in minutes, and I can't stand the feeling of it lapping at my sides. After my bath, I rearrange my pile on the floor, curl up into a ball of my own, and force myself to think.

I can't do twelve more days like this. Or is it eleven?

Why can't I mate Trevor in secret? We could leave, go camping in the foothills, and come back once everything is settled.

People would talk if we both disappeared. Shifters gossip. What are they saying about me now? That I have moon sickness? Or maybe Dad's allies are spreading the truth around. If Geralt Powell gets credit for abandoning his pups, maybe Dad gets credit for forbidding me from mating a low ranker.

Why is this happening to me? I've always done what I was told. I keep my head down and do my work. I always arrive on time and stay late if I'm asked. I was always told if I worked hard, if I went above and beyond, everything would be okay, but it never has been, and it isn't now. My wolf is hurting. She's scared.

I drift off, and sometime later, I wake up to the doorbell buzzing. I hear my mother, and then another female. I don't recognize her. I can't make out her words, but she's pleading. My mother is sharp and short.

I try to untangle my legs from the sheets and scrub the bleariness from my eyes.

The female raises her voice, more urgent, beseeching. My mother's wolf snarls, and the door slams. There is a sudden silence. I've only managed to push myself up on my shaky arms.

My wolf wants me to stand and investigate, but I don't trust my legs. They're as numb as my brain.

I've been sitting half-propped up for a few minutes when there is a brisk knock and my bedroom door flies open. My mother strides in, wrinkling her nose.

"Oh, Izzy." She sighs at the sight of me on the floor. "It reeks in here."

I don't have a window. This room is intended to be an office. If I had a bedroom, I'd have a window, but the bedroom is Dad's study, so there's not much I can do but circulate my sweaty stink with the box fan that Aunt Catrin sent down for me.

Mom takes one look at my stripped mattress and pulls out my desk chair, primly seating herself on the edge, pressing her legs together all the way to her ankles. She's wearing her good slacks with the sewn-in creases and beige pumps even though she didn't go to the office today.

"Who was the female at the door?" I croak. I have a water bottle, but even though I'm parched, I keep forgetting to drink.

She ignores the question. "You can't lie around, wallowing on the floor. You've got to get up, get in the shower, brush your hair."

"I just had a bath." An hour ago. Or this morning? Yesterday? Time is blurry.

Mom scowls. "This isn't doing anyone any good."

What good am I supposed to be doing? My arms and legs are rubber, and my brain is Swiss cheese.

"I don't feel well." Being sick has never gotten me out of school or practice or chores before, but it's the truth.

My mom purses her mouth and smooths her bob even though there's not a strand out of place. Her hair behaves. It wouldn't dare not to.

"You need to bear up," she declares. "Think about my great-grandmother."

I swallow a groan and tuck my knees to my chest. I'm not wearing underwear. I can't stand the feel of the elastic, but if I'd known she was going to come in here, I'd have managed to pull on sweatpants.

"It took her family fifteen days to cross the Atlantic, crammed in steerage, cheek-to-jowl with humans, starving and terrified of discovery. What do you think the humans would've done if they'd heard a howl? If one of us slipped and showed fang? The pups were kept muzzled in the cabins. Humans didn't know about us back then. They would've seen us as monsters, and we would have never seen New York Harbor."

I paid attention in history class. The packs in our part of the world came over by steamship and fled the city as soon as we caught a whiff of the raw sewage. We made a new home in the mountains here, far away from humans. At first, our people hid in caves, ignoring the threat growing closer and closer, until the Great Alpha Broderick Moore led us out of the dens, forcing us to abandon the old ways and learn to live beside humans, so we would never have to live in secret again or face fear and want.

Even with my brain as thick as mud, I could recite the story. It never struck me as such complete bullshit before. Never face fear? Who were they talking about? Not me. I've been afraid of my father's wolf for my entire life.

Before I can follow the thought, Mom continues, "Our ancestors did what they had to do, and they were better for it in the end. Stronger. Can you imagine making a new home in a cave?" Her mouth pulls back into a grimace. "Having a pup in a dirt cave?"

Is this supposed to be a comfort? Is this *encouragement*? I gape at her slack-jawed as I clutch a soggy sheet to my agonizingly swollen breasts.

"Do you think those mothers wanted to muzzle their pups?" Mom draws herself up, her collarbones stark above the neckline of her silk blouse as she thrusts her shoulders back. "As a female, you do what you have to do. To *survive*. To protect the pack. To protect your *family*."

The words should make sense. The order is right. The ideas have been drummed into my head since I was born—success demands sacrifice. Nose to the grindstone. It's not about you; it's about the pack. There is no *I* in team.

I should instinctually agree, but in this moment, the words are gibberish. We're not a baseball team or soldiers. We're wolves—*animals*—and this heat is killing me.

"I can't do twelve more days," I tell her, tears welling in my eyes, sticking on my lashes and blinding me.

"What are you talking about? End of quarter is only ten days away."

Ten? I lost a day somewhere. Or more. I've been lying in this pile of limp, damp sheets forever.

"When is Trevor coming?"

My mother's lips peel back in disgust. "Don't worry about that. His father is handling him. At least that male understands the stakes. That overbearing female he mated —" Mom shakes her head and sucks her cheeks in. "She refuses to accept that this is the way it is. She doesn't have a choice, though. None of us do. This is bigger than any of us. And it's only a few days, for goodness' sake."

What is bigger than us? Uncle Howell explained it all to me—probably the first time he's spoken to me like an adult —so it must be true, but for the life of me, I can't remember any of the specifics.

"I need Trevor," I try again, my voice breaking. She's my mother. If she could only understand how bad it feels, she'd help.

"You need to pull yourself together." Her brown eyes go hard and dark like wet stone. "What do you think will happen to Trevor Floyd if he puts a spoke in the wheel of his betters' carefully laid plans, and Madog Collins ends up fending off a challenge? Do you think Uncle Howell and your father are going to welcome him into this family with open arms? People disappear, Izzy. You know that. You don't want to mess around and find yourself knocked up with a pup whose father 'went for a walk' like the scavengers say. Do you?"

My tears are falling now, streaking down my cheeks. No,

of course I don't want anything bad to happen to Trevor. "But Mom, it hurts. It hurts so bad."

"Life hurts." The words roll off her tongue. That's her answer, and I should have expected it. If I say I'm tired, she says everyone's tired. If I say I'm nervous, she says you should be. She's not going to help me. Why won't the part of me that expects her to just die?

"Enough of this," she says, standing and dusting off her immaculate slacks. "Go wash yourself. Brush your teeth. We'll get you another one of my pills, and you'll feel better." She frowns at my room and wrinkles her nose. "When all this is over, we'll need to do a deep clean. At the minimum, the carpet needs steam cleaning."

She shudders and leaves, but she doesn't shut the door all the way behind her. When her phone rings moments later, I hear her say, "Catrin? What are they saying?" And then I hear her bedroom door click shut.

I don't have a clock or a window. What time is it? It feels late, but Dad's not home yet. It might be Friday. At the end of the week, he always goes for drinks after work with the males he's trying to schmooze. But would he go out when I'm home like this?

Of course, he would.

I don't waste another second. I grab the bed to hoist myself upright. When I'm steady enough, I drag on gray sweatpants and an oversized white T-shirt and creep down the hall, past Mom's closed bedroom, through the living room. My wolf rises to her feet, ears perking. We don't hear or smell Dad.

We need space. Sky. Wind. We need to get out of here.

Mate, my wolf whimpers.

No. We're not allowed. Remember what Mom said. I'm dangerous to him.

We can't be inside here any longer, though. We'll feel better with fresh air in our lungs. We'll be able to breathe again and calm our racing heart. We'll get a second wind, and then we'll be able to hold out for as long as we have to.

Trevor brought us sodas and got us an apartment of our own. He made jokes, and he kissed so sweetly, and if I wouldn't have gone with Dad, Dad's wolf would have torn him to pieces. I know it. Trevor's a good male. Mom's not making idle threats. I can't let him get hurt. I can wait. I just need air.

I quietly let myself out the front door, leaving it slightly ajar so Mom doesn't hear it close.

I take the elevator because I don't trust myself on the stairs. My wolf wants to go outside, but she wants to get Trevor first. I'm afraid that she won't let us leave, but for some reason, once we pass his floor, she chills out about going to him. For the entire ride down, I pray we don't stop. I look moon sick. If anyone sees me, they'll definitely call my parents.

I go all the way to the basement. There's an exit by the gym that leads to street level. Brynn and her friends use it when they sneak out at night. They've never invited me— I'm too much of a rule follower—but they tell me all about it.

I hold my breath for the thirty feet from the elevator to the emergency exit. Even though the doors to the gym are closed, the stink of male sweat seeps out along with the sound of clanking weights. The scent has grown even more rancid. Even though I'm not inhaling, my nostrils burn, and my eyes water.

My wolf urges us to flee faster, and I do, dashing down a back corridor and pounding up the flight of concrete stairs that lead to street level.

As soon as I clear the Tower, I drag air deep into my lungs, and my wolf surges to the border between us, yapping with excitement. This is right. We've thrown our bridle and saddle, slipped our leash, and until this moment, we didn't even realize we wore them.

I'm scared. I'm always scared—I'm *made of* scared—but I'm also something new. I'm high, soaring, uncaged.

I've never seen the world like this before. I run toward the Academy, sticking to the alleys, and despite the gross water trickling down the sloping pavement and the grubby green dumpsters, it's an exquisitely beautiful night.

Dusk must've not been too long ago because the scent of dew hasn't totally obscured the hint of sunshine lingering in the air. The moon is full and low, its seas like bruises on a fat, pale fruit.

I'm not allowed out alone after dark. Only low rank females who aren't going anywhere hang out at the marina or walk with their friends along the promenade on Friday night. I stay home and hit the books, staring at my blank, eggshell walls. I'm not allowed to tack up posters. When it's our turn to move up, we don't want to have to waste time repainting.

But what does all that matter now? I'm outside. My wolf closes her eyes and lets the night wind ruffle her fur.

I pump my legs harder, racing away from the buildings and the lake, and when I hit the Academy, I jog along the perimeter until I reach the woods that spread all the way to the foothills. I don't know where I'm going. My wolf and I are soaking in the moonlight, our lungs and thighs aching, free and surefooted, and I've never, ever felt this way before, not even in my dreams.

This is the right direction. This is the way I'm supposed

to be going, through this ditch, past this cluster of beech trees, across this dry creek bed.

My sneakers pound a rhythm on the ground, and a hundred other sounds join in a chorus, the crickets swelling and fading—crescendo, fortissimo, diminuendo, pianissimo—the bullfrogs honking their parts right on time. My heart thumps along in perfect measure.

I'm not surprised when I round a bend and Trevor is there, standing under a massive white oak, its gnarled trunk knotted and mossy and as wide around as a shed, the moon shining through its thick branches. That's exactly where he should be.

I run right to him, stopping only when he doesn't move, not a twitch except for the fire blazing in his eyes.

"T-Trevor?"

He looks rough. His skin is sickly gray like mine, his jaw dark with stubble, his curls sticking up at all angles. His hands are clenched in fists, and he seems bigger. The short sleeves of his maroon T-shirt dig into his biceps, and the hem rides up, showing the carved V pointing into his loose gray sweatpants.

Heat bursts through me, spinning pinwheels in my belly, surging out to the tips of my fingers and toes, spilling into my chest. Without thinking, I clutch my breasts to hold the feeling in, groaning in the back of my throat.

Trevor's wolf rattles his chest, and my wolf prances, calling out to him, howling her need. Why is he standing over there, his face so bleak? Why doesn't he wrap us in his arms?

"Go back," he says, his voice guttural. Strangled.

The bond sings, then roars, stoking a craving in me, a vicious, jagged longing. I fold my forearms over my breasts and press down, as if that'll keep me together, ease the ache.

I can't think straight.

I need a nest.

I glance around. We're in a small clearing, and there's not much to work with—paper thin, brown leaves that survived the winter, thick green moss, a rotten log. It won't do. I need warmth. Softness. I pace, searching for what I need, knowing it's not here. My nest, for what it's worth, is back in my room in the Tower. We should go there.

No, no, we can't. We'd be caught. I do need to go back, though. I'm not allowed out here. Why again? I can't remember.

I stare up at Trevor. I've wandered close to him, and for the first time, I notice the bruise circling his left eye and the crack in his swollen bottom lip.

"What happened?" I ask, stepping closer, raising my hand.

He ducks his head away, hissing, "No. You have to go back. I didn't mean for you to come out here."

Tears spring into my eyes. "Why not? It hurts, Trevor. It hurts so bad."

He growls in agonized frustration and grips the back of his neck. There's no doubt—his arm muscles are bulging much bigger than they were. Delicate silver stretch lines glow against his tanned skin. "Izzy, it's not safe. I'm— I can't —It's too hard to hold back. You have to leave. Now. Before —before something bad happens. *Please.*"

My tears reach my mouth, salty from my sweat as I lick them away. Trevor's throat rattles, a sound of pain and warning and terrible desperation.

I know I'm not supposed to see him, but why? I want him to kiss me again and hold me and smile gently and tell silly jokes. Make me feel safe. Wanted.

"Help me," I beg. "I can't take it anymore."

He squeezes his eyes shut. "You can, Izzy. You *have to*. Go back now."

"My wolf wants out, and I hurt." I clutch between my legs to staunch the terrible pulsing ache down there. "Why can't I be here? I can't remember. Do you?"

"Izzy, please. Please go." He grabs the oak behind him, digging his claws into the bark, slicing the moss and sending a lush, earthy scent into the air. He's so anguished and beautiful, like the print of Saint Sebastian tied to a tree and shot with arrows that hangs in the art studio at the Academy.

I reach out to touch his jaw, to tilt his tormented face down so he's looking at me instead of up at the moon. My fingertips graze the bristle under his chin and slip to trace the vein throbbing in his neck. I'm going to bite him right there, and then he'll be mine, and whatever is wrong will be fixed.

His wolf rumbles, rattling his ribs, and I smile. For the first time in my life, my fangs descend, pricking the inside of my lower lip. I run my tongue over the pointy tips experimentally and moan. They ache to sink into flesh.

I've never wanted anything before except to escape notice and get along, but now, I want everything—the moon, my wolf, freedom to run, the male in front of me. *My* male.

I step closer so that when I inhale, my sore, heavy breasts touch his chest. Every muscle in his body goes as tight as a stretched bow, flexing, swelling. I want to lick the hollow at the base of his throat. I want to sink my claws into the meat of his forearms like he's digging his into the bark of the tree.

"Go back, Izzy. *Please*." He's desperate, pleading, but he's wrong. I'm supposed to be here. He's supposed to touch me.

"Why?" I curl my fingers around those hard forearms,

and they're like steel, like stone, except I can feel the blood rushing through his veins slug against my palms.

"Izzy, you have to focus," he pants through jagged breaths, drawing my gaze back to his face. "If we do this now, they say they'll strip my dad of his rank. They'll take his job, and my brothers', too. We'll lose our apartment. They say the scavengers won't even let us stay in the bogs once they're done with us."

"Who says?" I ask, but I know. Dad. Uncle Howell.

"We just have to wait, Izzy. Not much longer. We can do it." I watch him muster up a smile, but it's nothing but clenched teeth and sunken eye sockets.

Tears roll down my cheeks. "I can't."

I don't want to admit it. I want to be strong, too, like him. I reach for bunched chest muscles that cover the place where the bond connects us. His wolf snarls. I pat his pecs to calm him.

"Izzy," he begs. "I promise it'll be okay. Go back now, and I'll follow, and in a few days, we can be together, and it'll be so good, I promise. I'll make shelves for your dolls. I'll make them beach houses and convertibles and whatever you want. I promise. But you have to walk away now."

"I don't really have dolls." Aunt Catrin bought me one when I was little, and I named her Isabel because I always wished I'd been named that instead of Isolde, but Baby Isabel got donated to the charity shop years ago. Dolls are for pups.

"Izzy, focus." Trevor's voice drops, and I can hear his wolf. I want to meet him so bad. "I'm losing it, baby. I can't hold on. Please. You have to go back now." His voice is mangled with wolf, and his eyes are blue-black with pain.

"Okay." I lean forward to take another breath of him. Just one more. Then, I'll be able to go.

He groans, and his need burns in the bond, so I have no choice but to rise up on my toes, rub my cheek against his, and mark him with my scent to comfort the wolf thrashing inside him, because it's wrong to leave my mate alone and suffering. As I tilt my head back, my hair falls away from my exposed neck. Cool air dances across my hot skin.

A tortured moan sounds in my ear. Trevor's stubble scrapes my jaw. His teeth scrape along my jugular. The tang of copper fills my nose. Yes. This is what we both need—to belong to each other for real. For good.

And then Dad will destroy his family, and it'll be my fault. Trevor will hate me, and he'll be stuck with me forever.

I don't know where I find the strength, but I hurl myself away from my mate. My wolf fights me, but I'm stronger. I take one step back. Then another. I stumble.

Trevor bellows, an unholy roar. No, not a roar, a word. "Run!"

Then a bloodcurdling howl rings out. I blink up, frozen with fear, and Trevor—is not Trevor.

The black of his pupils bleeds into the blue and then the white until his eyes are voids. He twists his neck and as he howls at the moon, his fangs tear through his bottom lip as they descend. His biceps burst from his shirt sleeves, his muscles lined with raised veins.

He's still in his skin, but he moves like a wolf, swiveling his neck to stare me down like prey, his nostrils flaring as he scents the air. There is no hint of awareness in his face. Or pity.

He is an animal, and he is starving.

I run.

My wolf rises inside me, directing energy to my calves and thighs and lungs, but my feet are human and too used to resting under desks. I trip on nothing, and that's all he needs.

He's on me. His weight slams into my back, knocking me to my knees. I topple forward, and I reach out to catch myself, but it's too late. He tackles me to the ground. My wrist snaps. My face hits the dirt, bounces, and hits again. This time my chin cracks on a rock. I scream.

A rough hand seizes the back of my neck in a vise grip, pinning my upper half to the ground. Claws rip through my sweatpants, slicing and slashing the soft skin of my hip, my butt, the back of my thigh. The tips of the claws wrapped around my throat pierce my skin. If I inhale, his claws dig deeper into my skin, and there's dirt in my mouth. I can't breathe, and I can't spit the dirt out. My wrist throbs, but I can't free it.

The air is cold.

I am fear, all fear, silent, screaming fear.

His wolf howls in his chest, and in the furthest corner inside me, my wolf presents, her limbs shaking, her rear legs incapable of holding her rump lifted. She whimpers, but so quietly that only I can hear.

Be still.

Don't move.

Don't breathe.

I can't. I won't.

This isn't really happening.

Oh, God.

It is.

It's happening.

It hurts.

His thrusts shove me forward, and my arm is caught under my stomach, so my broken wrist rolls, over and over, and I scream, but my lungs are crushed, and the sound is muffled. Snot drips from my nose in strings, so I can't see or breathe or wipe it away, and there's nothing I can do to help myself but rub my face in the dirt.

I feel his hot breath on the crook of my shoulder and brace myself, but there is nothing my body can do to protect itself—I'm trapped, overpowered—and his fangs plunge into my neck, tearing flesh, piercing to the bone. I fight, I swear I'm fighting, but I can't move my legs or my arms or my head, I can only bend and buck my spine, and it does nothing but push him inside me deeper.

He rips his teeth from my neck and roars. Warm blood splatters on my bare back. My blood.

The thrusting stops.

A terrible pressure swells inside me.

His knot.

Be still.

Be quiet.

It'll be over soon.

The punishing grip disappears from my neck. The weight eases off my back.

It's silent except for our ragged breathing, his and mine, and my wolf's low whine, and his wolf's anguished howl.

He backs off, just a little. His knot tugs against my battered flesh and stings. I whimper. He bends forward over me, his shadow falling across the moonlit ground where my cheek rests against the dirt. He wipes carefully at my face with the hem of his sweat-soaked maroon shirt, his hand shaking like an old man's as he sops up snot and blood.

Pain shoots up my forearm from my wrist. I want to pull my arm out from under me, but I'm too scared.

Trevor lifts himself off my back again. The knot tugs, but this time, I smother the whimper of pain. Then, he leans over me again, and cradling my head with one hand to lift it, he slips his folded T-shirt under my face for a pillow.

I'm shaking, my teeth clattering, and my wrist throbs. There is something stuck inside me, and I'm too terrified to look up. If I close my eyes, maybe I could shut the whole thing out, but then I wouldn't see danger coming, but it's already come, hasn't it? The worst is here, and there's no way out.

He's calmed down, and he's not hurting me anymore, not much. It's almost over. Soon.

My legs go numb, but I can still feel the knot stretching me. How am I going to run when I get free if I can't feel my legs?

The question pounds over and over in my brain, insistent and critical and unsolvable, when his knot finally shrinks enough to slip out of me. He immediately scrambles backward, leaving me alone in a heap on the ground.

I can't run.

I can't even stand.

I don't have the strength.

Let me, my wolf whispers as she struggles to her paws.

I grab the offer with both hands and gratefully let go. She limps forward, staggering through the border between us, taking our body for the first time even though she's as battered and broken as I am. The second that her legs form, they buckle, and she collapses to the bloody, matted grass and clawed-up dirt I'd been lying in.

Trevor staggers forward, and as gently as he can with his wildly shaking hands, he picks up my wolf and cradles her in his arms like a bride. My wolf tucks her foreleg to her chest to keep it still, but the pain from my broken wrist still throbs with each step he takes.

My wolf feels my pain like her own, but her body doesn't

show my injuries—there is no chunk taken from her shoulder, no blood dripping from between her legs.

Trevor carries me what feels like forever, through the woods, along the fence that borders the Academy, across a muddy worksite with nothing but a poured foundation and concrete and rebar columns. The mud sucks at his boots.

He didn't have to put them back on. He never took them off.

It's not until he turns onto the main avenue that I get the courage to peer up at his face. My stomach lurches into my throat and sticks there, suffocating me, while he stares straight ahead.

His eyes are blue-gray again. There is dried blood caked in the corners of his mouth. Tears course down his cheeks.

He turns at the infirmary and carries me up the sidewalk, silent, his steps slow and careful. We aren't even to the doors when there's a shout, and then everything happens in fast-forward. A swarm of people emerge from the building, rush toward us, and skid to a halt when Trevor's wolf lets out a howl so eerie and mad that the air instantly fills with a fog of fear and aggression.

The medics surround us in a semi-circle, hands raised, the males casting calculating looks at each other, while Trevor carefully lowers my wolf's body to the ground and steps back. I look up, nursing my limp forearm, but he doesn't even glance down.

"I hurt her," he sobs.

"I see that," the oldest male says in a calm, deliberate voice. "What happened?"

"Get me away from her," Trevor begs.

"Okay." The old male nods to the others, and they converge on Trevor, boots thudding on the pavement around me while I huddle on the concrete. He doesn't resist when they seize his arms and drag him away.

My wolf wheezes a thin, weak cry. He hurt us, but his wolf is her mate, and she doesn't want to be left here alone.

Trevor's spine stiffens, but he doesn't turn his head.

She cries for him again, louder, summoning the last of her energy.

He keeps walking.

My wolf collapses, at the end of her strength, leaving my naked human body behind on the sidewalk.

"Trevor," I cry one last time as a nurse squats next to me, pity and horror in her eyes. He doesn't turn around.

"Oh, sweetheart, what did he do to you?" she murmurs, setting her metal first aid kit next to me and flipping the latch open.

I don't know what to say, so I keep my mouth shut, and she considers my mangled body, her hand hovering in the air with an alcohol swab. She doesn't know either how to even begin fixing this terrible, horrible thing.

4

TREVOR

'm a monster. The knowledge screams in my brain.

I can't think.

I let the medics get me away from her, but then I fight. I have to get away. I can't escape them as a man, so I shift. My wolf gets us away from them, but as soon as he escapes, he wheels around to go back to her. I wrench him out of our body and collapse to my knees, keening, retching.

I hurt Izzy. It wasn't me. I would never hurt her. Never. But they were my claws. My fangs. My ears. I heard every single scream and cry and didn't stop. I would never do this thing, but I did.

I pound my chest, trying to beat the agony out, but I can't. The shame shreds me, rends me to pieces, and it should be unbearable, but every second is a fresh horror, every thought is a knife plunging into raw flesh.

There's blood on my hands. Under my nails. I rip them out with my teeth and spit them onto the ground.

I hurt her. Am I feral?

It's a mercy to put a feral down.

I wipe my mouth, stagger back to my feet, and race

through the woods, faster and faster, mindless at first, but then a destination rises in my mind.

I weave through trees and leap fallen logs. Rocks chew the soles of my feet, limbs whip my face, and the pain isn't nearly enough, not nearly what I deserve. The horror chases me, nips my heels, swipes its razor-sharp claws across my back, bowing my spine.

Izzy nuzzled my cheek, marking me.

I shoved her face in the dirt.

I told her to run, she did, and I chased her.

It was my fault, my fault, my fucking fault.

She came to me, and I was weak. I failed her.

I'm a piece of shit.

I'm a monster.

I slow to a jog when I near the access road to the High Rise's loading dock. I dodge the cameras and slide under the rolling door of Bay C. Maintenance never remembers to secure that door. The bay is empty except for a custodian, a scavenger named Nevitts, but we're cool, and although he looks shocked, he doesn't make a move to stop me.

This late, there aren't many people working, mostly bored guards, scrolling their phones. I stick to the western stairs, farthest from the security desk. I force myself to sprint up as fast as I can, pushing harder and harder until my side stitches and my calves cramp. By the tenth floor, I'm slowing. By the twenty-fifth, I'm crawling up the steps.

The burn in my muscles is nothing to the roaring pain in my head.

Izzy is so small. She weighs almost nothing. I crushed her. I put my—my stomach heaves, but there is nothing left.

I hurt her.

I tear at my hair, tears blearing my vision. I do the last

flight of stairs by feel, bursting through the emergency door onto the roof.

The tarred roof scrapes the bottoms of my raw feet. The pain is not enough; no penance will ever be enough. There is no possible way to make this right.

After I bit her, her fear surged into my chest. She was afraid that she was going to die. That I was going to kill her.

There is no way to take it back. No way to reverse time and throw myself off this building before I become the worst thing a male can be.

I fucked everything up. I made the wrong call every single time. I didn't bust through her apartment door and take her away the night she told her parents. I let Dad convince me to let him negotiate with Mr. Owens, father to father. I let her family put me off with threats, let them make a coward of me until I became an animal. And worst, worst of all, when I scented her on the wind, I didn't run as far and as fast as I could. I waited under that tree. I knew she was coming, and I knew how close I was to losing it.

It's all my fucking fault.

I jog past the air handling unit I fixed last year to the edge of the building. I step up on the tarred lip and stare down at the plaza. A thirty-floor drop is enough to smash anyone to pieces, even a shifter. The fall wouldn't be long. Seconds. If I dive, my head would explode on contact. The screaming would end.

Down below, streetlamps cast circles of light on the stone pavers below. Otherwise, the planters and benches are cast in shadow. There is only a sliver of a moon tonight. The dark lake laps against the bulkhead.

Izzy's wolf was trembling in my arms, peering up at me, confused. Betrayed. Her brown eyes are tattooed on my brain. She was in pain, and I'd hurt her, and she didn't understand. Neither do I. How could I do it? How could I not stop it?

What I did is a howl in my brain, fire licking my skin, serrated knives sinking deeper and deeper, tearing my flesh from my bones.

I am not this thing.

I *cannot* be this thing.

I straighten my spine and draw in a last, deep breath of cool evening air, searching for the trace of Izzy's scent clinging to my skin. Sage, rosemary, and thyme. She smells like peace. Like home.

I don't know what happens after you die, but so help me, whatever the next world is like, I'll make it home for her. I'll build her shelves. I'll build her castles. I'll find Fate and make her tell me how to fix what I've done.

I close my eyes and lift my arms.

Behind me, a metal door slams against a brick wall.

"What did Nevitts say?" I hear my dad say.

"He said—" and then Mom must see me because she screams, "Trevor!"

"Stop!" Dad roars, the word instilled with all the dominance he possesses. I feel the impact and shake off the command easily. My dad is a good male, but he's not a powerful one.

My oldest and youngest brothers, Tarian and Llew, race toward me, skidding to a halt when I sway on the roof's edge.

"Oh, baby," Mom cries. "Don't. Please, don't."

"Shit. Don't do it. For fuck's sake, Trevor," Tarian shouts, hovering a few feet away, not daring to come closer.

"Just walk away," I hiss. "Get Mom out of here."

"We'll figure this out, son," Dad says, approaching

slowly with his palms raised. "Just please step back. It's okay. We'll figure this out together."

"Please, Tarian," I ask again, my voice cracking. "Mom doesn't need to see."

"Now you stop right there, Trevor Floyd!" she shrieks. "You stop this very minute. Think, damn it. *Think*. What happens to Izzy if you do this?" She stalks closer, and unlike Dad, she keeps coming, her eyes wild. "Listen to the bond, baby. It's already there. If you die, what happens to her?" Tears stream down her face, and she shakes, but her voice is ferocious. "Listen to the bond, baby. Please."

Listen? It's all I can hear. Izzy's pain beats at my heart. Her fear scores my brain, scraping the nerves. Her shame stabs me through the gut.

How can I live with the shame?

"Let me go," I say. My toes curl over the edge.

"Don't you dare, Trevor Floyd," she snarls back, her own wolf gravel in her throat. "I didn't raise a coward. Listen to your wolf. *Listen to him.*"

She has no dominance, but still, her words turn my fractured mind to my wolf.

He's howling in his cage, desperate to fight, to protect his mate, to comfort her, but he's trapped, torn from her, powerless, but he still cries for her like he has the right. Like he's her mate and not her rapist.

His voice doesn't falter. If there is an infinitesimal chance she can hear him, in this dimension or another—even if there is no chance in hell—he'll howl for her to let her know he's here, she's not alone, never alone, as long as he has breath in his body. Guilt flays him, too, but he is stronger than I am. He will live with this for her. He will do anything for her.

He inhales and howls again.

A small sharp ache stabs just underneath my sternum, so subtle I almost miss it, but I notice because this pain isn't mine.

It's hers.

I feel her.

She hurts. She's lost and scared.

"Listen," Mom urges, prowling closer.

I can't leave Izzy to hurt alone.

My weight shifts back to my heels.

Before I can make another move, my mother shifts and leaps for me. She sinks her fangs into my shoulder as my brothers grab me from both sides and drag me from the edge. They wrestle me to the ground, and my father's wolf throws his bulk on top of me, pinning me to the tar roof.

When the struggle is over, I'm flat on my back with my parents' wolves crouched above me, my brothers on their knees at my sides, their shoulders heaving, all of us gasping for breath.

Above us, the sky is pitch black, not a star in sight, the only light a scythe-like sliver of cold moon.

I can't feel Izzy's pain anymore.

All I can feel is my own, and the horrible, crushing knowledge that I have to live with this, every moment of every day, for the rest of my cursed, wretched life.

THE NEXT FEW days are a blur. I'm thrown into a cell. Mom and Dad visit. Their faces are gray.

My body is nothing but crushing weight and unbearable pain. My thoughts fight each other like ferals, mindless, senseless, mad.

There are no sheets on the steel cot, no case on the plastic pillow. No sharp edge. No window, no glass pane, no mirror. The fluorescent light overhead never goes off, but that's fine. I don't deserve comfort.

They feed me. I don't eat. They take me to the showers. I stand where I'm put until they drag me out. They don't give me clothes until the day they take me to the room where the Council meets.

Again, I stand where I'm put, this time behind a wood table. Mom, Dad, and my brothers are there. They sit on benches behind me. Now, their faces are white as sheets, except for Mom's. Hers is red and swollen.

The Council sits in front of us on a dais with the alpha, Madog Collins, in the middle. I'm introduced to a silver-haired male in a suit. I instantly forget his name.

Everyone talks and talks. Dad, my supervisor, the guys from Facilities, my friends, my brothers, Mr. Owens, Howell Owens, the alpha's second, the medics from the infirmary. Voices are raised. Mom weeps in her chair, her fist shoved in her mouth. I can see her from the corner of my eye.

I did this.

I hurt her, too.

I hurt everyone I love.

I don't know what they say. My ears ring with the screaming in my head.

Howell Owens and the silver-haired male argue bitterly, gesturing wildly, interrupting each other. The silver-haired male slams his palm on the table. Howell steps toward him. Madog barks at them to stop and calls them up to the dais to huddle and argue more, but quietly.

In the end, Madog orders me to look him in the eye and says, "Trevor Floyd, you are hereby exiled from Moon Lake pack and all its territories, entities, and interests, for now, and forever." His face is grim—conflicted—but his voice booms.

Mom bursts into fresh tears and clings to Dad. Dad hangs his head.

I did this. I failed them all.

How do I live in my skin another hour? Another minute?

Two males I don't know grab my upper arms and lead me out of the room.

Mom cries, "Trevor! No!" She lunges for me. Dad holds her back. My brothers stand at the bench and watch like sentinels as I leave.

I want to call to Mom and tell her not to cry, not to worry, that I'll be okay, but my lungs can't draw air, my tongue doesn't work, and it'd be a lie anyway.

The males take me through windowless hallways to the loading docks. "Don't think about running," one says to me before he shoves me out the door.

I don't. I can't think at all. Flashbacks gore my brain, stabbing the soft tissue, turning it to pulp. The night air had been wet. When Izzy ran, the backs of her ankles flashed white in the dark. When I bit her shoulder, my fangs scraped bone. Her blood filled my mouth so quickly, I couldn't swallow it all. It gushed down my chin.

I fold over and puke.

"Too late for that now," a male says and drags me the rest of the way to a waiting van.

He throws me in the back. Another male climbs in after and squats, blocking the rear doors, and glares at me like a steaming pile of shit. I am. Worse than that even.

I glance around. There's nothing in reach but a spare tire. A chicken wire screen separates us from the driver.

We pull away from the Tower and drive north. A few minutes after we leave Moon Lake in the rearview, my wolf wakes up, howling. He feels the distance growing between us and Izzy and races back and forth inside me, frantic, mindless with the need to stay close to her.

He launches himself over and over at the boundary between us, but he's trapped. He has no chance against me, against the power of my guilt and shame.

Exile is good. I'll never be able to hurt her again.

Never have to look her in the eye.

Never have to look anyone I know in the eye anymore.

We drive for hours, stopping a few times for the males to piss by the side of the road. They don't let me out. They give me an empty peanut butter jar to use.

We're still heading northwest, gaining elevation. Are they going to drop me in the no-man's-land between Quarry Pack, Salt Mountain, and North Border where the ferals live?

How quickly will the ferals kill me?

Or will I lose the rest of my mind and become one?

The male guarding me never takes his eyes off me, like I might attack him at any moment, but I've never felt smaller or weaker, not even as a pup. My new bulk is a joke. I'm a shell of who I used to be.

I'm a stain.

When we arrive at our destination, the sun is setting. The male watching me jumps out the back and barks, "Get out."

We're standing in the shadow of Salt Mountain. Above us, a pocked dirt road rises into the hills with mismatched shingled roofs and smoking chimneys sprouting among the trees. Our way is barred by the rusty gate to their pack territory. For some reason, it reeks of young male piss.

An older blond male waits there to greet us. He has a

younger blond male with him. Their matching faces are angular and cold.

"You Munroe?" my guard asks.

The older male nods. "This him?" he asks, his ice blue eyes narrowing with contempt as he looks me up and down.

My guard grunts.

"Does Madog want him dead?"

"He didn't say that. He said leave him here."

Munroe sniffs. "I guess he works behind a desk?" His lip curls with derision.

My guard shakes his head. "He's low rank. He's in facilities. Some kind of mechanic."

Munroe takes a second look at me. "What kind of mechanic?"

He's asking me, but even if I wanted to answer, I can't speak. My throat is too tight, my tongue too thick, and every word I know is a scream.

"He fixes shit," my guard volunteers. "Supposedly, he's good at it."

"That right? You fix shit?" Munroe asks.

No. I fuck shit up beyond repair. I destroy lives. I hurt the people I love. I should be put down.

"He don't talk?" Munroe snorts. "He's got that going for him, I guess."

"We good?" my guard asks, clearly done with the conversation. The driver didn't even get out of the van. It's clear they don't like being on foreign pack territory.

"I guess so."

My guard doesn't need to be told twice. He hops into the van's passenger seat, and they pull off, tires squealing.

The three of us are left alone, staring at each other. The young male breaks the silence.

"What did he do?" he asks.

"His female and her people wouldn't let him mount her," Munroe says. "So he went into rut and attacked her."

"Why the fuck would they do that?" The young male glares at me like he's trying to see what's so wrong with me, but he's not going to be able to see the weakness from the outside.

Munroe jaw tightens. "Who knows why those fuckers at Moon Lake do anything they do. They wear suits and sit at desks all day, trying to figure out new ways to sniff human ass. I tell you this, though, he should've put that bitch on her hands and knees as soon as he scented her. He wouldn't be in this situation if he hadn't listened to a female. The minute you give them an iota of power, they will stab you in the back. Every single time. Mark my words, Leith. Every single fucking time."

My wolf growls at *put that bitch on her hands and knees*, but he's too deep down for anyone but me to hear. The talk turns my stomach—all of it does—but if I could speak, what would I say? I *should* have taken her away. I should've made the decision she couldn't make. I was weak and wrong, and she is paying.

Leith nods as if Munroe is only telling him something he already knows. "What are we going to do with him?"

"He can fix shit. We'll drop him at the Camerons."

"Increase their numbers?" The young male questions his elder like he has the right, and Munroe lets him.

"That wolf's no fighter," Munroe sneers. "If he was, he wouldn't be here."

Without waiting for a response, he turns and begins the hike back through the rusted, leaning gates and up the rutted dirt road leading to the collection of squat concrete building and dilapidated clapboard houses that cluster along the river flowing down the mountain.

Leith stares at me. "You can run if you want," he says. "I won't chase you. The ferals will get you by dawn if you stay in one place and make some noise." His tone is light, and his eyes are dead.

Then he turns and follows Munroe.

Behind me, in the wilderness that sprawls in all directions, unearthly howls rise as if Leith summoned them.

It would be easy to let my wolf take our skin and do nothing as he bolts back to our mate through the feral-infested woods. Take our body back and let them tear us to shreds.

My mother's words ring in my head. *If you die, what happens to her?*

Izzy will never have to look at me again. She won't feel the male who raped her in her chest for the rest of her life. She'll be free.

Or is that wishful thinking? They say mates don't tend to survive long without each other. Grandma Floyd died within days of Grandpa Floyd. She refused to eat or drink. Mom said it was the grief that killed her.

Surely, Izzy wouldn't grieve for me. She'd be grateful.

How sure am I? Enough to risk her life?

I glance over my shoulder at the woods and then back at the mountain. Leith has already caught up with Munroe, yards up the road.

I don't have the energy to take a step in either direction. I want to lie down here in the dirt and pray a feral is hungry enough to brave the stench of wolf piss to come and drag me off. Take the chore of breathing away from me. Shut up the screaming in my brain for good.

But somewhere miles away Izzy exists.

So I force myself to take one step up the mountain, and then another, away from everyone I ever loved.

THEY LEAVE me with an old female named Shona at a huge house that looks like it's one strong gust of wind away from collapsing in on itself. Easily a dozen males lounge around a fire in a metal trash can out front. In the living room, a few more males are slumped on a sagging couch, snoring and farting. Two gaunt females bustle silently in the kitchen, scrubbing dishes and wrapping leftovers.

Shona leads me through the house to an enclosed porch in the back. In the corner, something tore the screen, and it hangs open like unzipped pants, letting mosquitoes in. Wood is stacked against the house's wall, and an old, yellowing chest freezer chugs like it's about to die. Either the compressor is failing or the condenser coils are filthy.

"You can sleep out here," she says. "I'll fetch a blanket."

I can't muster a thank you, but she doesn't wait for one, either.

I step through the creaky screen door and sit on the concrete blocks serving as steps to the patchy yard. A stiff breeze blows from higher up the mountain, and bedsheets snap on the line. Power lines run from the house to a half dozen outbuildings, none of them made the same, all of them leaning or sagging or missing slats of siding or shingles. The full moon is high and far, far away.

I don't belong here.

I don't belong anywhere.

The wind carries the males' shouts and laughter and the fading scent of turkey and cornbread stuffing. I can't bear it. I take off, ducking around the clothesline and jogging past the only outbuilding with a light on. I don't know where I'm going. Away from here.

I find the river that the town seems built along. A trail runs beside it. I jog uphill until my lungs burn, and I clear the last cluster of houses. The river curves, and the trail becomes stepped as it winds through a thick wood until it ends at a grassy field that slopes to a sandy beach and rocks that jut into the river.

On the far side of the field, a huge stone furnace stands in shambles as if it's being harvested for raw materials. Old tires are stacked or half-buried nearby like an obstacle course. The whole place smells like strange wolves and stale smoke.

I trot the rest of the way down to the river and kick off my shoes. The moon is bigger now. Closer. Its reflection ripples with the current.

I walk out on the cold, wet rocks that stretch nearly to mid-stream. Except for the rushing water, it's quiet. The screaming in my head echoes in the silence.

I'm exhausted, but I can't sleep. The nightmares have taught me not to lie down or close my eyes. In my dreams, I see Izzy's bare back and the thin line of her spine. I watch my claws plunge into the flesh of her hips and her blood run from her pale flesh to dribble into the dirt.

I'm a coward. I didn't fight hard enough. All the things I swore in my mind— that I'd love her, protect her, make her smile, never leave her alone, never let her go—I failed to do.

I let go. I left. And there's nothing I can do to make it right.

The weight of it is a mountain. An ocean.

My hand rises to rub the pulsing ache in my chest.

How do I live the rest of my life with this?

How does she?

How can I let her carry the weight alone?

I'm not brave, I'm not strong, and I've lost the right to

any claim on her. But how can I abandon her, too, after what I've done?

I close my eyes and press both palms to my chest. For the first time since the roof, I listen closely to the bond.

At first, I can hardly find it. The connection is more of a ghost, a blur, or a glitch. My brain is so beaten, so deaf from the screaming, that my attention keeps slipping, and it slides through my fingers, but I try, again and again, and eventually, I figure out how to focus and keep hold of it.

My pain fades. Izzy's agony replaces it. She's hurt. Scared.

Ashamed.

I stand on a rock jutting into the river with tears streaming down my cheeks as her pain flows into my chest. I welcome it. If I can take it from her, I will. I open myself completely, my arms rising to my sides of their own accord.

My muscles tense until they cramp. My teeth clench. I use every ounce of focus and sheer force of will to draw her pain into my body. It feels like letting your brother punch you in the gut with all his strength, but a thousand times worse. It's like taking fire without flinching, like standing still while a wolf rips into your neck.

Like I tore into Izzy's.

Her despair slices my insides to shreds, and the pain is a relief to me, but it doesn't help her. Her misery keeps flowing, relentless, pitiless.

It's not enough.

I'm failing her again.

I can't.

I won't.

The moon shines from miles above, so lovely despite the horrors it gazes down on. So distant, so useless.

Can Izzy see the moon from where she is now?

Would it make her feel better to see it? Females love the moon. As a bonding gift, males buy their mates necklaces with a charm of the phase of the moon on the night they met. I had it in my mind to buy one for Izzy. I'd dropped by the jeweler and priced it out.

The unholy racket in my brain threatens to distract me, but I've got the moon in my sights now. I don't know how to do what I want, but I'm not letting that stop me.

I'm going to give Izzy the moon.

I stare at it until my eyes blur. I imprint it on my brain until it belongs to me, and then I channel it to the bond and send it sailing like a folded paper boat in a stream. I pray, harder than I've ever prayed.

I send the moon's perfect roundness, its glow, the shadows of its seas. I send its glimmer on the water. I send its quiet. Its distance.

And then I listen.

Did it work? Maybe. I can't tell, not with any certainty, but I think maybe the pain is a little less sharp, maybe it's cutting a fraction less deep.

So I turn my attention to the moon's reflection on the water, focus with all my might, and send her the calming rush of the river and the flickering glitter of moonlight.

For a few hours, I shove my shame and self-loathing deep down and do the only thing I can for her other than pray, until I fall asleep, exhausted, on the rock.

I send her the beautiful things in the world.

Because the memory of her is the only beautiful thing left in mine.

5

———————

IZZY

Far away, in another world, a machine beeps and fluorescent lights glare overhead, but it's dark where I am. I'm asleep, I think, but not deep enough to escape the pain. This is a dream, and my body still hurts.

My wolf is curled in a ball on a cold, damp rock. Her nose is tucked to her chest. She shivers and shakes. A cold breeze riffles her fur. We're alone, scared and hurt. Our mate did this.

Why. Was he bitten? Is he feral? Moon mad? She has her eyes closed tight, but she can feel the outside yawning around us like a void and the moon floating every inch of two hundred and fifty thousand miles away.

She's angry at me. I ignored her and stayed away until it was too late. Now we're here, alone, and nothing will ever be right or good again. Our mate is our enemy now. He hurt us, ripped us to pieces, betrayed us, and dumped us on the ground for other males to tend. How could he do it? How could he leave us like that?

She whines and shakes, and she can't get warm.

Then her ears prick.

A click of claws on stone. A whiff of pepper, thyme, and sage. Our mate! Her heart leaps. And then she remembers.

He hurt us.

He *abandoned* us. *Twice.* He left us on the concrete side-walk, and before that, weeks ago, in the building that stinks like the fake pine and lemon that humans use to cover their tracks, he left us with the angry male who fathered us. Our mate doesn't want us. In the woods, he told us to leave. To run.

My wolf curls tighter. The fur along her spine prickles, and a low growl sounds in her chest.

Click, click, clack. He's coming closer. Slowly. Tentatively.

She whips her tail, warning him to stay away.

Click.

Clack.

He whines. He wants her to look at him.

She shoves her muzzle deeper into her chest. Traces of his fresh pain and grief still reach her nose.

Not fair! *She* is grieving. *She's* in pain. She lifts her snout and snarls at him over her shoulder.

Sinking to his belly, he lowers his head, laying it flat on the rock. The wolf is as pretty as his human, with bluish-gray fur sprinkled with wheat the color of his hair and the same blue-gray eyes. He blinks at her mournfully. She tucks her muzzle back to her chest and closes her eyes.

He's sorry, more than sorry—destroyed. What good will that do? She hurts so bad. She's so alone. He didn't stop this.

He crawls closer on his belly. She wants to turn on him, slash him with her claws, tear his flesh with her fangs and rip his heart from his chest, but she's too fragile, too broken, too exhausted to move.

First, she feels the absence of cold. He's blocking the

wind with his body. Then, a minute or an hour or a day later —there's no time in the dream—she feels a slight warmth on her back. She tries to snarl again, but it comes out as a sad, small whine. His chest rumbles as he closes the distance between them and curves his body around hers. His rumbles vibrate against her spine. If he means to soothe her, it won't work. Nothing can help.

Whining low in his throat, he nudges her muzzle with his cold nose. She blindly snaps her teeth. He left before. Why won't he leave now? His presence hurts. He's trying to block the bond, but he's a foolish male who thinks he can control nature, and don't we all know now that's impossible? His grief flows into her chest as his warmth sinks into her skin. She wishes she could drown in it.

He nudges her again and nips the tip of her ear. She twists her head, ready to snarl, ready to bite. He lifts his head and howls. *Look. The Moon.*

She glances up. Oh. The moon. How did it get so close? It's huge and hanging so low in the sky, the tops of the trees on the far side of the river cast black shadows on its bottom curve like veins. Everywhere the current ripples, moonbeams scatter shiny pearls. It's a dreamscape. No moon is that big, no night air is this crisp.

He lies his head back down on the stone. Exhausted, she rests hers on the crook of his neck. They both watch the moon as it slowly wanders westward. They're torn to pieces, lost, hurt, and scared. She's too tired to fight him, so they lie there, far away, in another world, together in the dark.

6

───────

IZZY, THE PRESENT

If you stare at the white walls in my bedroom long enough and let your eyes slide out of focus, the walls ripple. I first noticed it during the weeks after I came home from the infirmary when Mom let me stay in bed all day. In the early days, I stared at the ceiling, but when she made me sit up and stacked my missing work from my final courses on a lap desk, I stared at the wall and watched the waves.

There's no window in my room.

That was fine with me before Trevor when I was busy with school and my internship and piano and tennis. And it was fine with me after Trevor. I needed the dark. Mom would flick the light switch on with a huff, leave a tray with food or a basket of clean laundry, and as soon as she left, I'd drag myself out of bed and flick the lights off again.

I slept as many hours as my body would let me, and for some reason, I didn't have nightmares—I had the most beautiful, vivid dreams. Magical dreams. The black outline of a mountain peak against a background of scattered stars.

Purple asters bathed in moonlight. A soft brown doe with white spots grazing in a field of wildflowers beside her mother.

I can't say they were a comfort. I always woke with an aching pain in my chest, but they were the only not-horrible thing in my life, and that was something. I still have the dreams, but not every single night, and they don't leave me so bereft in the morning. Maybe because I've managed to numb everything—the good and the bad. The windowless room sure helped.

When my parents gave up on me finishing my internships and decided it'd be best that I work from home, I didn't need a window. I got a computer with the internet so I could work for accounting, doing billing. I was always good with numbers, so that was fine.

No one said I had to stay home, but they let me, so I did. It was easier than seeing the pity in everyone's eyes, better than trying to put people at ease while they think about how my own mate nearly killed me in a rut.

And it was easier than taking the elevator past the twelfth floor and wondering who is living in 1248 now.

Easier than passing the fifth floor and wondering if the hall in front of Trevor's old apartment might still smell a little like gravy.

Easier than being reminded by stairwells and soda cans and work boots that I had a mate, and he was kind, until I drove him into a rut and ruined both our lives.

Dad got the promotion—they weren't going to give it to someone else when his poor daughter was ripped to shreds in an infirmary bed—but they never moved us to a higher floor. Maybe if they had, I'd have gotten a room with a window, but they didn't, so I stare at a screen or at the walls.

And I wait.

For *something*.

Not for Trevor. He's never coming back.

Not for someone to tell me what happened to him. All they'll say is that I never have to see him again. If I push, they say don't upset yourself.

Not for someone to tell me what to do with myself now, how to get out of this room—this hole—and live life again.

Uncle Howell visited me the day I got home from the infirmary. He said no one blamed Trevor or me. It was an unfortunate tragedy. No one's fault. No one saw it coming, or it would never have been allowed to happen. When we were alone again, Dad told me that Uncle Howell was being kind. If I'd listened and stayed inside, I wouldn't be where I am.

No one visits anymore. Brynn and Teagan did in the beginning. I think Aunt Catrin made Brynn, and Brynn dragged Teagan along, and they made a habit of coming after work for a half hour so they could be fashionably late to happy hour. But then, last year, the whole pack kind of fell apart.

Cadoc Collins, the alpha's heir, mated a scavenger named Rosie, and when that romance ended with a showdown between him and his uncle, Cadoc led every scavenger in the bogs out of Moon Lake just like his grandfather led our ancestors out of the dens.

Apparently, scavengers did the bulk of the work needed to keep basic services running, so everyone got assigned a second job that they're calling "public service." Brynn and Teagan don't have time to visit now. They spend the hours after their day jobs in the High Rise cafeteria doing food prep.

Since I don't have to act okay anymore for visitors, I

spend a lot more time sitting on the edge of my bed and staring at a wavy wall until my head hurts. When I've had enough, I lie down, and if my mom asks why I'm in bed, I say I've got a migraine, and she's usually too frustrated with me to expend the energy to nag me about making myself useful.

Today is a Tuesday.

It's been five years since the terrible night, as I call it in my head.

The terrible night feels like yesterday and like something that happened decades ago to someone else. I'm no different than I used to be, but also, I've never been the same since.

I have an inbox full of action items that I could knock out in a half hour if I focused, and then I'd have the rest of the day to do whatever I want, but there's nothing I want to do.

There's no reason I shouldn't log on to my computer, clear some invoices, take a nap, shower, help make dinner, trudge through all the things I'm supposed to do. Today is a day like every other one.

There is no *reason* today should be different from yesterday.

Last night, I had a new dream, different from the usual moon or a river or bright green moss on a fallen log. I guess my subconscious is obsessed with the beauty of nature since I spend my life indoors.

I wonder what the weather's like outside today.

The weather was perfect in last night's dream. For the first time, I saw a crystal blue pool in a huge cavern with these gothic stalactites and stalagmites. Overhead, a natural skylight let in the sun. It was beautiful.

The cavern reminded me of the Old Den that we visited

on field trips back in primary school, but that cave was dusty and dim. This place was magical. The sun streamed down like liquid gold.

I feel like I haven't seen the sun in years. What did it even feel like on my skin? The memory of warmth from last night's dream is stronger.

Deep inside me, my wolf stirs, dragging herself up to sit on her haunches as she yawns. She still sleeps most of the day away. Lucky her. She never hits that point where she's slept so much that she can't sleep anymore.

I look down at myself. I'm wearing navy leggings, white ankle socks, and a blue plaid shirt two sizes too big that falls past my knees. I can hide my hands in the cuffs and my neck in the popped collar. It's my new uniform. Oversized flannel and soft pants.

I'm not wearing shoes. I rarely do. My sneakers are in a cubby in the closet.

I could put them on and go see what it's doing outside. It's March. The weather could go either way. Lion or lamb.

My wolf rises to her feet. She's interested. She's always bolder than me. At night, she takes our skin and runs through the wildflower fields and green forests in our dreams.

She watches me closely, her narrow eyes bright and eager. She wants to leave, but she thinks I'm going to chicken out.

She has good reason to doubt me. I haven't decided to go for a walk since that night.

It feels like it should be a momentous decision, not something you just do on a random Tuesday.

I'd have to pass Mom to leave. Is she home? I stand up and tap the touch pad on my laptop to see the time. It's one o'clock in the afternoon. Mom will be at work.

I'd have to take the elevator down to the lobby. There'll be people, and they'll stare. Maybe whisper. Everyone in the pack either pities me or blames me, but they all know what happened on the worst day of my life, and I bet they have all sent up prayers of thanks that they're not me.

And I'm going to walk past them and out the front doors with nowhere to go?

I blink, suddenly aware that I'm not sitting in bed or staring at the wall. I'm standing beside my desk. It wouldn't take much effort to reach out and slide the closet door open. I don't even need to take another step.

I don't have to be that brave. Just a tiny bit.

I open the closet. Instead of my sneakers, I grab fur-lined boots that I can just slip on. It might be too warm already for them, but they're comfortable, and they remind me of walking the Academy paths, books clutched to my chest, taking it slow and soaking in every second of freedom between classes.

Am I really going to leave this apartment? By myself?

I do have my boots on.

I glance at my bed. It's unmade. I could get back in and crawl under the covers. There's no reason I should push myself right this minute. Outside is always there. I can go out tomorrow. I've told myself this same thing a thousand times. No one is making me. No one blames me for hiding myself away. Mom, Aunt Catrin, Brynn, and Teagan have all said at some point that they can't imagine what it must be like to have gone through what I did.

That makes sense because I couldn't ever explain it.

My wolf sighs, lowers herself back down, and rests her chin on her front paws. She thinks we're going to give up.

Well, what does she know? Why shouldn't I go out?

It doesn't have to mean anything. No one will know if I get to the front door and chicken out.

Like I'm a puppeteer, I command my feet to move. I will my hand to twist the knob, will myself to walk through the living room and out into the hallway, and oh—my heart stutters. This is where I caught Trevor's scent and followed it down the stairs. The ache is a blade stuck in my chest.

I want to go back in time, grab his hand, and run.

I'm so alone.

I can't fix that, so I decide to be just a little brave instead. I walk out the front door and down the hall. I push the button for the elevator.

It's surreal. I haven't done this without Mom or Aunt Catrin in years. The elevator arrives. The bell dings. I get on. The doors shush closed. My wolf hops back to her feet, her whiskers quivering. No turning back now.

Of course, I could. It'd be so easy. I haven't seen anyone yet. No one will know that I tried and failed.

But maybe I'm not going to fail today. Maybe I'll keep going. Why not?

By the time we get to the lobby, my wolf is at full attention. When I get my first lungful of fresh air, she stands stock still, alert and listening for danger, but as I cross the marble courtyard, she bursts into motion. She dashes to the border between us and then races in figure eights inside me, yipping with unbridled excitement. She wants me to run. She wants the wind in her face.

My lips quirk.

After the terrible night, she never came out again. She never even tried. She's not trying now, but she is ecstatic to be along for the ride. I set off down the sidewalk, and she howls in delight.

I'm actually not sure if she *can* come out, even though Abertha, the wise woman, reassured me that my wolf is fine.

The first night I spent in the infirmary, Abertha came by. She kicked Mom and Aunt Catrin out and asked me if I wanted a pup. I threw up in the bean-shaped plastic dish the nurse had left beside me on the mattress and burst into hysterics.

Abertha hollered for boiling water and a cup, and after she scrubbed my face clean with a handkerchief that smelled like weed and patchouli, she pressed a pill into my palm and brewed me a pot of chamomile tea. She told Mom that the pill was to calm my nerves. She told me I didn't have to worry about anything but healing.

Every evening during those early days, Abertha came and sat beside me for hours. Someone found her a rocking chair, and she rocked, slowly, back and forth on the high heels of her black granny boots.

She told me all kinds of things—that Fate feels cruel because she's tempering steel, that time heals all wounds, that she knew nothing she said would make anything better, but she'd keep talking just in case.

She said that my wolf wasn't broken, she was scared, and she'd come when she's ready. Abertha said everything happens in its own time.

Abertha talked for hours, day after day, rocking, her silver hair glowing in the moonlight that shone in through a high window, and she was right, nothing she said made anything better, but I didn't feel alone.

I wish I understood how she was able to sit with me when everyone else bailed as soon as they politely could, how she had no problem looking me in the eye when no one else could, but the questions didn't occur to me 'til years afterward, and I didn't see much of her after I was discharged. She won't enter the High Rise or the Tower. She says they stink of betrayal and avarice, and it messes with her sinuses.

Thinking of Abertha reminds me of the infirmary, and as I stride toward the lake, my steps take on purpose and direction.

I leave the tall buildings of downtown behind and follow the promenade along the water, passing the Academy to the left, and the statue of the Great Alpha Broderick Moore's wolf, larger than life, gazing into the distance, with his foreleg raised as if he's about to run off the pedestal.

Now the scavengers live in the dens he left to come here. We hear through the grapevine that rogue shifters from other packs are finding their way there, too.

Is Trevor there?

Where did they send him?

Did he go feral? I don't think so. I'm sure I'd feel that even though I keep the bond muted. I figured out how to do that early on. I don't think about it.

It's weird I don't think about the bond, but I think about Trevor every day. I search color swatches on the internet and try to find the exact blue-gray shade of his eyes. I picture his smile, close my eyes, and trace my own lips so I don't forget the shape. I take him out of a box in my brain and put him carefully back a dozen times a day.

But I never, ever talk about him.

Mom acts like he's the kind of devil that shows up if you say his name three times. She always lowers her voice when she brings him up. Dad leaves the room if anyone even alludes to what happened.

I'm supposed to hate him. Fear him.

I'm afraid when I remember that night, and I hate what

he *did*, but I don't hate him. I don't even know him. I never got the chance.

The loss is a weight, but for once, it doesn't sap all my energy. I stroll along the empty promenade and fill my lungs with the breeze coming off the lake. There is no one around. Everyone's at work.

Before the brick walk turns to gravel, I veer off onto South Street. I don't have a clear plan in mind. I follow my gut, and I'm sure it's my imagination, but I feel a sensation like wind at my back, urging me onward. I pass Food Services and the off-site Facilities Maintenance compound.

My heart thumps faster as I get further from the water and closer to the woods. I know where I'm going—back to the scene of the crime. Not to the clearing where it happened. I'm not nearly brave enough to go there, but the infirmary.

I spent enough time there five years ago. Shifters mend quickly, but as Abertha explained, my body had too much to do, dealing with the loss of a mate and the physical injuries. The worst was the bite Trevor took out of my shoulder. A human plastic surgeon had to assist our healer to recon-struct the muscle enough so my shifter healing could take over.

I try not to look at the scar, but sometimes, when I shower, I catch sight of it in the mirror, and I'm transfixed. It's too jagged to be a mating mark, but it's in the right place.

Did Trevor want to claim me or kill me? I can't make up my mind. Did he even have conscious intent, as lost as he was in the rut?

I wish there was someone I could ask, but I'd sooner stick a poker in my eye than talk to Mom or Aunt Catrin about it.

My head is so busy that I arrive at the infirmary before I

realize it. I don't remember much from the night Trevor brought me here, just the pain and how desperate I was to get away from him and how heartbroken I was when he left me.

The infirmary is bigger in my memory. In reality, it's a simple, one-story building with white siding and a concrete ramp leading to the front double doors. Next to the entrance, there is an enclosed bulletin board with a little slanted roof with a bunch of faded flyers posted.

FLEAS ARE EVERYONE'S PROBLEM.

Reminder: Report Workplace Injuries Promptly to Human Resources at x4567.

You're a Shifter, Not a Superhero—Wear Your Safety Gear.

I pretend to read as I sweat bullets and breathe through a wave of delayed panic. What am I doing here? This is stupid. Unnecessary. I have work I need to do at home.

So, I can walk to the infirmary. Am I brave now? Am I fixed?

Suddenly, the doors fly open and slam the siding, and I nearly jump out of my skin.

Abertha struts out like a diva through a stage curtain. She's wearing a white doctor's coat over her customary flowy skirt. The fake gold coins sewn into the flounces tinkle as she moves. "Oh. Izzy. Good. You're here." She peers up and down the empty street. "Are you the only one?"

"Only one?" I croak. The scene suddenly becomes surreal. There is no one else in sight, and no noise, either, no cars or birds. The whole block feels like a ghost town.

She glances around and sniffs. "Well, time is money. Come on in. Let's get started."

"Started with what?"

"Orientation," she says like I'm being dense.

"Orientation?"

She thumps the glass covering the bulletin board, pointing to a neon green flyer that I hadn't noticed.

NURSING AIDE ORIENTATION. TUESDAY. 2 PM.

"Oh. I'm not here for that."

"Are you sick?" she asks, not like the infinitely patient Abertha from when I was hurt, but like the scary, crotchety witch I always thought she was when I was a kid, before I knew her.

"I'm fine. I was just—" Just what? Going for a walk? For the first time in five years? My cheeks heat. I have no idea what I'm doing.

"Well, you're here, and it's Tuesday at 2 p.m. It's nursing aide orientation time. Come on. Time's a-wasting." She turns, her skirts twirling, and disappears into the building.

Despite her age, she walks with a dancer's grace. She doesn't move like a grandma, maybe because she doesn't have children.

"Come on, Izzy. Time waits for no woman," she shouts out the door.

I could go home. I could tell her that I'm sorry, but I'm tired, and it wouldn't even be a lie. I'm bone weary from a leisurely twenty-minute stroll. Today doesn't have to be the day.

But it could be.

"Procrastination is the thief of—" Abertha stops mid-holler as I step into the infirmary.

The painfully familiar smell hits me first—antiseptic, latex, and that gross pink hand soap they use—and triggers my memories hard. The cold seeping into my forearm from the IV. Holding my pee because it burned, and I didn't want to ask for help getting to the bathroom. The nurse spraying my hair with a squirt bottle, slowly working dried clumps of blood out of the strands.

My gaze sweeps the space. Nothing's changed. There's a registration desk to my right and a waiting area to my left. Patient bays line the walls and computer and supply stations are clustered down the middle of the room. All but one of the curtains are open, so there is only one patient.

Except for a nurse stocking a cabinet, no one is around. Boisterous, joking voices filter from the break room in the rear. That sound is etched into my memory, too. My room was close to that door.

Abertha nods at the nurse and strides with purpose to the only bay with the closed curtain. Thankfully, it's nowhere near the one I was stuck in for nearly two weeks.

As she nears the bay, she whistles like a human calling a dog, waits a few seconds, and throws the curtain open.

A sleepy-eyed pup, a male no older than five or six, struggles to sit up in bed. "'Bertha," he says, scrubbing his eyes.

He's missing a front tooth, his arm is in a sling, and ash blond curls stick out from the white bandage wrapped around his head like a sweatband. He looks so small in the big cot. The scent of his misery hurts my stomach. I glance around for his mother, but he's alone.

"Did you bring me something?" he asks Abertha plaintively, swiping at his nose.

"No, 'nice to see you?' No 'how was your day?' Straight to 'what did you bring me,' eh?" she grumbles gently as she digs in a well-concealed skirt pocket and plucks out a small, brown ceramic buffalo.

The male's sad, tired eyes widen.

"Guess where I got this?" Abertha asks.

"The store," he guesses, reaching for his present with his good arm.

"Nope." Abertha places it in his palm. "I got it in a box of Tetley's tea."

"You're joking." His brow wrinkles.

"I'm not." She crosses her heart. "I was just as surprised as you to find him in there. Seemed an unlikely place for a buffalo."

He examines his treasure, somber and serious, like the buffalo is the important thing, not the boot on his lower right leg or the IV in his thin arm.

My heart twinges. He is such a little guy. He can't weigh more than forty pounds. "What happened?" I whisper, anxiety stealing my voice. Did someone hurt him?

"Harri here had the inspired idea of riding the Great Alpha Broderick Moore, but he miscalculated how slippery a bronze statue can be. By all accounts, he fell off like a pinball. Got his ankle twisted up with Broderick's leg, broke his arm when he landed, and cracked his head on the pedestal for good measure."

I gasp.

Harri balefully bares his teeth. "I broke a tooth, too, see?"

"I do see," I say, collecting myself, willing my nerves to settle down. No one hurt him. He's in good hands, and he'll be okay. Pre-shift pups heal slower, but they're still sturdy. "That must have hurt."

"It did," he nods. "I'm in trouble now."

"I'm sure you're not."

He shakes his head like I'm sadly mistaken. "Dad told me the next time I screw up, I've got to go live in the bogs."

"He didn't mean it. That's just a thing parents say when they're mad." Mine said the same to me all the time.

Harri sighs. "No, I've done it now. Sometimes sorry doesn't cut it." He says it like he's heard it a hundred times. My dad would always say, "You're always sorry. Words won't cut it this time."

I don't know what to say to reassure him. His round, solemn eyes are breaking my heart.

"This is Izzy," Abertha interjects, finished with her cursory examination of Harri's injuries. "She's new. I'm going to teach her how to change a bandage. Are you okay with that?"

"Okay," Harri agrees, already distracted by his buffalo.

"Follow me," Abertha says and leads me over to the supply closet. The nurse has disappeared, and the voices from the break room are even louder. The place feels so empty.

I was never alone when I was here. Nurses woke me up every few hours to check my vitals, and people were in and out of my room constantly once I was well enough for visitors. Everyone dropped by—former instructors and people I worked with at my internships and basically anyone I ever had a conversation with at the Academy.

Some of them meant well, but most of them seemed more interested in either doing the expected thing or getting the dirt firsthand. Either Mom or Aunt Catrin held court at the foot of my bed during the day and accepted folks' expressions of horror and dismay on my behalf. I wasn't talking much at that point.

"Here," Abertha says and hands me a roll of gauze and some medical tape.

I glance over at Harri. He hardly makes a bump under the sheets. Why isn't anybody keeping watch over him?

"Where is his mother?" I ask quietly.

"The High Rise," Abertha murmurs back. "It's the end of

quarter. Mom and Dad can't be spared. They've got an IQ report to finalize."

"10-Q." I know it. It's the quarterly financial report that gets filed with the human SEC.

"10-4 right back at you, good buddy," Abertha says, winks at me, and heads back to Harri.

"Ready for a fresh wrapping?" Abertha asks him.

He nods, his focus on the buffalo that he's trotting over the hills his knees make. His relative calm lasts until the exact moment that Abertha unwinds the bandage enough that she's pulling off the gauze that sticks to his hair with dried blood. Tears gather in his blue eyes, and his lower lip wobbles. He tries to be brave, but climbing onto a huge wolf statue is one thing, and having your hair tugged out by the root is another.

His hands dig into the sheets as he gulps down breaths, visibly trying not to cry. Males are taught young to hold in their tears, but they don't usually master it until they're older than Harri. He fights his hardest—screwing his eyes closed and mashing his lips together, but he loses the fight, and as fat tears dribble down his cheeks, the bitter scent of his distress singes the air.

Immediately, a memory bursts into my brain, but not one of the usual ones that plague me—not the dirt in my mouth or the broken bones in my wrist grinding together. Not the view of Trevor's back as my wolf lay limp on the pavement in front of the infirmary.

A vivid picture of Trevor sitting next to me on the counter in apartment 1248 flashes in my head. I was lightly drumming my heels against the cabinets beneath me because of my nerves. I glanced down and saw that Trevor was drumming his heels, too. The memory slips between my ribs, plunging into my heart. Something sharp and hard, something like guilt, leaks into my chest like ink.

Trevor didn't know what he was doing any more than I did. He was trying to be cool and confident, but he was young, too.

Why am I thinking about this now?

I shake off the memories and sink to my knees beside Harri's cot. Abertha has paused, giving him a break. She's only about a quarter way done with the bandage.

I'm not sure what to say to comfort him. I've never been in this position before. He's opened his eyes, and he's looking at me like I have the answer.

I guess I do. I've been in that bed before while a strange female changed my bandages.

"It's going to hurt," I tell him. "But only this much." I hold my fingers an inch apart. "And it's not going to hurt any worse than it already has, okay?"

He nods and sniffles.

I dig deeper. "It won't take more than two minutes max. Look up there." I point to the big clock with the white face and black numbers and the word Standard above the six. Like the smell in the air and the texture of the sheets, the clock face is also burned into my memory. "See the thinnest hand? The quick one?"

Harri nods again.

"By the time it goes around in a circle twice, Abertha will be all done. Okay? It'll only hurt for that long, no longer, and it won't get any worse."

"Are you sure?" he asks.

"I promise."

"Okay," he says and grabs my hand.

I squeeze it tight. "Okay," I repeat.

Abertha unwinds the rest of the gauze, doing her best to

hold his hair to give his scalp a break, while Harri and I intently watch the clock. She finishes at the exact moment the second hand ticks onto the twelve for the second time.

Harri blinks at me. "You were right."

"I was." Something loosens in my chest.

"Want to see my buffalo?" he asks, his tears already forgotten.

"Sure."

I admire the buffalo, and then Abertha shows me how to rewrap Harri's head. Harri's eyelids droop as she tells me about his arm and ankle, how the treatment of fractures differs between shifters and humans, and how pups, the aged, and the heartbroken take longer to heal.

After Harri falls asleep, Abertha walks me around the infirmary, showing me what's in all the cabinets and closets. The medics and nurses eventually emerge from the break room and offer us a slice of cake. It's someone's birthday.

We both decline, and Abertha says we've done enough for the day, and she'll walk me back to the Tower. Harri is still asleep when we leave. That's good.

We make our way back slowly along the lakefront promenade. The work day is over, and we're walking against the flow as people stream from the High Rise and head to the marina for a drink or the shops and restaurants downtown. Everybody is busy. Everyone has a purpose.

About a block from the Tower, Abertha veers off to linger at the low wall that prevents pups from tumbling into the lake. The sunset has caught her attention. I stand next to her, and we both gaze across the lake to where the sun is sinking below the top of Salt Mountain.

"You did well today," Abertha says, breaking the silence.

"I didn't really do anything."

Abertha sighs, long and loud. "Do you know how much

I'd get done in a day if I didn't have to undo all the bullshit that first wolf did?"

"Which wolf?"

"That first wolf who decided that rank was a thing, and he wanted to be on top of it, and he was going to undermine everyone's natural confidence to do it."

"Who was he?"

"I do not know, but I guarantee, he was male, and he was unsatisfied with the size of his dick." Abertha snorts and then takes a deep breath. "Never mind that. Let's circle back. You, Izzy Owens, did well today. I suspected you had the makings of a good healer, and you'd come to it when the time was right, and I'm pleased to discover that yet again, I'm right."

"I just followed you around and listened."

"First of all, don't knock the ability to listen. Second, you proved that you have the instincts of a true healer."

My cheeks flame, and I can't meet Abertha's eyes. I've never been able to take a compliment, and I think that's what she's doing, even though she sounds like her usual salty self. I'm too shy to ask her what she means, so I'm happy when she explains.

"If you listen to humans, or our people who trained with humans, they'll convince you that knowledge is the key to healing. To them, it's all about diagnosis and treatment regimens and standards of care. Pain is a symptom, and not an important one. Doctors will even tell a patient that their pain isn't as bad as they say."

"How would they even know that?"

Abertha shrugs. "Well, if knowledge is the key to healing, and you know everything, I guess you know how much a person does or doesn't hurt. A real healer gives the brain its due, but she pays equal attention to the heart and gut, and she will tell you that pain isn't 'the body's alarm system' or a number on a scale from one to ten. It's a *power*, a destructive power, and its damage isn't incidental. You knew that, so you tended to Harri's pain, and your instincts were solid. You told him how bad it would be and when it would end."

Of course, I did. "Anyone would do the same, right?"

"Would *anyone*?" She pierces me with her hard gray eyes, and I know she's thinking about our long evenings alone in the infirmary, the nurses tiptoeing in and out as quickly as they could, my mother gone as soon as visiting hours were over, even though she was allowed to stay.

"I can't be a nursing aide. I already have a job. I work in accounting."

"Doing what? Going clickety-clack all day?" She mimes typing on a keyboard.

"I work from home. I don't leave much." I'm not sure why I'm arguing. The idea that I'd just up and switch jobs was ridiculous a few hours ago, but now, it's got a shininess to it.

"You left today."

"I have no idea why," I say softly, watching the evening breeze blow gentle ripples across the surface of the lake. "Why today? I didn't have a plan. I didn't know anything about orientation." I glance over at Abertha. "Nothing happened or changed. It's just a random Tuesday."

She nods. Her expression is serious, but her eyes are oddly warm. "Yeah, that's how it happens. You fall into a deep, dark hole, and then some random Tuesday, for no particular reason, you decide to climb out. That's a power, too."

"Climbing out of a hole?"

"*Deciding*." She smiles, flashing her gold tooth. "So are

you going to be my apprentice, Izzy? I'll warn you ahead of time, the job pays jack shit, and there's a lot of bodily fluids."

My parents will never agree. Mom is always nagging me to get out more, but she doesn't mean to do menial work among lower ranked wolves. I'm not sure why exactly Dad will lose his mind about it, but I have no doubt he will.

That should be enough for me to make an excuse and scurry back to my room, but it's a random Tuesday, and by some miracle, I dragged myself out of a deep, dark hole today, so instead, I say, "What are the hours?"

And I decide to change my life.

7

———

IZZY

I was right. Mom and Dad were dead set against me giving up my "prestigious" position working for accounting from my bedroom. They basically shouted me down every time I brought it up. I didn't stop bringing it up, though. I'd drop it as soon as Dad's wolf showed his fangs, but I kept trying.

I wasn't getting anywhere until one day, I ran into Abertha on my now daily walks along the lake shore. I explained to her that I was working on it, and she said, "I want you to know, what I'm about to do, I wouldn't do for anyone I didn't truly believe was going to make my life a butt-load easier."

And then, the next day, Dad got a call from Uncle Howell who told him Madog Collins heard that I wanted to work at the infirmary, and he should let me.

For the next year, I apprentice with Abertha when she's in town, and when she disappears on her mysterious errands, I do grunt work around the infirmary—stocking shelves, mopping floors, and laundry. So much laundry. It's not fun or

easy work. Mom thinks it's beneath me and lets me know every chance she gets, telling me that my hands are chapped and my clothes stink like pine cleaner as if I don't know.

I'm not a big fan of the grunt work, but healing clicks in a way that piano and tennis and accounting and corporate communications never did. It's like the deeper I go inside myself, the better I get at doing the outside work.

Like, for example, one of my first lessons was about medicinal plants. Abertha and I would trek through the woods for hours, searching for the big three—dragon's tongue, ashbalm, and wolf's bane. We rarely got lucky, but when we ended the day empty-handed, she'd say, "Good work today. We're narrowing it down. We'll have better luck tomorrow."

That was when I still had trouble leaving my room some days or holding it together all day. I'd beat myself up about it, and then, inevitably, the next day Abertha would say, "Let's go hunting."

Eventually, I learned the lesson. Failure isn't the end of the world. You're narrowing it down. Your chances will be better tomorrow. And they were. I hate going home now. I like it better at the infirmary where I'm useful.

I've learned so many things—how to sit quietly with someone who's hurting and let my presence be a comfort. How to crack a joke when the fluids get embarrassing and how late-night radio and singing along together and sharing a snack eases pain. How to clean a wound and bathe a hot face with a cold washcloth and which teas are best for fevers, which are best for frights, and which are best for heartbreak.

With my small paycheck, I buy a crossbody bag for the tools of my new trade—tissues, tweezers, throat drops, and tiny curiosities like the animal figurines that apparently come in tea boxes, although never in a box I've bought.

I realize what's happening—Abertha is teaching me to heal myself—but I also love what I'm doing. I'm good at it. After they're discharged, when I pass patients on the long walks I take now, they'll say hello, and there's no pity in their eyes. I'm not a tragedy to them. I was a helper.

And then, on a random Thursday, after a year as her apprentice, Abertha tells me I've learned everything I'm capable of understanding—which doesn't sound like a ringing endorsement, but from Abertha, feels like high praise—and that I've graduated to healer, and my first official task is to cover for her and go to Quarry Pack to make a swap with their alpha female.

My parents are totally against it, but they don't dare interfere with anything Abertha wants since Madog made it clear that he backed her when it comes to me.

I haven't left pack territory since an Academy field trip to Old Den. I was nervous then, surrounded by packmates, and that was before my life skidded into a brick wall. I'm terrified now. I'm not ready. I've had no time to prepare.

That's what repeats in my head as I follow Abertha to a bus behind the sportsplex. She's arranged for me to hitch a ride with fighters going to train with Killian Kelly, the alpha of Quarry Pack. I pray I don't run into him. I've never met him in person, but I've seen video. He tears huge males up in the ring like a pup biting the heads off gummy bears.

I sit in the seat right behind the bus driver, and as I expect, the males leave me alone and respectfully avert their eyes. Young, unmated males are especially careful around me. They've obviously been told to steer clear.

I wouldn't want their attention, but still—it makes me feel lonely.

Ironically, I was less lonely when I spent all day by myself in my bedroom. Now, I'm surrounded by mates who love each other and pups and families, and every day, the fact that I'll never have that is hammered home.

It's not like I want a male, per se.

I want to sit on the steps, sipping a cold soda, and feeling one thousand percent alive.

I want to close my eyes, hit a button, and start over again on a countertop under a vent in apartment 1248.

I'm so distracted by the memory that I don't have time to work myself up about meeting Una, the Quarry Pack alpha's mate. Even if I had, I would've relaxed right away.

She greets me with her pup when I get off the bus. Raff, a male about two years old, races to and from her like the kid's toy with the rubber ball and a paddle, rebounding off her legs like a bumper car.

He's wearing a miniature version of the muscle shirt and athletic shorts that seems to be the pack males' uniform. Una's style is much more earthy. Her thick, braided hair dangles almost to her waist, and she wears a long, flowy skirt like Abertha's and an almost ethereally calm expression.

"Welcome to Quarry Pack," she says, smiling. "Got my drugs?"

I hold up the jar of dragon's tongue that we're trading for what Abertha told me are "assorted herbs, for fun and profit, and mushrooms both edible and magical."

She shuffles forward to take the jar. I've heard that she limps, but it's not as noticeable as people make it sound.

"Lucan will stow your things in the bus," she says, gesturing to a snaggle-toothed male with an overflowing basket. He gives me a friendly jerk of his chin and bounds onto the bus. My stomach tenses, and it takes me a second to realize that I'm unsettled because he made direct eye contact. He doesn't know to treat me like I'm damaged. It feels strange, but not bad.

"Well, now that business is done, we have the rest of the day to ourselves while the males smack each other around." Una doesn't seem to mind. She actually seems delighted by the prospect. "Would you like to see our bees first?"

"Absolutely." The day is taking on a real magical quality. The weather is mild, the trees are a fresh, spring green past the worst of the pollening, and Quarry Pack itself is charming— a rustic camp with wide paved trails leading from its quaint woodsy cabins and low whitewashed buildings.

"Ready, pup?" Una asks.

"Mama, up," Raff says, lifting his arms in the air.

As soon as Una picks him up, Raff starts to try and take the dragon's tongue from Una.

"That's not for pups," she tells him firmly.

He actually growls and tries to peel her fingers off the jar.

"Raff! No!" She seems genuinely surprised that her pup's not listening, but even though he can't be more than twenty-five pounds, I can smell his dominance.

"No, Mama," he says adamantly. "Daddy says you don't carry. Remember?"

"Oh." Una flushes and shoots me a glance. "Killian's always telling him to take care of me." She smacks a kiss on Raff's forehead. "Thank you, baby, but this is glass. Mommy carries glass."

"Daddy says no," Raff repeats, and he leaves off trying to take the dragon's tongue, but by his tone, he thinks Una will regret her choices. He has "just wait 'til Daddy finds out" written on his face.

Una sighs and calls, "Lucan?" The snaggle-toothed male trots over and grabs the jar. "Happy?" she asks her son.

He smacks a kiss on her cheek and smiles. "Good Mommy."

The Kellys show me all around their territory—the beehives, a greenhouse with a mysterious locked back room, and the terraced garden where they grow the flowers and herbs for the potpourri, perfumes, and lotions that they sell at their store in the local human town. *And* to ship internationally, Una tells me with obvious pride.

After the tour, we have lunch, and then sit on her porch and sip sun tea that she brews herself. Her pups play with their friends in the grassy commons in front of her cabin, and it feels like a summer camp you'd see in a TV show or movie, complete with the gnats and crickets. Time feels slower, but not in a bad way. I thought being away from pack territory would be nerve-racking, but this is the most relaxed I've felt in years.

"Any news about Cadoc?" she asks after we've polished off a few lemon cookies. "He trained here a few years back, not long after Killian and I mated. We were surprised when he broke with Moon Lake. He seemed like a very" —her nose wrinkles as she searches for a word—"straitlaced male. He certainly didn't seem like the type to lead a rebellion."

Straitlaced is an understatement. He's quite a bit younger than me, but he never seemed *young*. At the Academy, he was always the voice of authority, even before his wolf came.

"I guess you never know about a person," I say.

Una hums in agreement.

"Old Den is doing well," I tell her. "Apparently, they're overflowing the actual dens, so they're doing a lot of construction."

When Cadoc first led the scavengers out of Moon Lake, there was no communication between the packs, and there was talk of war, but then Madog came back from the mysterious mission that had taken him away when the fight between Cadoc and Alban Hughes went down.

Slowly but surely, Madog has been putting things to rights, and now a few council members have made diplomatic trips to Old Den. They issue official statements afterward, but the good tea comes from the folks they take with them.

"They've been taking refugees from Salt Mountain. Males as well as females."

Una rounds her eyes. "Really?"

I nod. It's extremely unusual for a pack to accept a male from another pack. I didn't believe it myself at first, but we've heard the stories a few times now.

"We haven't been to Old Den in a while. There was a bit of an—shall we say *incident*—last time we traveled, so Killian's put a moratorium on me leaving pack territory."

"An incident at Old Den?"

She shakes her head. "No. North Border."

I really want to ask what happened, but even though Una feels like a normal, everyday female, like a person who I would've been friends with at work or the Academy, the hulking, hard-faced males posted about a yard away in every direction don't let me forget that she's an alpha female, and I'm not going to pry into an alpha female's business.

My brain searches for a change of topic, and for some reason, it returns to Old Den.

And how Old Den has taken in males from Salt Mountain.

Why would a male leave his pack?

Because he was exiled?

Even though I'm sitting in a rocking chair, I feel the strange sensation of wind at my back again, like I did the day I ended up in nursing aide orientation.

A question pops out of my mouth. "When you visited Old Den, did you meet a male my age named Trevor?"

My throat constricts the instant the name leaves my mouth. I haven't said it aloud in five years.

Inside my chest, my wolf cracks an eye open as if she wasn't dead to the world a second ago.

Una's forehead scrunches. "You know what—yeah. Last time we were at Old Den, Cadoc was showing off this pump they've installed to improve plumbing—apparently it was a big deal—and he introduced the males working on the project. One was named Trevor. He was really reserved. The only reason I noticed him was because while the rest of us were talking, he was making sure an old male in a rocking chair drank his water. That's what made me remember him. It was funny to me that they'd dragged a rocking chair out to a worksite so they could keep an eye on an elder. I thought it was sweet."

My heart beats faster. I feel raw. Exposed. Like I've stepped out of the shower into the cold. "Did he have curly hair and blue eyes?"

"I'm sorry. I don't remember." She smiles apologetically. I can tell she wants to ask me why I want to know, but she doesn't pry. She has a healer's way about her. I wonder if she studied under Abertha, too, before she became an entrepreneur.

"Have you visited Old Den yourself?" she asks, gracefully changing the subject herself.

The conversation continues from there, and it's a pleasant, easy visit. No one bothers me on the bus ride back to Moon Lake, probably because all the males look like wrung out dishcloths, and half of them pass out before the bus even leaves Quarry Pack territory. Training must've been brutal.

I deliver the basket of herbs and 'shrooms to Abertha's cottage before I head home. She's not home, and from the size of the gravity feeder she left out for her cat, she's off on one of her adventures.

I take my time walking back to the Tower, enjoying the glitter of moonlight on the lake. That's one of my most frequent dreams—moonlight on water—although now that I think of it, I haven't had that one in a while.

The entire time I'm making my way back to my parents' apartment, and all night, as I toss and turn instead of conking out like I usually do, and for the rest of the weekend, I wonder about the male named Trevor at Old Den.

Una could be wrong. She must meet hundreds of shifters.

There are a lot of names like Trevor. Travis, for example. Trent. Tristan.

It's too much of a coincidence that I would think to ask, and she'd have met him. I've read about how susceptible witnesses are to the power of suggestion.

I'm still thinking about it on Monday morning as I make my way to the infirmary for my shift.

What would Trevor be doing at Old Den? The pack didn't even exist when he left Moon Lake. It's more likely another Trevor, a relative of the old male. Males don't tend to care for other males unless they're related, and that's only if there's no female around to do the work.

How would Trevor have ended up at Old Den?

Where did he go? Or where was he sent? Why did I never *really* try to find out what happened to him? I asked Mom and Dad, they told me to leave it alone, and I did.

Because I do what I'm told. Like I did when they told me to wait to mate him.

Like I did that night when Trevor said *run*.

Chills run down my arms, and I tug my sweater tighter.

Why am I torturing myself with this? Even if it is my Trevor, what would that matter?

He's not really *my* Trevor, is he?

Yes.

Yes, he is.

I stop in my tracks, right at the foot of the ramp leading to the infirmary doors, with my water tumbler in one hand and my lunch bag in the other. My wolf wakes up, her eyes wide and bright. She never gets up this early.

It's not her voice that said *yes, he is*.

It's mine.

And I'm right. Trevor Floyd is my mate. He did a horrible thing, or a horrible thing happened. I've never really decided how to put it, but however you put it, he's my mate.

Fate made him for me, and me for him.

And then she fucked everything up.

Or did she? It wasn't all on her, was it? I listened to my parents and Uncle Howell and stayed away. Then, when I was too far gone to think straight, I snuck out. He begged me to go back home, and I didn't.

Trevor wasn't the only one to blame—that's the cold, hard truth—but other things are true, too.

I did what I was told. I was loyal to my parents. Of course, I was. They'd trained me to obey them.

Every piano practice that bored me out of my mind, every tennis practice when I was exhausted from school, and every argument I had to swallow to keep Dad's wolf appeased taught me how to ignore my own interests and needs and thoughts.

Of course, everything blew up. My parents raised a powder keg.

Each realization lands on me like a blow, knocking the very last remnants of denial and indoctrination out of my brain, until I'm standing in the middle of the sidewalk, clutching my water bottle and lunch bag in my shaking hands while my heart cracks on a random Monday morning.

I lost my mate, but he's still alive, and even if he hates me, he's mine.

My heart feels freshly ripped from my chest. I'm not sure why.

Inside the infirmary, someone drops a tray loud enough to be heard through the doors. I blink, dragged back to reality, and as I gaze around to get my bearings back, my eye catches on a neon green flyer on the enclosed bulletin board with its little slanted roof. I read it, expecting an advertisement for nursing aide orientation—which must be due since there hasn't been one since mine over a year ago, and we are perpetually short-staffed—but instead, it reads MOON LAKE – OLD DEN GOODWILL EXCHANGE.

As I stare at it, I feel that strange wind blow at my back.

Well.

If I was waiting for a sign—

There it is.

8

IZZY

With the notable exception of dealing with Mom and Dad's epic meltdown, signing up for the goodwill exchange is easy. I fill out a form. I go to an orientation where a council member explains that our mission at Old Den is to advance the three Rs—rapprochement, rapport, reconciliation—through the three Ss—skills, service, and support.

Moon Lake is sending people with medical and mechanical skills—for some reason *not* referred to as the two Ms—and Old Den is sending us scavengers who, if I understood the council-speak correctly, are going to engage in talks with our leaders about normalizing relations. No one seemed optimistic about that. I imagine at this point, the scavengers would rather skin their own wolves than rejoin this pack, especially since they've already hauled all their homes out of the bogs.

My parents think the whole thing is a farce, and that the pack is better off without the scavengers. Of course, they say this in between complaining about the extra hours they

have to work and how everything from trash removal to building maintenance seems to be falling apart.

When I first told them what I was planning, they forbade it. They said if I left, I wouldn't be welcome back in *their* home. Then, the next night, we had dinner at Uncle Howell and Aunt Catrin's.

Dad told them how I applied, like the crazy mess I am, but that of course, I'd thought better of it. Uncle Howell got really flustered. Apparently, the program is Madog Collins's pet project, and he's been really concerned at how few people have signed up. If I bow out, he'll notice, and he'll want to know why, and that is the kind of attention we don't need now that things are so precarious.

Mom and Dad couldn't say anything after that, and now, two weeks later, I'm in a van driving down a dirt road, hours from home.

My stomach is a barbed wire ball of nerves, and I've already sweat through my collared shirt, even though it's a lightweight cotton, and it's only June.

I'm terrified. I've never not had a room to hide in. I've never not had a routine. Hopefully, they'll tell me what to do right away. All the unknowns have me on the edge of panic. The only thing keeping me somewhat steady is the weird kernel of fluttery warmth in my chest. I can't quite nail down what it is—one second it feels like anticipation, the next like hope, and then sheer terror.

Luckily, the three other "ambassadors," as the council is calling us, are not the talkative type. One is a nurse from the infirmary. She prefers human methods, so we don't work together often. The other two are males from Facilities. Did they know Trevor?

Is he going to be there? If he is, what do I say when I see him?

Does he hate me?

I'm almost tempted to search out the bond, but what if I do, and all I sense is disgust and regret?

He must wish that I wasn't his mate. He must curse Fate.

What if I see him, and I flash back to that night and run for my life again?

What if he chases me?

My heart thumps harder and harder, and by the time we get to the end of the dirt road we've been bouncing along, I jump out of my seat. I'm the first one down the steep steps, and when I see why we stopped, I'm so thrown that I stop in my tracks, causing the male behind me to leap to the side so he doesn't plow me over.

The male whistles, catching sight of what surprised me. The road hadn't ended, per se. There are several huge felled trees laid across it so that we can't pass.

On top of the trees, three males and a female are perched. It takes me a second to recognize them, but when I look closer, I know them from Moon Lake, but they have *changed*.

The male who looks most like I remember is Cadoc's second, Seth Rosser. He's wearing khakis and a T-shirt, and he's standing straight with his legs planted and his shoulders back. Typical Seth. He's younger than me, but like Cadoc, he always had the authority of someone a lot older.

The rest of the welcome committee has gone back to nature. Nia, Pritchard, and Bevan are scavengers, so they've always let their wolf hang out, as Mom puts it, but this is next level. Nia still has the partial perma-claws—she's got them painted bright red rather than her usual black—but now she's also sporting wolf ears that poke through her black hair, and she's got them pierced from base to tip.

I was always fascinated by Nia. She kind of stomps

through life, but not like she's angry. More like she's Godzilla and everyone else is Tokyo.

Nia is sitting on the topmost log, drumming her combat boot heels against its bark. Her mate, Pritchard, squats beside her. He basically looks like someone shoved a wolf into a shirt and pants, kind of like humans squeeze their dogs into sweaters. His feet are paws. His head is more muzzle than face.

Nia and Pritchard mated really early, and they were never really *together*, at least while I was still going to the Academy. I can't tell if they're together now. He's sitting close to her, but not too close, and in every mated pair that I know, the male is dominant, and that is not the vibe I'm getting from them.

The fourth member of the welcoming committee, Bevan Nevitts, is strolling back and forth like the log is a balance beam. He's the only one who waves and smiles as we pile out of the bus, flashing his gold teeth. His tail is sticking out of his drawers, and as he turns, everyone can see that instead of bothering to sew a hole, he's cut the rear of his pants from waist to crotch and pinned the seam partially back together with diaper pins. The kind with yellow ducks on the heads.

It's a look.

"Good trip?" Bevan hollers down.

At the same time, Seth orders, "Get your luggage and come around this side." He points to a narrow trail that's been cleared through the dense woods to skirt the downed trees.

Seth casts Bevan a dark look, and Bevan raises his palms in the air, grinning. "Sorry, boss. Forgot that I was supposed to forget my manners."

Seth's jaw tenses. He ignores Bevan and barks down at

us, "We leave in five."

Then he steps off the back of the blockade and disappears on the far side. The others follow him.

We all turn back toward the bus, only to hear the screech of the doors closing. The bus driver has already taken our bags from the stowage compartment and piled them in the middle of the road. We gape as he proceeds to reverse the bus straight back out the way we came. The woods are encroaching on the road so much, there's nowhere for him to turn. Tree roots are breaking through the packed dirt. The road is going back to nature, too.

As the sound of the bus's engine grows fainter, the knot in my stomach grows. This is it. I'm doing this. There's no going back now.

My mom's voice echoes in my head. *"You have never succeeded at anything you started. Do you think it wise to fail in a cave somewhere in the wilderness surrounded by strangers?"*

I set my chin, and I'm the first to grab my duffel bag and the tote I've stuffed with my various cosmetics, toiletries, and sundries.

The others follow my lead, the males from facilities helping the nurse with luggage, but they don't offer to help me with mine. I don't expect them to—unmated males always treat me with that weird combination of pity-tinged respect and superstitious wariness. When we all round the blockade, though, and Nia sees that I'm carrying my own bags, her mouth curls with contempt.

"Izzy's bags too heavy for you delicate flowers?" she asks. I had no idea she knew my name. I'm surprised. I was pretty forgettable in school. I made a point of blending in.

The males look down and shuffle their feet.

Bevan bounds toward me, careening to a halt about

three feet away. "I'll take those, milady," he says and thrusts out his arm in my direction.

He's treating me with kid gloves, too, but more like I'm venomous than cursed, and it doesn't sting so bad as the usual ten-foot-pole treatment. I can't help but smile as I hang my bags on his forearm. He's such a hyper person, you'd think he'd be wiry, but he's actually pretty muscular, especially for a scavenger. He doesn't even have to flex to hold my bags up.

He gives me a goofy bow and goes to strap my luggage onto the back of a four-wheeler. There are several ATVs waiting for us, including the dual-sport bike that Nia is mounting.

Bevan and Seth mount four-wheelers. The nurse hurries to double-up with Seth, grabbing him by the waist and giggling about how it's her first time, and she's so nervous and excited. Seth's jaw is so tight that his teeth must ache.

The Moon Lake males watch me, waiting for me to make my choice. I don't want to spread my legs and sit so close to another male.

I don't want to hold another male's waist. I know touching another male won't erase anything. It's not like there's psychic energy left on my fingers from when I touched Trevor's face, and my thumb pressed into his stubbly jaw, or when he held my hands at his side.

But still.

If there were, I wouldn't want it to rub off.

And that's silly and stupid, and everyone is waiting for me to make a decision. I break out in a sweat. My collar is too tight and scratchy. My gaze sweeps the scene as if I'm looking for an escape and catches on Nia.

She's smiling and patting the seat behind her butt. "Wanna ride with me?" She arches a pierced eyebrow.

It feels like an out. I take it.

It's not until my butt is perched on the narrow ledge, my front plastered to her back, and the rubber soles of my Keds propped on thin, stubby metal pegs that I realize what I've gotten myself into.

The four wheelers are actually designed to seat two people with full-sized butts. This is basically two females sharing a banana seat.

Nia revs the engine. Pritchard hops onto the other dirt bike and pulls even with us, flashing Nia a sharp-toothed grin.

"Loser sucks the winner's dick?" he somehow manages to say around his descended fangs.

Nia cocks her head as if she's considering, and while Pritchard shifts in his seat to free his tail, she reaches back, grabs my arms, and wraps them around her middle. "Hold on tight, Isabella Cinderella," she mutters.

I open my mouth to say my real name is Isolde, but before I can say a word, she peels off, kicking up a cloud of dirt. I get a face full, and for the next several seconds, I'm too busy sneezing out dust particles to freak out.

Nia whoops and leans forward. I lean with her. I'm her backpack now. I don't dare move a hair on my own. What if I tip us over?

We're not wearing helmets, and the trees encroach even more into the road the farther we get from the barricade. Nia slaloms left and right, avoiding roots and rocks and ruts carved from rainwater. Pritchard catches up before we've gone a few yards, but for some reason, he can't seem to pass us.

My heart is thumping in my chest. Wind rushes in my ears, whipping my hair against my cheeks. Everyone but

Pritchard falls far behind until I can't even see them when I work up the courage to turn my head and look back.

I'm terrified and wide awake and somehow, I'm not falling off the bike. The road and woods are mostly cast in cool shadow from the canopy high overhead, but here and there, the sun sneaks through gaps in the leaves and dapples the ground. As we race, we sail through the sunny spots, warmth bursting onto my face and disappearing in a flash.

I squeeze Nia with my thighs as tightly as I can and lift my chest a little off her back. The wind snaps at me harder, but I don't mind. The forest air smells dark and deep and lushly green, like something out of dreams I had as a pup.

I'm still afraid, but that's not the thing I am *most*. I'm alive. That's what I am.

We hit a straightaway where there aren't any washouts or rogue tree tentacles, and Nia opens up the throttle. Pritchard does, too, coming within a few feet of our rear wheel, but for some reason, he's still not able to pull even with us.

Nia must worry that he will, though, because she shouts back, "Hold on! Detour!" And she veers off the road, up an embankment, into the woods.

I hug her tighter than I've ever hugged anyone before. We bounce so hard, my teeth click, even though I've got them clenched together as hard as I can. She weaves between tree trunks, nimbly picking her way through obstacles, cursing a blue streak when her tire spins out or she hits a bump too hard, and we get air. I hold on for dear life. There is nothing else I can do.

We don't shake Pritchard. He's still on our tail, although he's fallen further behind. He's picking his way more carefully. Nia plows ahead like confidence is everything.

She might be right. By the time she intercepts the road again, Pritchard is so far behind us, I can't see him. I only know he's there by the fading sound of his engine.

Nia is all grins, and she actually slows down to a leisurely pace for the last leg of the trip to Old Den. I vaguely remember the terrain from Academy field trips, but the woods seem denser and greener and somehow *wilder* than they did back then.

We've lost the others, too. It's just Nia and me when we swing around another log barricade—this one with guards in wolf form stationed on top—and the road opens to a grassy clearing about the size of a basketball court. Nia pulls up to a row of hard-used dirt bikes and four-wheelers and parks. I slide off the back onto wobbling legs.

Nia hollers, "Whoo!" and slings an arm around my shoulder. "Looks like I'm getting my dick sucked."

The people around the clearing stop what they're doing and stare our way. We seem to be standing in the middle of a kind of commons. Paths emerge from the woods and converge on the commons from the east and west, and opposite from where Nia and I are standing is the round entrance that leads into the Old Den.

This area was a gravel parking lot when I was a pup. Now it's covered with thick grass, and the mouth to the Old Den is decorated with an arch strung with woven ropes of wildflowers. Peering down one of the paths, I can just make out the corner of a red cottage among the trees, a fairy tale house with a steep pitched roof and white gingerbread trim along the eaves.

To our left, a group of males stand around, poking a fire burning in a rusty metal drum. A few females sit with their babies on a blanket under a pine tree. Back by the vehicles, two males stop working on a disassembled ATV to gawk at us. Everyone is staring.

"Let's go pay our respects to the bossman," Nia says with a reassuring smile and nudges me with her elbow.

I wipe my sweaty palms on my navy-blue capris. I already don't fit in. I'm dressed like an accounting intern in my white collared shirt. Everyone I see is wearing mismatched hand-me-downs like scavengers, even the two or three higher-ranked people I recognize from the Tower. Even though the weather isn't at all hot, several people aren't wearing shirts, including two of the females hanging out on a picnic blanket.

At least my hair fits in. It's a wild mess. I run my shaking fingers through it, working out the knots, as I follow Nia across the commons.

I'm nervous, but the adrenaline from the crazy ride with Nia hasn't faded yet, and it's giving me a little extra courage at the prospect of meeting my new temporary alpha. I'm straightening my shoulders when I see him.

Fate gives me no warning. No lightning strike or gut feeling.

I'm walking toward the Old Den entrance, and then, all of a sudden, Trevor Floyd strides out, straight toward me, carrying a load of two-by-fours by resting the planks on his shoulder.

Time stops. Sound fades like someone shoved cotton balls in my ears. My wolf leaps to her feet, fully awake in an instant.

I clutch my chest. I feel him. Shock. Loathing. Horror.

I whimper.

The two-by-fours clatter to the ground. My gaze drops with them, and then travels helplessly back up his body, logging every detail, every change.

He's wearing tan work boots, just like he wore before. His faded blue jeans are frayed at the hems and ripped at the knee. They ride low on his hips, but they're tight over his thighs. He's wearing a worn leather tool belt with a hammer hanging at his side. His white T-shirt clings to his broad chest. His biceps stretch the sleeves.

My insides are caught in a mixer. I can't untangle what's happening—can't sort his feelings from mine. Is this fear his? Is this grief?

I can't catch my breath. There isn't room enough under my ribs for my lungs to expand.

My face in the dirt. My airway clogged with snot.

The memory crashes over me, cranking my heartbeat, fast, too fast, triggering every nerve in my body. My body primes to run. The acrid scent of terror erupts from my pores.

My wolf bounds forward, howling, throwing herself into the boundary between us, crying for her mate, trying to drag us closer to him with the force of her longing and loneliness. She isn't afraid.

I raise my eyes to Trevor's face. He's grown up. I didn't realize it until this moment, but when I compare the face in my memory to the one in front of me, he wasn't a full-grown male before, but he is now.

My lower lip trembles. I frown to stop the wobbling and blink to force back the tears.

His cheeks and chin are scruffy with stubble—his face was smooth before—but his curly, wheat blond hair hasn't changed at all. His blue-gray eyes aren't darker, but they're deeper somehow, like the quarry lake with its smooth surface that reflects the sky but goes down twenty stories deep.

Holding his gaze is like holding my palm over an open

flame, but I can't look away any more than I could pluck out my own eye.

Another picture flashes in my head. Those beautiful eyes bleeding pure black. His fangs ripping through his bottom lip. His head swiveling on his neck as he scented the air. I whine. The stench of my fear burns my nose.

Trevor jerks as if his body took a hit, his tanned face blanching gray. He raises his palms in the air and backs away, faster and faster, past the males poking the fire and the females on the blanket. When he reaches a maple tree at the edge of the woods, he leans on it with one hand, bends over, and pukes behind the trunk. Then, without a glance in my direction, he disappears down the path toward the fairy tale cottage, leaving his two-by-fours lying on the ground like pick up sticks.

Everyone is watching. It's theater in the round. He exited stage left, and I'm left here alone, and a dozen strangers are waiting with bated breath for a cue that the scene is over.

My hands curl into fists. I'm not going to cry.

I hate crying. Crying only ever pissed my parents off even more, but I've never been tough, even when it would've saved me trouble. My eyes fill with tears.

"Oh, girlfriend," Nia murmurs and wraps her arm around my shoulder. I'd forgotten she was standing next to me.

"Shit, you're here early," a female says from the den entrance.

Rosie Kemble and Cadoc Collins stroll out, heading for us. Could this get any worse? Rosie's brown eyes are brimming with concern while Cadoc frowns in the direction where Trevor disappeared. Because Trevor belongs to his pack now? And I'm an outsider who made him puke and drove him away?

Because I'm a walking tragedy, a living reminder of something no one ever wants to think about?

Because under the pity, there's the thing everyone whispers, but only behind closed doors—she did this to herself. She knew what would happen, but she forced Fate's hand anyway and ruined two lives.

I shouldn't be here. I glance over my shoulder at the bikes. I wouldn't even know how to start one. Nia kind of stomped on a pedal.

Nia hugs me tighter, reminding me that she's still there. "That was my bad. Pritchard bet me he could beat me back to the den."

Rosie shakes her head and arrives in front of us. She stops a few feet away. Cadoc stops further back, almost like he's her bodyguard, not the alpha.

"Pritchard knows he can't beat you," Rosie says.

Nia's lips curve in a funny smile. "He never will as long as he keeps letting me win."

"I think this calls for a cup of tea, right?" Rosie offers me her hand.

I take it, but only after getting my hand thoroughly wet by wiping away my tears, like I really was raised by ferals like Mom always said. My face heats. This is maybe the worst first impression I've ever made.

Rosie squeezes my hand and keeps a tight hold of it, drawing me toward the den.

"You okay, babe?" Cadoc asks as he gathers the two-by-fours.

"Yeah. I've got this," Rosie says. "You go after Trevor."

Before Cadoc walks away, he bends over, bumps her forehead with his own, and nuzzles her temple. His wolf rumbles in his chest. He doesn't want to leave his mate.

I hear the four-wheelers approaching in the distance. I

need to pull it together. Instead, I sniff harder, and the tears come in sheets. The spigot is broken.

I let Rosie lead me into the den, down the narrow tunnel, and then into the huge cavern that used to be empty except for excavation sites marked off with wooden stakes and string and the occasional orange cone.

Now, the place reminds me of the craft fair held every May on the great lawn in the middle of the Academy, but instead of booths, there are little tableaus—a female stirring a pot over a fire, males bent over a workbench, packmates perched on overturned buckets watching an old-timey television, the kind shaped like a box.

"You have cable?" I say without thinking. My brain is slow from crying.

"Cable in a cave? That's nuts." Nia's tone is teasing. "We've got satellite."

We weave between centers of activity, and unlike outside, most of the people are too absorbed in what they're doing to take notice of me. When we pass a cluster of elders, they call hello to Rosie and raise their gnarled hands in greeting. Their faces fall when they see my face, and a thin male with almost no hair on his spotted head shouts, clearly distressed, "Flora, why is that female crying?"

A chubby female with glorious wavy hair pats his hand. "It's okay, Granddad. Rosie's got her. She'll be okay."

"Rosie?"

"You know Rosie. The alpha female."

His craggy face scrunches. "The one with the wolf?"

"The one with the wolf," Flora confirms. I know what he means. Rosie's wolf is the size of an elephant, and ever since she chomped off Alban Hughes' head, she's been *the* wolf.

"The female will be all right then." The male relaxes,

sinking back into his chair. "Why don't you go make sure, though?"

"All right, Granddad." Flora smooths the quilt covering his bony knees. Is this the elder Una was talking about, the one that Trevor fussed over?

At the thought of his name, my eyes well with tears again. He saw me and puked. He hates me. Our mating is irreparably broken, and how messed up in the head must I be to think there's anything to salvage? I was going to be professional and collected, and I'm having a meltdown in the middle of strangers.

While I sink into despair, Nia and Rosie herd me past the pool and into an alcove decorated like a booth in a fancy Italian restaurant. Nia slides into a highbacked, curved bench upholstered in burgundy velvet and pulls me down after her. Rosie squeezes in next so I'm sandwiched between them.

"I'll be back with a pot of tea," Flora says, disappearing toward the cooking fire we passed on the way inside.

Two mismatched wooden chairs sit across the table, which is covered by a white fabric shower curtain. I wouldn't have known it wasn't a tablecloth except the metal grommets bumped my thighs as I scooched in.

Beyond the chairs, we have a perfect view of the pool. I truly thought it was magical when I was a pup. Sunshine streams through the natural skylight above it, and by some chemical process that the instructor explained but I never quite understood, the stalactites clean the rainwater. An underground river feeds it as well, so it's a perfect clean and clear blue.

A blonde female in a bright yellow bikini is standing in the shallows, massaging the scalp of a beefy male sitting in front of her. Even though he's kneeling, his head still almost reaches her chin. He's twice her size, but she's not the least bit afraid of him. His eyes are closed. She's chatting to him, and he's smiling dopily, blissed out.

Trevor stared at me like I was a ghost, and not the gothic kind, but the jump-scare, bent-neck, hole-where-her-nose-should-be kind.

I drop my head into my hands. What was I thinking? How did I think this was going to go?

The truth is I didn't think. I took the ropes that Fate or Abertha threw me with no plan, bumbling along through life with no urgency, like Dad always accused me of doing. Did I figure there would be a neon green flyer posted on a bulletin board with what I should say to Trevor?

I stifle a sob, but my shoulders still shake. Nia hums like a mother to a hurt pup, Rosie sighs, and they both shift even closer to me. Their arms press against my side. Nia smells like motor oil, and Rosie smells like baby food—specifically strained peas—and it's so oddly comforting. I'm not used to being so physically close to females.

"Well, the worst is over now." Nia breaks the silence. "They always say you feel better after you throw up."

Rosie hisses, "Not helpful."

"You were supposed to have gotten Trevor away from the den already, so we could ease them into the first meeting," Nia hisses back.

They had a plan?

"Abertha said this has to be handled *delicately*." Nia is still whispering, even though her mouth is right next to my ear.

Abertha. That explains it.

"Well, Rae asked him to fix her radio, and I didn't want to *order* him to leave. That would've been suspicious." Rosie gives me a comforting pat on the back. "And everything is going to be fine. We ripped the Band-Aid off."

"Damn, Rosie, you're starting to sound like me," Nia laughs.

"And you sound like me. Delicately? Since when do you handle things delicately?"

"Since the witch recruited us for this mission." Nia sounds absolutely serious. "Don't tell me you didn't get the sense that this is a test. Mark my words—she's planning an *Avengers Assemble*, and this is how we prove ourselves. Whatever she's up to, I want to be on the original team. I don't want to be added at the end for comic effect like Ant Man or something."

I have no idea what Nia is talking about, but she is distracting me from my meltdown. I manage to sit up straight and wipe my face. I have no choice but to use the sleeve of my cardigan. If Mom saw, she'd have a conniption.

"Your imagination is running away with you. Abertha just wants us to be supportive," Rosie says and smiles at me gently. "She cares about Izzy. And Trevor."

"Abertha knows Trevor?" I ask. My sinuses are so swollen, I sound like a goose.

"She brought him here, with Alec's Granddad and the other Salt Mountain refugees," Rosie explains. "Alec is Flora's mate. And Flora is the lady with the tea." As if on cue, Flora arrives, sets a crowded tray on the table, and then sinks into a seat.

Nia grabs an oatmeal cookie from a heaped plate, sticks the whole thing in her mouth, and proceeds to pour all of us a cup of tea.

Flora takes over the explanation. "Things are apparently getting a little hairy at Salt Mountain now that Leith Munroe is alpha. It was decided that it would be best to evacuate the more vulnerable folks—the elders and the sick and the young unmated females who don't have male relatives. Abertha led the group here. Trevor carried Granddad all the way. He took out a pack of ferals that was stalking them, too."

A small glow warms my chest. It feels strange to be proud of him, but still—I tuck the story away so I can take it out and consider it more later.

Nia sets a steaming cup of tea in front of me. The floral pattern on the chipped saucer doesn't match the pattern on the cup, and the flowers on the cup don't match the flowers on the teapot. The dessert plate she passes me piled with cookies has a blue and white Chinoiserie pattern, with, for some inexplicable reason, pterodactyls and a rampaging Sasquatch running through the classic temple scene.

"Here." Flora passes me a bottled water. "Drink this while your tea cools. You need to hydrate."

Rosie plucks an orange from a bowl on the tray and peels it with her thumbnail. "Trevor's been here for a few months now, and Cadoc says he doesn't know what we'd do without him. Alec is so busy rehauling our infrastructure, he doesn't have time to fix all the little things that break in a given week. Trevor has really come in clutch. He fixed my pocket watch."

"He rewired the kill switch on Pritchard's bike," Nia adds, nabbing a peeled orange slice from the pile Rosie's started.

"He's supposed to be fixing my rabbit's hutch as we speak." Flora blows on her tea.

"What happened to Harriet's hutch?" Nia asks.

"I pried off a few of the slats like Rosie told me." Flora takes a sip.

"Why'd you do that?" Nia asks Rosie.

"That was the ruse to get Trevor away from the den when Izzy arrived."

Nia snags another orange slice. "Where's poor Harriet?"

"Keeping Miss Nola company, watching cop shows, probably." Flora gives me a smile. "Miss Nola raised me. She'll be so delighted to meet you. She loves Trevor."

My chest twinges. I can't be jealous, but that's what it feels like. "What did Abertha say to you about me?" I ask to change the subject.

I don't want to examine that twinge too closely. Would it be worse to be jealous of an elderly female because she actually knows my mate? Or to be jealous of my mate because everyone here seems to like him, and even though I'm useful to my pack now that I'm a healer, I can't imagine people thinking about me, let alone speaking highly of me, when I'm not around.

Rosie smacks Nia's creeping fingers and snatches up an orange slice for herself. "You want to hear everything she said?" she asks me. "Even the rough stuff?"

My stomach knots. I feel raw and fragile and so far out of my depth that I'm in the middle of the ocean. Still, I say, "Yes."

Rosie hands me the orange slice she saved. I clutch it a little too tight, but it doesn't squish.

"She said that when you mated Trevor, you were both young. Your parents and Howell Owens pressured you to wait, and threatened Trevor's family. Trevor went into rut and raped you. He was exiled to Salt Mountain."

I didn't think I had tears left, but I do. My eyes are aching in their sockets now. "Is that all?"

"She said you were brave. That you're unlearning, and that's a hard thing to do. She said when you got here, you'd know what to do, and we should help you."

I'm not brave. Abertha's right about the unlearning, though. Whatever I've been doing, it's the opposite of figuring things out. "I have no idea what to do."

"Well, what do you want?" Rosie asks.

I let out a ragged sigh. "Go back to the start. Do it all differently."

"What would you do differently?"

Memories rush over me, more feelings than pictures, but one image stands out—Trevor's stormy eyes watching me, tentative and wary and longing at the same time. "I'd talk to Trevor when he was staring at me in the parking lot. I'd stay with him when he brought me a soda."

They won't know what I'm talking about, but all three females look at me like I'm making perfect sense anyway.

"We have sodas in the fridge," Flora says. "You can take him one and tell him you want to start over."

"Oh, good idea." Rosie pops the last orange slice into her mouth.

Nia leans back and away a little so she can look at me better. She's not smiling like the other two.

"Can I ask you something?" she asks.

"Sure."

"It's none of my business."

I almost snort. Everyone knows my business. The worst day of my life is Moon Lake lore. "Okay."

"You might get upset."

"It's fine."

I figure after that preamble, she'll let it rip, but she takes a few seconds to choose her words. "Can you really forgive him for what he did? I mean, I understand that he was in rut. He was out of his mind and everything. But do you really believe that? Like deep down?" She pauses like she's frustrated that she's not putting it exactly the right way. "I mean, if it were me, even though I'd know in my head that he wasn't to blame, I don't think I could ever really trust him. How do you sleep next to a person, knowing they're capable of that, you know? How do you have pups with them?"

Flora's jaw drops. Rosie's eyes bug. Everyone tenses. You could hear a pin drop.

"What the fuck, Nia?" Rosie barks. "*Handle delicately,* remember?"

Nia ducks her head, but she doesn't break eye contact with me. "Sometimes you've got to lance the boil after you rip the Band-Aid off. Trust me."

I got hit in the solar plexus with a lacrosse ball once, during Human Sport class at the Academy. My heart stopped for a second, and the air whooshed out of my lungs. That feels like this.

I don't think these thoughts.

I don't ask these questions.

In my mind, there is Trevor with the blue-gray eyes who knows about feng shui and smells like gravy. And then, in a locked box that I store as deep inside as I can, there's the beast with the bleeding black eyes. He's always lurking down there, but if I don't look, he doesn't exist. He's the monster under the bed.

And that way of thinking *works.* It got me out of bed and out of my room. It got me here. If Nia had just kept her mouth shut, it would get me all the way to chasing down Trevor with a soda, and I'd magically know what to say to him, and we'd start fresh and end up happy ever after.

"It's not your business," I say through grinding teeth.

"I know," she says. The compassion in her voice pisses me off.

"Oh, no, you don't. Everyone thinks they know, but they

don't—they can't possibly— and they should be *grateful* they don't know, and mind their own damn business, but instead, everyone's morbidly obsessed with the story, like, like I'm a true crime podcast. I'm just a person. Why can't I have what everyone else has? Why can't I want what everyone else wants?"

The females listen with their kind eyes and commiserating faces, and I want to sweep the tea service onto the floor and flip the table and scream at the top of my lungs.

Instead, I blubber through fresh tears, "Everyone wants to talk about it behind my back, but they sure as hell don't want me to talk about it in front of their face." The dam has burst, and I'm not even sure what my point is anymore. "Can I forgive him? I don't know. Sometimes, I think I'm more to blame. Can I forgive myself? What do we do if we're both unforgivable? Die alone?"

Over in the pool, the burly male is rising to his feet. Water sluices off his hairy chest. He leans over to kiss the tip of the female's nose. They're totally absorbed in each other, completely oblivious to the fact that there's a female melting down a few yards away.

"I don't know if I can trust him. I can hardly trust myself. But I'm not sitting around anymore like my life is already over. I'm done with that." As quickly as they came, I run out of words. I straighten up, lift my chin, and sniff back snot.

"Here, here," Nia says and raises her tea cup.

I stare at it dumbly.

"Sometimes you've just gotta break loose and let the pieces fall where they may," Flora says, raising her cup.

Rosie lifts her cup. "We are the masters of our fate. We are the captains of our souls."

I remember that poem from the Academy. "Invictus" by

William Ernest Henley. "We're literally not," I laugh through the tears and clink my cup against theirs.

"Feel better?" Nia asks.

"Oddly, yes."

I still have no plan, and not a lot of hope, but it feels, for the first time, like I might have friends. It feels good.

Izzy is beautiful. She's still slight with bigger breasts and a rounder ass than you'd expect on a female her size. She wore the same office worker clothes, but her hair was messy from the wind, and her cheeks were pink. She always moved tentatively, like a mouse creeping across an open floor, trying not to be noticed, but she stood right in front of me with her back straight and chin up.

And I puked behind a tree.

One whiff of her fear scent and I was back at Moon Lake, staggering for the infirmary with her broken wolf in my arms.

For years, I've forced myself to replay every second of what happened, over and over again, until the flashbacks don't have the power to knock me on my ass. I figured out early on that I had to master the horror and shame, or it would flow through the bond to her in a moment of weakness. I can't afford to be weak.

I can picture every minute of that night without flinching, but her scent took me out at the knees.

I've got to get away from here, as far as I can, before I

mess her up anymore. I saw her eyes when I walked away. Her hurt was sharp as daggers.

I need to be shifting and running for the hills, but instead, I stride for Alec and Flora's cabin on autopilot. That's where I was heading when I came face-to-face with her in the commons. Did she even speak? My head was roaring. If she said anything, I couldn't hear. My nose caught her fear, and I loathed myself to the core again.

Where can I go? Not back to Salt Mountain. Leith is poison. He's cruel to his new mate, and the stronger males in the pack have taken it as permission to indulge their worst natures. I will never let the fucked-up priorities of high-ranking males turn me into a monster again. I'm not even risking it.

I doubt any other pack would take me. There is a no-man's-land in the triangle between North Border, Salt Mountain, and Quarry Pack, but it's feral infested, and if my experience on the trip here taught me anything, it's that I can't take on more than three ferals at a time. If we'd been attacked by four of them, or if they'd been able to work together, I'd be dead.

Once upon a time, I would've welcomed a swift death—and sometimes still, in dark moments, I think it'll be a relief when it comes—but if I die, Izzy will hurt, so I fight as hard to survive as a male who has something to live for.

I bring her face to mind again. Her eyes don't eat up her entire face like they used to, and she wasn't chewing on her lower lip like she always did. Maybe she still has the habit. I saw her for, what, ten seconds?

I picture her, tracing every detail to etch it in my brain. Her hair is the same length, but it wasn't tied back. She used to wear it in a low ponytail. Until that night, when my claws tore her rubber band as I jerked her head back, and then later, when she was trapped by my knot, and I gently pulled the strands out of the mangled, bloody mess I'd made of her neck, I'd never seen her hair down. Not until today.

My guts are racked with cramps, and I heave, but there's nothing left in my stomach. I gulp down a series of deep breaths, and then, bent over with my hands braced on my thighs, I force myself to remember. My claws. Her snapped hairband. The jagged gash in the crook of her neck. Her blood. Her limp body. Her gray skin.

I cast the images up over and over as my wolf huddles in a whimpering mess in the furthest corner of our self. It's punishment until I'm numb, and then it's protection. For a little while, my shame and despair are muted, and there's no chance it can hurt her through the bond.

I blow out a long breath and straighten up. I'm standing in front of the rabbit hutch behind Alec and Flora's cottage, and I have no idea how I got here.

I blink at the scene. Several splintered wood planks are flat in the dirt. A rabbit didn't do that. A gorilla maybe, or a bomb, but no rabbit.

I glance around. What do I do?

I never thought I'd see her again. I figured I'd know if she was close by, and I'd be able to bail. The bond would warn me somehow, even though the connection is spotty at best. If her emotions are strong enough, I can feel them, but most of the time, I get nothing but a dull gray static. If she picks up on what I send her, there's no sign.

Is she okay? In the second before I freaked out, she didn't look okay.

Rosie was there, though. And Nia. They'll take care of her. The females here are different from those at Salt Mountain or Moon Lake. They don't give a shit about rank, and they're not cowed by the males. Kind of the opposite. The males court their favor and give them the best of everything. Like Dad did for Mom.

It's good that Izzy's here. I need to get word to her that I'm leaving so that she stays.

I'm staring at a clearly vandalized rabbit hutch, trying to think of what to do next, when I hear a male approaching, his steps intentionally heavy.

"You dropped these," Cadoc calls out and comes to stand beside me. He eases a stack of two-by-fours from his shoulder and leans them against the hutch. "What happened here? Don't tell me something ate the damn rabbit." Cadoc scrubs his neck, and briefly closes his eyes as he blows out a long-suffering sigh.

I never had dealings with Cadoc's father in person, but Madog Collins is a legend, larger than life, a shifter version of James Bond combined with King Solomon and Iron Man. Cadoc is nothing like him.

Cadoc is one hundred percent about his people. If it concerns them, it concerns him. I've seen him fetch old Auntie Madwen her sunflower seeds, rip Danny Powell a new one for disrespecting his mother—and then let the pup get a few good shots in when they sparred. I saw him haul Dewey Kemble's drunk wolf out of the pool, towel dry him, and put him to bed by the fire. He's a good alpha. Izzy will be safe here.

"She can stay, right?" I ask. "I'll leave."

Cadoc's brow creases. "Izzy's only here for a few weeks. She's part of the exchange program."

I'm aware of the program, but I never considered Izzy might be one of the representatives from Moon Lake. Cadoc said only medics and tradespeople were coming. Izzy was interning in corporate.

Well, if it's only a few weeks, I can rough it. "I can patrol until she leaves. I'll stay away from the den."

It would be better if she were here to stay permanently. Old Den doesn't have Moon Lake's numbers or the high-tech security, but people don't just disappear. The males don't terrorize their pups, either, and if they did, the females would call Rosie, and her wolf would eat them, bones and all.

I've worried about that every day since I was exiled—males like Izzy's father don't change.

"Could she stay if she wanted?" I ask, my wheels turning. I could work something out where I run a shop off-site. Bevan would bring me things to repair. He's the kind of male who's always happy to help, even if he does tend to get lost on the way a lot. I could hunt between jobs, and send the meat back with him, too. "I can pay her keep."

"Trevor—"

I rush to interrupt him before he can say no. "You know I can fix anything. I'll set up shop past the border. I'll do repairs, hunt, patrol. Whatever needs doing."

"Trevor." Cadoc turns from the hutch to face me. He's a stone-faced male, so I have no idea what he's going to say until he says it. "You're not leaving. This is your pack. Izzy can stay as long as she wants, and no one is going to pay her keep. You're pack, so she's pack. But I'm afraid you're getting way too far ahead of yourself here."

My brain catches on the first thing he says. "I have to leave. It isn't right to make her—"

See me. Think about me. Remember.

"Trevor." He takes a second, glances at the sky, and then, like he's made a decision he thinks he'll regret, he looks me in the eye again. "She knew you might be here. She asked Una Kelly about you."

I open my mouth, but the words don't come. She meant

to come to me? Or was it that she didn't care that I was here? Or did she come to face me so she can put me behind her forever? Hope and devastation bloom in my chest as I break into a cold sweat.

"How do you know that?" I finally manage to ask.

Cadoc flashes a wry smile. "Female grapevine. Una Kelly told the witch who told my mate. I'd appreciate it if you kept it to yourself. I was sworn to secrecy." Cadoc snorts. "If only cell service was as reliable out here as the gossip."

I gape at the busted wall of the hutch and say, more to myself than anything, "What do I do?"

Cadoc crosses his arms and examines the missing slats, too. "Well, I'm not going to pretend that I know what you've both gone through. I can't even imagine. But going by my experience, the mistakes I've made in life, I'd say that you can't go wrong with listening. And patience. If she had the courage to come to you, you can hear her out." He scratches the back of his head. "Maybe stick to bland foods for a while. Bananas, rice, applesauce, toast. That's what the witch told Rosie to eat for the morning sickness."

I tilt my head back, close my eyes, and groan. "I'm never living that down, am I?"

"Never," Cadoc chuckles. "Pups will be reenacting the scene with their sock puppets around the evening fire for years."

"You could just whack me across the back of the head with that two-by-four now."

"Nah. You've got a hutch to mend. If something gets that rabbit, Flora will be devastated, which means Alec will be off his game, which means we'll fall behind on the drainage overhaul—yet again—which means the next time it rains more than three inches in an hour, we'll be in standing water, and guess who'll be bailing out an old cave like it's a sinking ship with every elder, female, and pup sitting on top every piece of available furniture, crying and shouting advice and complaining about how they're hungry and missing tea?"

I feel like Cadoc isn't describing a hypothetical. "Me?" I answer.

"Not you. You'll be scavenging the woods for a rabbit that looks exactly like Harriet while you concoct a plausible story about how she escaped and miraculously returned home."

I hope that's a hypothetical, too. Harriet is adorable.

"I guess I'll fix this hutch, eh?"

Cadoc grunts. He turns to leave, but before he goes, he stops and levels his gaze at me. "Like I said, I can't imagine what you've gone through, but I want you to know—in case it's doubt that makes you think you need to leave—the witch wouldn't have asked you to bring the others here if she didn't trust you. I wouldn't have let you stay around my mate and pups. And, say what you will about my father, if he thought you were a monster, there wouldn't have been a trial or exile. He would have slit your throat."

My lungs tighten. Six years ago, what he said would've dropped me to my knees, but I'm a different male now. A shell. I hear him, but I can't take the words in.

I give him a grim nod and take my hammer from my belt. I need to claw out these bent nails before I fit new slats.

Cadoc nods back and sees himself off.

Listening. Patience.

I ripped the meat of her shoulder from the bone. I ground her clavicle in my fangs.

What could she possibly want to do except curse me?

What else do I deserve?

10

IZZY

I'm asleep, but this cave-within-a-cave dormitory is new, this bunkbed is new, and so are the sounds of the other females snoring and tossing, so my sleep is shallow. This is a dream.

My wolf stands guard. There are too many unfamiliar sounds and smells.

And her mate is here. Close.

Not only his wolf. *Him.* She can't scent him—not with so many shockingly grubby females around—but she knows it all the same. He's not as close as the main cavern with its tempting pool, which she will be swimming in soon, but he's not much farther. Maybe he's sitting just outside the narrow entrance, his back propped against the mossy rock, his forearms resting on his bent knees. Guarding us.

Part of her is pleased, but most of her is angry. He should be here, with us, not skulking outside, leaving us alone in a strange place again. *He* should be the brave one, not her, not us. He's stronger, after all. If he wasn't, none of this would have happened.

Growling low in her throat, she bares her fangs when

the beaded curtains of the dormitory clink, and his wolf strolls in with a fat gray partridge in his maw.

He pads over and drops it at my wolf's feet, pride in his strut and the swish of his tail. For my wolf, it's a flash of red to a bull.

She picks the bird up by its head and tosses with all her strength. Its neck snaps, its body goes flying, and blood sprays across the woven rag mat covering the cave floor. She doesn't want it. This is a dream. She can't eat dreams. She wants real.

She snarls in his face, snaps at his muzzle, and then tears at the bleeding carcass, shredding it to pieces until it's an inedible pulp of feathers, muscle, bone, and organs. Then she hunches over it and howls at him while blood drips from her fangs.

She wants her mate. *All* of him. He broke this. He has to fix it. We came this far. Does he not want us? Is he disgusted with us, too?

His wolf lowers his head. His blue-gray eyes are sad. He turns and trots toward the door.

A fresh wave of rage rolls over my wolf. She stamps her paw in the bloody mess of partridge.

His wolf looks over his shoulder and jerks his head, asking her to follow him. She lifts her muzzle and with her head held high, she goes to him, surreptitiously wiping her paws on the rug as she goes.

He leads her down a corridor, through the cavern, past the pool and the banked fire and snoring wolves piled together in nests. Because it's a dream, blue moonshine, glittering with starlight, streams through the opening in the roof, and the den takes on the fairy-like feel of a miniature inside a shadowbox egg.

Then we enter the pitch-black passageway that goes

outside, and finally, emerge into fresh night air. His wolf stops. Mine stops beside him. Beside the entrance, just like we imagined, Trevor sits with his back against the den's outer wall. His knees are bent. His head rests against the rock, and he stares at the moon.

Pain is carved on his face and shines in his eyes, its weight bearing on the bunched muscles of his shoulders.

He is so beautiful, even in despair.

My wolf doesn't know what to do. She whines. His wolf inches over so he's pressed against her side. She leans on him. They stand together and watch Trevor stare blankly at the moon as he twirls a partridge feather in his fingers.

11

IZZY

"So is today the day?" Nia asks as she sails into the apothecary at noon in her Cookie Monster pajama bottoms with a cup of coffee.

I shrug. "Are you still in your pajamas?"

She blinks down at herself, feigning surprise. "Well, shit. Sure am. You know what they say—it's three a.m. somewhere."

We grin at each other. We kind of have a thing going where we bust each other's chops.

I shouldn't be surprised by the pajamas. Time is weird at Old Den. There are no standard working hours or meal times, per se. Things seem to happen when people get around to them, and honestly, everything seems scheduled around pots of tea. I've been here for five days, and it feels like I've heard "let's do that after a pot of tea" or "let's get this done so we can have a pot of tea" a hundred times.

Lucky for me, Rosie keeps fairly normal hours, and she's the one who's working with me. She says she was Abertha's apprentice back at Moon Lake, and I'm sure that's true—she knows the names of things and what they're for—but that's

pretty much all she knows. I had to throw out a trashcan full of milk thistle and St. John's Wort that was so old it wasn't good for anything but kindling.

I'm actually feeling pretty useful, which I didn't expect. The nurse from Moon Lake is assigned to their infirmary, one of the newly constructed cabins in the nearby woods, but I'm working in the Old Den itself, in an alcove under the skylight that's been set up as part indoor greenhouse, part apothecary.

Folks dip in and out of the nearby pool all day, in fur and skin, so there is always a background hum of laughter, yips, and splashes. It's nice, the opposite of Moon Lake's stiff silences that make you feel like you're walking on eggshells, or another shoe is about to drop.

It'd be downright peaceful except for Rosie and Nia going on about "Operation Soda Pop." They have a plan, and it's a simple one. I take Trevor a drink while he's at work. The problem is that's as far as their plan goes. Nia and Rosie aren't worried about what I say to him, or what happens next, or how I summon up the courage. They're focused on logistics.

They have Rosie's nephew Danny reporting on Trevor's movements, which has actually reduced a lot of stress. I'm not going to run into him by accident again. I've only seen him at a distance at meals. He grabs his plate, checks on Granddad Cameron, and bails. Nia says Trevor built a platform in the woods that he's pitched a tent on with the intention of building a cottage. He's settling in here. He's accepted.

Yet again, I find myself jealous. I really like it here. No one barks at anyone. No one ever bends neck, except sarcastically. Or playfully. Last night at dinner, for example, the blonde female from the pool, named Enid, stood, stretched her arms overhead, yawned, and cocked an eyebrow at her mate, Derwyn. Derwyn immediately bared his neck to her and crammed the rest of an enormous turkey drumstick into his mouth as he leapt from the table and trotted after her.

I was jealous of that, too. How quickly he came. How easy it was.

I've started counting down the days I have left, and when I think about it, a resentful ball forms in my stomach. Trevor is building his own cottage in the woods. I get sixteen more days until it's back to a windowless bedroom in my parent's apartment. I never dreamt of a cottage in the woods before, but now, for some reason, it sounds like the best thing ever, and I'm pissed as hell that he gets one, and I don't.

I know it doesn't make sense. I can't figure out how I feel, and last night's dream isn't helping. I can't remember it clearly, only feathers flying, and I woke up with my heart pounding and wet cheeks. Thankfully, the other females in the dorm were dead to the world.

Today should not be the day. There are no auspicious signs. It's not even a Tuesday.

But.

It could be the day. I could make it the day.

My heart beats a little quicker. My hands tremble and dirt scatters as I knock the fenugreek I'm repotting against its container. "I don't know where he is," I say.

Nia practically squeals. "Danny!" she hollers. "Report!"

Unsurprisingly, he doesn't do what he's told.

"Stay here," Nia says, "I'll find him and get a pop and be right back!" She hollers the last part over her shoulder as she races toward the part of the cavern where the young males watch television on overturned buckets.

I straighten my fingers to stop their shaking and focus

on the fenugreek. This doesn't have to be a big deal. What's the worst that could happen? He sees me, barfs, and runs away?

Or tells me I should leave. That he can't bear the sight of me.

Or I see him, it all comes rushing back, and I collapse into a weeping, mewling mess?

No. I already saw him. I freaked for a second, but I was okay. I can do this.

After giving the dirt around the fenugreek a few final pats and watering it, I wash my hands in the utility sink. I catch sight of myself in the shard of mirror propped on a nearby shelf. My eyes are so buggy, I look like a possum caught in headlights. My ponytail is neat, though, and there's no dirt on my face or my sky-blue collared shirt.

I'm looking for something to get into to keep my hands busy when Nia arrives with Rosie in tow, wielding a soda, the red kind, but without a cherry on the can. Rosie's wearing her pup, and the pup is peeking out of his sling at me with sober interest.

"He's working on the old peeps home," Nia announces, slapping the soda can into my hand.

"The elder cottage," Rosie corrects. "We're building a dorm for the elders so they have a place to go if the den floods again."

"If? More like when," Nia mutters. Rosie and her pup both frown at her. Nia is unapologetic. "I'll take you there," she says. "This is so exciting! I knew today would be the day."

"I didn't," it's my turn to mutter.

"Oh, come here," Rosie says and draws me into a hug. I have to stick my butt out and bend so I don't squish the little alpha heir who's still watching me with the sober consideration of a grown dominant male. It's his father's expression, and it's really funny on a baby's face.

Rosie pushes me back and smiles, her eyes misting. "Go get 'em," she says.

I try to smile back, but I don't think I quite manage it. The baby's brow furrows.

"Well, no time like the present!" Nia chirps and grabs my hand. "Let's go rip the Band-Aid all the way off."

Nia is a force of nature. She plows through the busy cavern, and as if they're not even conscious of it, her pack-mates shift out of her way or pause to let her through. Everyone except Pritchard. He catches sight of her from where he's lazing as his wolf by the big fire, rises, shakes himself off, and pads after us at a distance.

I am so curious to know what the deal is between them, but I don't feel comfortable enough with her yet to ask. I think we're getting there, though. Like we could become friends, real friends, not just females who form an alliance to protect our rank, like my friendship was with Brynn and Teagan.

I guess I could have made real friends back then, too, if I'd been braver and surer of myself. But then, I wouldn't have been Izzy Owens. Some people are born brave, or they're raised to be. I was born cautious and raised to be well-behaved, and that's a different thing.

I follow Nia out of the den and down one of the paths leading into the woods, and my stomach knots and my heart thumps like I'm breaking the rules. I've got that dread. My skin has that tight, prickly feeling. I'm stepping out of line.

I hold the soda tight. My sweaty palms and the condensation on the can are a slippery combination. Every few yards, Nia shoots me an encouraging smile, and I grimace back. It's the best I can do.

Oh, shit. What am I going to say?

I've tried so many times to script out the conversation in my head, but I can't get past, "I brought you this."

It'll come to me, though. It has to. Right?

My heart pumps faster, my steps slow, and Nia has to wait for me to catch up at a fork in the trail. "Not much farther," she says.

All the blood drains from my head to my feet. My ears whoosh. Every nerve in my body is on high alert. Pritchard's wolf steps on a branch a few yards behind us, and my pulse shoots straight up like the puck in the strongman game at the carnival. Ding.

Nia grabs my hand and squeezes. "You're not alone."

I nod. Clearly not. Pritchard is back there freaking me out.

Nia leads me the last few yards, down a side path, and into a clearing with the skeleton of a cottage. Only half the frame is standing. Trevor is kneeling on one knee in the center of the wood floor, nailing down the subfloor.

He's not wearing a shirt.

If I had breath in my lungs, he'd steal it. He's perfect. The swell of his biceps, a shade paler than his tanned forearms. The light catching on the blonder strands of his hair like sun dappling the bark of a tree. He glances up, his blue-gray eyes instantly storming.

My stomach clenches. My wolf trots forward, ears perking.

He slowly rises to his feet, his hammer hanging at his side.

I swallow, and nothing works. My mouth is bone dry, and my throat sticks. Nia digs her elbow into my side. I look over, blinking. She bugs her eyes emphatically at the soda in my hand.

Yes. Okay. Right. I know my first line.

She slowly backs away as I hold up the can and make myself say, "I brought you this."

His gaze focuses on the soda. His brow wrinkles. I see the exact moment he remembers that night, and then the dawning horror as he remembers the *other* night. Every muscle in his body stiffens. The corners of his eyes crinkle in pain. He looks like I punched him in the face. No, like I plunged a knife into his gut. That's not what I wanted.

This isn't working, and I don't know what to say next because what could you possibly say next? There are no words, there will never be any words, this is a terrible, stupid, useless mistake.

His clenched jaw tics as he stands, frozen perfectly still. His chest doesn't even rise.

I raise my palms in the air. I don't mean any harm. I'm just a walking, talking decaying albatross.

Behind me, another twig snaps, and I know it's Pritchard or Nia, but in the silence, it has the effect of a gunshot. I yelp.

Trevor startles and drops his hammer. It hits the plywood with a ringing thud. My nerves are strung so tight that I scream. Fear floods my system, and my wolf, who had been avidly watching the proceedings from the very edge of the border between us, senses an opening.

She leaps. I'm distracted. For the first time since that horrible night, she thrusts herself into our skin.

I'm vaguely aware of the pain as my bones crack and rearrange, but mostly, I'm mesmerized by the expressions breaking across Trevor's face in waves. Alarm as he scans the clearing for the threat. The realization that the threat was him. Devastation. Despair.

I shake my head, opening my mouth to explain, but I'm

inside now, and my wolf has her own mind. She races up to the cottage construction, jumps to prop her forepaws on the foundation, and begins to yip and snap at Trevor as if she hasn't seen him in forever, and she has so much to tell him —so many bones to pick with him—that she can't stop for breath. Her tail swishes like crazy as she tries to push herself up to the platform, but she's too small, and can't get enough leverage.

Trevor's brow knits. His wolf sees his opening. Trevor's irises blow up, and seconds later, his wolf surges from his skin, bursting through the seams of his jeans and wriggling loose from his toolbelt. Immediately, he howls and bolts for my wolf, his paws skittering on the plywood. I brace myself, crab walking back as fast as I can, away from the boundary between us. My wolf stretches her spine, straining toward him, yowling at him like he's a wayward pup.

He leaps down to our level, and she attacks him, butting him with her forehead and burrowing her snout under his chin, howling and yipping, prancing as she knocks him off his balance. He tries to mark her back, to sniff and lick her face, but he doesn't have a chance against her. She's a fur tornado. He chases her with his snout, but she's half his size and turning him in circles.

Eventually, he gives up and sprawls on his back, panting, and lets her sniff and nip and jump on his exposed belly with both front paws, oofing a little each time, content to lie there and sneak a lick in when her face comes close enough to his happy, gaping mouth.

They know each other. How? Through the bond? I've dreamt of his wolf over the years, but I never remember much, and what I did remember faded quickly once I was awake. Does she think she knows him because we dreamed about him?

Whatever the reason, she's comfortable enough to stick her nose *anywhere*, and she's as mad as hell that he's been gone and equally ecstatic to see him. Inside, my face burns, but she's shameless.

Luckily, she's calming down, settling into the work of nuzzling him from tip to tail, but every few minutes, she seems to remember she's pissed, and she'll growl and snap a few times. Each time, without fail, he bares his neck, and then twists himself to nudge her until she's coaxed back to her grooming.

His wolf is so chill. When my wolf takes a momentary break and rests her head on his chest, I can hear his heart pounding a mile a minute, but he doesn't make any sudden moves or dominate her with his size. I've seen my mom's wolf groom my dad's. If she stops before he's happy, his wolf nips her. I've seen him draw blood.

Trevor himself was chill, too. In the very beginning, he didn't push. He let me come to him. I was so snobby, ignoring him those first few days, acting like I was better, and he never let it bother him, not that he let on. Did it hurt him, though? Is that why he was so angry in rut?

My blood runs cold, and inside my wolf, I huddle further away, but if she can feel my unease, she doesn't care.

She's finally content that she's covered every inch of him in her scent, so she lays her chin on his belly and watches him watch her. His tail lazily slaps the ground. A chickadee *chick-a-dee-dees* on a branch high overhead. Only one *dee*. That means the danger isn't too bad, probably only the two wolves messing around underneath her.

My wolf dozes for a while, exhausted by her enthusiasm. When she wakes a few minutes later, Trevor's wolf is still watching her, his mouth curving dopily. She yawns and stands, and he clambers to his feet. While she shakes out her fur, he trots toward the woods and barks at her to follow. She does without hesitation.

She trusts him implicitly. He's big enough to protect her, and there is no doubt in her mind that he'd defend her with his life. She has no picture in her mind of his eyes bleeding black, no muscle memory of his claws piercing her hip flesh.

I shudder inside her. As he trots off between the trees, I watch her run with him, and it feels like a movie, and I'm in the back row. No, I'm up in the projection booth, peering through the little window. It's safe. But lonely.

He leads her deeper into the woods, the trees growing closer together the farther we get from the old den. She follows at his heels as he weaves and ducks and dashes, showing her all kinds of treasures—a blackberry bramble that smells faintly of red fox. A hollow log that reeks of possums. A hole under an aspen tree with the scent of old rodent layered with fresh garter snake.

Pausing at a shallow, quick running stream, he yips at her to drink. She does, and then yips back at him to do the same. After they've both had their fill, he leads her on along the marked boundary of Old Den's territory. At one point, he urges her up a steep hill to show her a crack in a rocky outcropping, and then spends three solid minutes alternating between howling at the cave entrance and casting her an impassioned, threatening glare that should, by all rights, have her baring her neck.

She doesn't. She smells the long-gone bear who must've slept there over winter, and she doesn't appreciate being treated like a pup with no sense. She trots toward the cave opening just to mess with him, and he clamps his jaws around her back leg, gently pulling her away while whining a plea around his full mouth.

She lets him, but she makes herself dead weight so it's as

hard for him to drag her as possible. He spends the next ten minutes nosing at her leg as they continue on their explorations, double and triple checking that he didn't hurt her with his fangs.

She's basking in his attention. If it wanders for even a second when a crow caws or a leaf rustles, she whines, and he immediately trots closer, brushing her side and nuzzling her face, laying his scent thicker.

He isn't submissive, though. He grumbles at her when she gets a few feet ahead and he feels she's ventured too far, and if he doesn't like the looks of the nook or cranny that she's investigating, he'll growl at her, and she'll back off right away. She's bold, a hundred times bolder than me, but she does trust him, and if he doesn't like the looks of something, that's good enough for her.

As the sun sets, our wolves keep going. Neither of them has any interest in turning around. They're alone in the world and perfectly content. He catches a fat squirrel for dinner and lets her have the legs and backstrap, making do with the ribs and organ meat.

One by one, the stars come out, and the woods fill with croaks and flutters and hoots. I've never been outside at night in the woods like this. I'm on edge, jumping at every noise and checking that Trevor's wolf isn't worried. My wolf, on the other hand, is having the time of her life. Her nose and ears sharpen as the darkness grows, and she treads along in the path he's blazing, happy to take it all in.

He doesn't take us beyond Old Den territory, but we meander for hours until her paws ache and her pace slows. My wolf doesn't want the night to end, but she's tired. She begins to whine, and not long after, he finds us a leaf-filled ditch next to a large, rounded stone, partially hidden by a chokecherry thicket.

She turns a few circles and plops herself in the middle, curling into a ball. He lies down beside her, and she snuggles up to his side, tucking her snout in his furry haunch. Seconds later, she's out like a light, and I follow not much later, lulled to sleep by the chitter of crickets and the rise and fall of our mate's body as he breathes.

I WAKE up butt naked in a pile of old, brown leaves in Trevor's arms. He's naked, too. We're both naked.

In an instant, every muscle in my body tightens. He startles awake. We're lying on our sides, our fronts pressed together, breast to chest, thigh to thigh, so I watch from an inch away as realization dawns in his eyes, followed immediately by panic.

"Don't anyone throw up," I squeak through my locked jaw. I don't mean to joke; it just comes out.

He squeezes his eyes shut, draws in a deep breath, and then exhales. His breath heats my cold neck. I'm warm where our skin touches, but everywhere else is numb.

We're naked. Alone. On the ground. He's hard. He's poking my stomach. I tense tighter, the scent of my fear bursting into the crisp morning air. His wolf growls in his throat.

This is the moment when he's going to let go.

Jump up.

Run.

I feel his muscles prime to bolt.

But he doesn't. He loosens his hold a fraction, but he leaves his arms around me, and draws another deep breath, and then another. Each time he inhales, his hard nipples poke my soft boobs.

He does angle his hips away so he's not poking me quite so hard, but otherwise, he doesn't move. His thighs stay pressed to mine. Our calves are shuffled—his, mine, his, mine. Our feet are tangled. Mine are kind of hooked under his, the tops of mine pressed to his soles.

I've never been this close to a person before.

Except for that night.

But that was different.

I know that. The chemicals in my body don't.

My heart and lungs and muscles are primed to fight or flee, and by all rights, my lizard brain should be pulling the trigger, but for some reason, I hang on the precipice of a freak out instead, teetering but not falling, one second, and then one second more.

Trevor inhales slowly. His chest lifts, and his belly rises against mine. Then he exhales just as slowly—one, two, three, four—with his lips slightly pursed like he's blowing through a straw. I have no choice but to breathe with him. We're in this together. He's not letting go, and I'm not fighting.

He presses his forehead to mine, and in a raw voice, he chants, "Don't be afraid. I won't hurt you. I'll never hurt you again. You're safe. I'm stronger now. I'd die before I hurt you again. I'm so fucking sorry, Izzy. I'm so sorry. So very sorry. I didn't mean to do it. I'm so fucking sorry. You're okay. I won't hurt you. I swear." His tears drop on my cheeks. His wild curls tickle my face.

His looped arms have mine trapped at my sides. I wriggle them. He immediately relaxes his hold even more. I reach up and push his hair back. He backs his head an inch away and blinks at me. Pale lines radiate from his pupil and make his eyes more blue than gray. They're so clear. I can read them like a book. He's scared. Uncertain. Fascinated.

"I lost my clothes," I whisper like I'm telling him something he doesn't know. What he just said was too big. I can't take it on now, here, naked in a ditch.

His soft lips twitch. My insides jump like I've got bingo, and my face blazes.

"Me, too," he whispers back.

"What do we do?"

His brow wrinkles. "I don't think we have a lot of choices."

"How far away from home are we?"

I'm so close, I can see his pupils widen when I say the word *home*. Something low in my stomach pulls. Oh, no. I have to pee. I squeeze my thighs together.

"What's wrong?" he asks, immediately picking up on my discomfort.

"I—uh—" Don't make me say it. Read my mind. Please.

He has the grace to switch the conversation back. "We're about an hour's walk away. Less if we shift."

I check on my wolf. She's conked out. I give her a few mental pokes, but she's dead to the world. "I don't think my wolf has the energy."

"She wore herself out," he says, the corners of his lips curling again. I like his smile. It doesn't seem intentional. It kind of slips out by accident.

"It's going to suck without shoes." Scavengers go barefoot whenever they can, so they have tough soles, but I've never walked outside without shoes, not even as a pup. My mom would've lost her mind and called me a *bog rat*.

"I could carry you," Trevor offers. His cheekbones darken. It's funny. *Now* he blushes, while his dick has been poking me this whole time. The tip is actually kind of pulsing.

And now I'm blushing, too. "I'm too heavy. You couldn't carry me for an hour."

He scoffs. "Bullshit. You're super-compact. I could carry you one-handed."

"Super-compact? Like a car?"

"I mean, I wouldn't say you're as big as a *car*, per se, but if you were, I could still carry you." He pauses, his eyes dancing. "Maybe not one-handed, but—"

By some miracle, I giggle, even though I'm naked with Trevor and a bunch of dead leaves are stuck to my hip. I even let out a little snort.

A big, delighted smile straight-out *breaks* across his face, and the air in my lungs leaves in a whoosh.

"I—maybe—uh—we should—uh—I don't want to get up. You'll see me naked," I say in a rush, so discombobulated that what I'm actually worrying about spills from my mouth.

"Oh. Yeah." He winces. "I guess, I could, uh, not look?"

"Yeah. I won't look, either." I'm cringing so hard that I can't help but squirm—and then I realize I'm squirming against him naked. His dick jerks. He grunts, embarrassed. I freeze. "Sorry," I squeak.

He blows out a breath. "No. No worries. I'm good. You're good. Everything's fine. Don't be scared. I can control myself."

"I know."

He plows on, the smile and blush gone, "I'm not like that. Like I was that night. I swear to you, that was—I lost control, but I never will again. I'll die before I do. Okay, Izzy? I *swear* to you."

His voice has dropped to a raw growl. For the first time, I can smell *his* distress. I guess I've never been able to scent it over my own fear before. I hate the smell. It's not gross, or anything, but it needles me. I have to *do* something.

I brush his hair away from his face again, even though it isn't tickling me anymore. It feels forward—and I am *never* forward—but it settles my nerves, and his scent sweetens almost immediately. He pokes my belly harder, too.

"I don't want you to die," I mumble. I can't meet his eyes. It's too much to look at him and touch him at the same time.

He ducks his head, catching the hand smoothing his hair so I'm palming his cheek instead. "Did you know I was here?" he asks.

I glance up, surprised by the question, and I'm caught again. His eyes are windows. I can see everything. He wants me to say yes, so bad, but he's braced for me to say no. He's waiting for my answer with bated breath. His chest froze mid-rise, and it's pressing against my achy breasts.

"I knew you might be," I say.

"You came anyway." He's trying to school his face, but he can't. Not with those eyes.

I could nod and agree with his assumption that seeing him was a risk I decided to take. I don't have to let him in.

I don't ever let anyone in.

But that's not quite true anymore, is it? I talked to Nia, Rosie, and Flora. What was it I said? I want to go back to the start and do things differently.

Of course, that's impossible, but—I could start doing things differently *now*. I could decide. On a random whatever-day-of-the-week-this-is.

"I came to see you," I admit. "I was hoping you were here."

"Why?" There is panic on his face and in his scent. No, not panic. Dread. What does he think I'm going to say?

My panic rises in response to his, and my scent sours. Thank goodness no one else is here. We *stink*.

His body has stiffened.

I could dodge. Say something like "to talk." I could be less than fully honest, and he'd never know, and somehow, I could change the subject, and we could bumble on like virtual strangers forever.

But he's still holding me, even though he's so tense that the veins on his forearms have popped.

"You're my mate," I answer, quietly, staring at the dusting of hair between his pecs to avoid his eyes. "I know it's probably too late, that we can never—but if there's a chance—I want what other people have, you know? At least I want to *try*. I gave up on life for a long time. I don't want to give up for good."

Since I'm staring at his pecs, I miss his hand moving, so when he cradles my jaw, I startle. He jerks his hand away, but I'm quicker. I chase his palm down with my cheek and nuzzle him with my face like I'm my wolf. A faint vibration sounds from deep in his chest.

"I'm so fucking sorry," he says.

"Is that all you are?" My voice is sharp. I drop my hand. What am I doing? I don't talk back. I *never* have an attitude. I have a sense of self-preservation instead. Dad's wolf would've never let me live to adulthood if I sassed him.

I tense. Trevor blows out a deliberate breath and lowers the hand I was nuzzling so he can gently rub slow circles on my lower back. He's not close enough to my butt that I worry about him touching me there. He's right at the hollow that aches after a long shift at the infirmary. I blow out a breath, too.

"I'm scared, too." He gives a short, bitter laugh. "Absolutely terrified, to be honest. I don't want to fuck this up—

more than anything in the world, I *can't* fuck this up—and I have no idea what I'm doing. There's no manual, no one to ask, even if I could—" He pauses, and I think he's done, but then he adds, "But I'm also happier than I've ever been in my life."

I look him in the eye again. "You don't look happy."

"It's a terrified kind of happiness," he says, mustering up one of his shy, rueful smiles that makes my stomach dip, but I'm not getting distracted. I've got some moxie left, and I'm using it all up.

"You can ask me. Okay?"

Still smiling softly, he dips his head, flashing his bare neck. We're both quiet for a minute.

He stops rubbing my back so he can trace my middle spine with the tips of his fingers, up and down, up and down.

"I don't want what other people have," he finally says, just when I think we're done talking. "I want you."

My skin flushes, my heart skips, and since I don't know what to say back, I whisper, "I have to pee."

He chuckles like I told a joke, jumps to his feet, and holds out a hand. I take it. He's careful to keep his eyes on mine as I stand, much less gracefully than he did. I'm sore and stiff. I've never slept on the ground before.

His weight slams into my back, knocking me to my knees.

He tackles me to the ground.

My wrist snaps. My face hits the dirt.

My chin cracks on a rock.

"Izzy? Shit. What's wrong?"

My eyes slowly focus on Trevor's pinched brow, his frowning mouth.

"I'm cold," I say. "I want to go home." It's close enough to the truth.

I don't want to tell him that I remembered and every drop of hope that collected during our conversation drained away in the blink of an eye, and I'm afraid of him again.

That when I say home, I mean my windowless room with blank eggshell walls.

That I'm broken and a coward and this is never, ever going to work.

Instead, as he leads the way out of our hidey-hole, I grab his hand. He startles, but he squeezes me tight right away, and I don't let go all the way back to Old Den.

I make a decision. I hold on. Even scared and hopeless, I don't let go.

I immediately fuck things up, and I have no idea how, but I don't ask Izzy to tell me what happened. That absolutely feels like the wrong move. One second, we were talking, and the next, she turned white as a sheet and clammed up. It felt like a knife in my belly, but I breathed through it and distracted myself by looking for interesting things to show her. I don't dare open the bond, so I end up narrating our walk back like the world's worst trail guide.

"Spiderweb over there. Big one."

"Woodpecker hole."

"Oops. Someone lost a tire."

"Butterfly on that milkweed. Nope. That's a moth. Moth on that milkweed."

She does let me hold her hand, but she won't let me carry her. It's slow going, and her feet are obviously hurting by the time we got to the cottage where we'd left our clothes.

"Soda can popped," I point out. The dented can is laying empty by her abandoned shoes. She hums politely like she did with the spiderweb, the woodpecker, and the moth.

Her wolf is a tiny critter, so her shirt and pants are fine, but my beast busted through the seams of my jeans, so I have to stroll into the den shirtless in my boxer briefs. Luckily, the elastic stretched instead of ripped.

Everyone's eyes are on us when we get back. Old Den shifters do not believe in discretion. At Salt Mountain, if something didn't concern you, you had better keep your nose out of it. At Moon Lake, at least among the ranked wolves, it's bad manners to let on that you're snooping. At Old Den, there's no such thing as other people's business. Drama is shared as freely as the pool, the food, and the workload.

Izzy tenses as we enter the gauntlet, but she holds her head high.

"There's my boy," Granddad Cameron calls out when we pass. "Worried I was going to have to come after you." He cackles, and the elders he's sitting with crack up, too.

He's got his cup of water with a straw close at hand and someone brushed his hair. Good. Back at Salt Mountain, if I didn't get him straight in the morning, it might be lunchtime before one of the females had time to tend to him.

Here, work seems more haphazard in that there aren't bosses or a starting bell or things like that, but still, things that need doing are more likely to get done in a timely fashion. Everything is everyone's responsibility, and instead of no one doing it, like what would happen in another pack, shit just gets done quicker. I can't explain it. I didn't think our nature worked like that.

"Did you get lost?" Pritchard asks as he passes me on the way out, carrying a full laundry basket on each shoulder.

"Moss grows on the north side of the tree," Irv Nevitts adds, clapping me on the back. He's following Pritchard with a bottle of detergent. Not sure why Pritchard has to carry two baskets while Irv carries the detergent. No. Strike that. I know why. Pritchard lost a bet.

"Sun rises in the east," Conway Kemble volunteers.

"Sets in the west," that little shit Danny pipes in.

When our group of evacuees arrived from Salt Mountain, most of us were honorarily adopted into the scavenger faction, but I guess because I was ranked at Moon Lake, I'm considered a nob, so I regularly get my balls busted. I glance over at Izzy to see if she's bothered, but she's not getting tenser or redder in the face, although that might be because it's not possible. She's pretty tense and red.

When we're almost to the relatively empty far side of the den, we walk past Drona and Rae, two of Rosie's relatives, and they whistle at me.

"Fine catch you've got there, Owens," Drona says. "You could bounce a quarter off that ass."

"A keeper," Rae adds. "Don't let that one slip off your line."

Izzy squeezes my hand tighter, and for a split second, I think things are going to be okay. It got awkward and weird, maybe even bad for a while, but she's squeezing my hand, so we're still in this.

And then she mumbles something and flees down the corridor to the female dorm.

"Oh, sorry, Trev," Drona says.

"We didn't mean to embarrass her," Rae comes closer. "Should I go talk to her?"

"No. It's not on you. It's on me."

Rae doesn't seem convinced, but she pats me on the forearm, and leaves me staring down the tunnel where Izzy disappeared.

I don't know what to do. My wolf is howling for our skin. He sees no reason he can't bust into the warren where she's holed up and make himself at home until she deigns to pay attention to us again. He's been taking lessons from Pritchard.

There was a book Mom read us when we were kids that had a bunch of animals who did jobs and drove weird vehicles, like the worm drove an apple and the gorilla drove a banana. Anyway, on each page of the book, there was a yellow bug for you to find. That's Pritchard. If Nia's around, look long enough, you'll find Pritchard. Or his wolf.

The last thing I want to do is invade Izzy's space, though. She clearly needs time alone, and my wolf and I need to accept that.

Except I can't. I pace back and forth at the mouth of the corridor, and one by one, the females pass me to check on her, stone-faced on their way in, and with sad, encouraging smiles for me on their way out. I feel awkward, embarrassed, and underfoot, but I literally cannot bring myself to leave, not even to go stand by the fire or check on Granddad. Rosie is the first to visit. Nia comes by a little while later with tea. Flora comes by at lunch.

Cadoc drops by mid-afternoon on his break from work, and my wolf leaps to his feet, growling louder with every step Cadoc takes closer to the corridor like he has every intention of busting free and fighting the alpha. Cadoc is kind enough to ignore him. He comes to stand beside me, and we both stare into the dimly lit tunnel with our arms crossed.

"So how's the elder cottage coming?" he asks. He's not hassling me. This isn't Salt Mountain. If he's asking, he actually wants to know. When Cadoc gives an order or calls a person out, it doesn't come with a question mark.

"Good."

"You've got what you need?"

"I do."

"Need another set of hands? I could send Danny over." Cadoc lifts an eyebrow.

"I'm good." I'll keep the little shit busy if I have to, but given a choice, I'm not signing up to babysit a pup on the verge of his first shift.

Cadoc snorts. "Can't blame me for trying." He's quiet for a moment, and then he sighs. "Rosie says I'm supposed to tell you that Izzy's fine. She just needs some time. She'll come back out when she's ready."

I nod. A lump swells in my throat.

Cadoc lets out another deep, aggravated sigh. "She also told me to tell you not to tell Izzy that she told me to tell you."

I glance over. He grimaces. "I don't want to be saying dumb shit like that either, but here we are—I sound like a teenage female, and you're staring at a hole in the wall."

I nod. We sigh in unison.

We spend a few more moments considering the empty corridor together, and then Cadoc says, "Well, looks like you've got things handled over here." He claps me on the back and strides off toward the pool.

A sharp pain pierces my chest. Six years ago—hell, *one* year ago—I would've never imagined that I'd be so close to my mate, having a normal conversation with an alpha I respect, part of a pack, not an exile working my ass off for my keep. The shame is still there. I can't imagine it'll ever go away, but it's not all I feel anymore.

I have hope. I guess that's what hurts.

What is Izzy doing in there? I wish Rosie had told Cadoc to tell me that.

What if she comes out, and I'm the first thing she sees, and she turns white again?

I can't keep standing around like an idiot. I'm nearly crawling out of my skin.

Go to her. Hang your head, drop your ears, and show a little neck.

My wolf paces inside me, howling like if he's loud enough, I'll listen. He should know better by now.

I'm about to growl back at him when an idea pops into my head. I'll need human money and a ride. I scan the den, searching for a male who owes me a favor.

Pritchard's wolf is sunning himself on the small island in the middle of the pool. He owes me, but there's no way he's got cash. Same problem with Alec who's sitting on a work-bench, fiddling with a perfectly fine-looking pressure regu-lator valve while he surreptitiously listens to his mate as she reads aloud to the elders from an old copy of Reader's Digest. He might have Salt Mountain scrip left, but I doubt he's got cash.

Then Bevan wanders in from outside, eating a bag of cheese doodles. Perfect.

I intercept him by the fire, and he grins in greeting. "Trevor. What's up?" He raises a hand to high five me, real-izes his fingers are too cheesy, and knocks me with his elbow instead.

"I need a favor."

"I got you, man. You know I owe you for that still you fixed." He reaches into his pocket with his non-cheesy hand and whips out a baggie of weed.

I shake my head. "Not that kind of favor."

"Oh, right," he says, reaches across to his other pocket and pulls out a baggie of shrooms.

"I'm good on that. I need some human money. And to borrow a bike."

"Ah, man, you gonna run? That's a shame. Your female is

gonna be heartbroken. Who she gonna be looking around for all the time if you bail?"

"She looks around for me?"

"I assume it's you. You're her mate, right?" Bevan tucks his baggies back.

I tuck that nugget away for later. "I only need five bucks. And I'll only be gone a few hours."

"On a mysterious mission, eh? Cool, cool. No need to ask about the bike. Those are communal property. Except if you take one of the bikes that the nobs consider theirs, then you're stealing, and you have to listen to them bitch about it."

"Which bikes belong to the nobs'?"

"None of 'em. Like I said, they're all communal property. It's a crap shoot. If you come back, and one of 'em is pissed, then you stole it." Bevan shrugs. "Now, the money...I don't have it, but I can get it. Gimme ten minutes."

"Thanks, man."

"Hang out here," Bevan says, tilts his head back, empties the cheese doodle dregs into his mouth, and sneezes. When he's done, he takes off across the den to the area where the ranked wolves from Moon Lake tend to congregate and pulls Seth Rosser aside.

Seth doesn't seem friendly—even back at Moon Lake, he was not a friendly male—and his face darkens as he listens to whatever Bevan is saying. Finally, Bevan finishes his spiel and cocks his head, waiting for an answer. Seth scowls, but eventually, he takes his wallet out and shoves a wad of bills at Bevan.

Bevan grins, flashing his gold teeth, and then reaches into his weed pocket, digs deep, and takes out a simple woven cord bracelet with odds and ends like bottle caps and shells hung from it like charms. Seth immediately shoves the bracelet into his own pocket and turns back to his group of Moon Lakers.

Bevan bounds back to me. "All right, all right, the day is looking up," he says, counting his stack. It's at least a hundred bucks in small bills.

"All that for a bracelet?"

"All that for that specific bracelet," he says and hands me a ten. "Keep the change. Treat yourself to something special." He laughs and saunters off, and I head for the bikes.

It's a long-time habit for me to fly under the radar as best I can and avoid pissing people off, and I try to figure out which bikes might be spoken for, but there's no way to tell. I end up taking the one in the worst condition, and make a mental note to replace the sprockets and clean the rusty chain when I get back.

I'm not really sure where I'm going, except for southeast. A human road abuts the territory boundary there, and I figure if I follow it long enough, I'll find what I'm looking for. I've got a full tank of gas and five extra dollars, so I'm fairly confident I can make this happen.

My wolf isn't privy to my plans, so when I drive away from the den, he loses his mind, howling and launching himself into the border between us.

No.

Stay.

Don't leave her again.

Never again.

I try to breathe through it, try to cast pictures of my goal into his mind, but he's past listening. I have to pull over to get him back under control, and I'm struggling, until I feel a sharp tingle sensation in the bond. My wolf and I both freeze. For the past six years, there has been nothing but radio silence from our mate. I communicate, but it's like the radio signal that NASA sends into space. I could very well be transmitting into the void.

My wolf perks his ears. I focus on the place near my heart where the bond connects.

Izzy's wolf yaps.

It's not a real, audible yap. It's more of an *impression* of a yap, but it's clear as day. She wants to know what the ruckus is about.

Now my wolf is in a quandary. The last thing he wants to do is alarm or upset her, but he is alarmed and upset. I will him to chill out, desperately tossing images at him of us returning to the den to stand guard by the corridor to her nest. He doesn't trust me, but he's stuck. He lets out a reassuring rumble.

Izzy's wolf yaps again to let him know what she thinks about him worrying her over nothing.

For the next few minutes, I stand alone by the side of the road, straddling a busted dirt bike, while my wolf and I listen with bated breath to hear whether our mate will speak to us again through the bond. She doesn't, and we continue on our way, my wolf wary but calm, my heart filled with hope.

13

IZZY

I don't mean to be a drama queen. Back at Moon Lake, when I hid in my room, everyone would pretty much leave me alone, so I didn't feel like I was a hassle. Here, I had more visitors in one day than I think I ever had for the whole time I hibernated back home.

Rosie came first to make sure I was okay, and then there was a procession of food. Nia brought tea and cookies. Flora brought turkey sandwiches for lunch and ate with me, and then a little less than an hour later, Enid, the blonde in the bikini from the pool, brought me a lemon bar fresh from the oven.

A little after Enid leaves, my wolf senses a disturbance in the force and yips, but her agitation is short lived, and I don't investigate too closely. I can't handle anything else jump-scaring me from my subconscious. Not today. Tomorrow, I'll decide to pull myself together, but I'm giving myself today.

Drona, Rosie's older sister, brings dinner along with her daughters Avalon, Sara, and Kadi. The girls seem to think I'd been gone longer than overnight because they spend the whole meal catching me up on the gossip, starting with how Rosie yelled at Cadoc to hunt me down when I wasn't back by nightfall, and how Cadoc refused, and Rosie was so mad she shifted, and her wolf's head banged the den ceiling, so Cadoc commanded her wolf to shift back, and then he made Rosie wear an ice pack until she threatened to spend the night in the female dorm and fall into a coma from a concussion in her sleep and die, so Cadoc finally let it go.

The girls then recount every argument between Rosie and Cadoc from the very beginning when Rosie rejected Cadoc for being too snobby, so he slept on a ledge outside their trailer in the bog until she gave him a chance, which he then screwed up. Drona doesn't say much. She just listens to her girls, bemused, and plays with her bracelet, a child's craft with bobbins, corks, and bottle caps as charms.

I'm stuffed and exhausted by the time Rosie pops back in with a cup of chamomile tea, and I'm asleep before any of the females who bunk in the dorm turn in for the night.

My wolf wakes me up. At first, I think I'm having one of those lucid dreams that I can't really remember in the morning, but the seams on the plastic mattress are too pokey, and the air is too thick with very specific female scents for me not to be awake. Old Den females don't shave, and they prefer things all-natural, so when they gather together, things get a little organic, for lack of a better term.

My wolf is on her feet, her tail swishing like a metronome on 200 BPM. She senses her mate.

I can't smell him, and I might not know him well, but I'm sure he would never come into the female dorm without invitation, and honestly, I can't imagine him doing it *then*, either. He's kind of bashful, but in a masculine way, like a cowboy in a movie who's been out on the range a long time.

My stomach does a weird flip, catching my wolf's excitement. I lean over the side of the bed and crane my neck to see if I can make anything out through the beaded curtain that serves as a door to the dorm. The corridor seems empty.

My wolf whines and paws at our insides. He's out there. She's certain.

It can't hurt to check. If he isn't there, I can just take a trip to the latrines. Decision made. I slide my feet into my slippers and pad down the aisle between the bunks, my heart picking up its pace. I feel like I'm sneaking out, but there isn't the nagging dread of when I was younger, creeping through my parents' apartment, only the swirl of anticipation in my belly.

I *want* to see Trevor. I'll be disappointed if he's not there. The lightness I feel isn't just excitement. In a way, it's also relief that maybe everything isn't ruined or lost, not yet.

I part the curtains, peek out, and my heart soars. He's there, a few feet away, sitting on the ground with his back against the wall, his forearms braced on his bent knees. He was staring down, but as soon as he hears me, he lifts his head and gives me a rueful smile.

He holds up a soda can. An offering.

Oh, it's not just any soda—it's the kind with a cherry on the can! Where did he get it? In the planning of Operation Soda Pop, Nia asked me if I wanted to bring him "brown soda" or "clear soda." Those were the choices.

I pad over, and before he can stand, I sink down beside him, stretching my cotton sleep shirt over my knees, creating a cocoon for modesty.

"Hi," I whisper.

"Hi," he replies softly, pops the top, and passes me the can. As I take a sip, the fizz tickles my nose, and I remember the stairwell, his pinky close to mine but not touching, and how it felt like electricity was arcing between our hands.

We're closer now than we were then. My arm rests against his. I'm sitting cross-legged in my cocoon, and my bent knee is tucked under his bent leg. The closeness feels different. I'm hyperaware, but there's also all these other feelings, good and bad and mixed, inexplicable and barely suppressed. He belongs to me, but he's a stranger. He hurt me, and I've missed him. Terribly. It's an irretrievably tangled knot, but it isn't a hopeless ruin.

"Where'd you get it?" I ask, nodding at the can.

"A human settlement. About an hour away."

"What were you doing there?"

"Finding you a cherry cola." He flashes another bashful smile. His smoky lashes dip, brushing his cheeks. He's so beautiful, like Michaelangelo's David, but with sadder eyes.

"Thanks," I say and take a bigger sip. It really doesn't taste anything like cherry, and it's not nearly so good since I'm not dying of heat, but it's still sweet, all the same.

"I'm sorry," he says. "For earlier."

I stare at the can gripped in my hand. "You didn't do anything."

We're quiet for a minute because we both know he did, but that's not what we're talking about, but also, it *is*, isn't it?

This isn't the time or place. It's late. We're sitting in a public corridor. Anyone could walk by. And why dig up the past now? What good can it do?

Still, I ask, very quietly, "When you did it, did you *know* you were doing it?"

He tenses, and his lungs catch. For a second, neither of us breathes. Then he exhales slowly. Intentionally.

"Yes and no. Afterward, I remembered everything I did. In the moment, I wasn't there." His voice has dropped a register, but he speaks very deliberately. "My wolf wasn't there, either."

"Was it like something took over you?"

"You could put it that way. It wasn't like I had it in me to do that, and the rut let it out. I swear, that...it isn't in me." His jaw tightens. He stares at the rock wall across from us, stricken, but clearly determined to answer my questions. "If I were there at all, I would have found a way to stop. I swear to you."

His shame is so heavy, I can feel its weight. Not through the bond. In the air. It's unbearable, but my instinct isn't to look away or change the subject or comfort him. I want to slice into it. Tear into it with my teeth.

"I was aware the whole time," I say. "I felt everything."

His hands curl into fists. The veins in his neck pop, pulsing, but he remains very, very still, and he listens.

"My face was in the dirt. I couldn't breathe. You broke my wrist, and then my arm got trapped under me. The bones rolled together. I could *feel* it." I swipe my nose with my sleeve. "You dug your claws in me. Why did you do that? I couldn't move. You were so much stronger. You didn't need your claws."

Tears stream down his face. "I don't know," he says.

"You bit me." I yank down the collar of my sleep tee. I'm crying, too.

He looks at the angry red marks on my shoulder, at the dents they make because so much flesh was too mangled to heal. He doesn't want to. It kills him. But he looks and doesn't look away.

"They had to bring in a human doctor to reconstruct the muscle. I had stitches. Like a human."

"I'm sorry," he says. "I'm sorry. I'm so fucking sorry." Like a litany.

"And then you left me," I go on, my voice breaking. "You left me on the ground for other males to deal with. Like I was ruined. You *left me*." Now my voice is shaking with rage. I didn't know I was angry. I had to protect myself for so long from my parents' story—that I fucked up by leaving the apartment. If I had only listened to them, none of this would have happened. *I* did this to myself.

I spent all my energy protecting myself from their blame that I never even considered that I might be *furious*. "Why didn't you come back for me? Send me a letter? *Something*?"

"I was ashamed."

"I was *hurt*. I was *alone*."

"I didn't want to remind you."

"Do you think I was ever able to forget?"

I'm hissing at him. He rumbles his replies, his pain roughening the words. There is so much rage coursing through my veins, I can't believe I'm still sitting here, but I am, pressing even tighter to his side, our heads tilted even closer.

"No," he answers, his head high, ravaged eyes meeting mine. "I know that."

"I never, ever hated you. Do you know that?"

His brow creases. He gazes at me for a long moment. I keep my head high, too.

"I missed you every second of every day," he says. "I—" He pauses. Whatever he was going to say, he thinks better of it. "I thought about you all the time."

"I wouldn't let myself think about you." I say it to hurt him, but my rage is burning itself out, and my heart aches when he flinches. I shrink into myself, tucking my knees to my chest and wrapping my arms around them. "Everyone stared at me, so I didn't go out. They pitied me for being so stupid. They thought I brought it on myself. I thought so, too."

"No—"

I don't let him finish what he's saying. "All my life, I always thought what I was told to think, and then after that night, it was like I was a broken puppet, and everyone dropped my strings, so I just lay there because all I was really made of was other people's expectations." I scrub the last of my tears from my eyes. "I'm not a puppet anymore. *I* picked myself up. *I* came here. You can feel sorry, but that's not what I need from you. I want a mate."

I can't look at him. I've never spoken like this to anyone before, let alone a male, one who I know can hurt me.

But he won't. I know that, too.

For a long moment, he's silent, and then, finally, he says, "I understand." He stands and holds out his hand. "Come on, mate. It's late. Let's go home."

My heart leaps. With surprise. And fear.

And hope.

14

TREVOR

I am absolutely unprepared for a mate. Psychologically. Emotionally. *Logistically*.

I've been living on a raised platform with an overhang I threw together to protect Granddad Cameron and me from the rain. When we got to Old Den, I didn't know Alec had made his way here, and for a minute, we figured Granddad would stay with him, but Nola, the female who raised his mate, can't tolerate an unmated male in the house, not even an old stray like Granddad.

That was fine with Granddad. He likes the bachelor life. He's in for a change.

When Izzy said she wanted a mate, I brought her right to my lean-to. She's sleeping on my bedroll, which is only a few moth-eaten quilts on a canvas drop cloth I salvaged back at Salt Mountain. Granddad is snoring up a storm on his cot. I'm sitting on the edge of the platform in the morning drizzle. There's not room enough under the overhang for three.

I need a bed. Table. Chairs. Three more fucking walls, at a minimum.

The weather's warm enough now, but I'll need a fire-place by winter, which means brick or stone. I earn my keep, and I can earn hers, too, but communes don't produce their own drywall and fiberglass insulation. Building materials cost money.

My throat tightens as the list grows in my head until Izzy lets out her own delicate snort and snuggles deeper under the blankets. The only visible parts of her are the top of her head and the bare left foot she's stuck out for temperature regulation. My lungs expand, and the thud in my heart eases. She's here. It's all good. Better than I ever prayed for.

She'll wake up soon, and so will Grandad. I don't want either of them out in the damp. I quietly slip down and go fetch breakfast. Everyone is acting very, very natural.

"Hi, Trevor," Enid chirps when I arrive at the long tables where the pack eats in random shifts.

"Hey there, handsome," Rae says as she passes with a pan of biscuits.

"Sleep in?" Arly teases, following with a pot of coffee.

"Good morning, Trevor," Drona calls.

"Hi!" her daughters chime in unison, waving.

At least Danny does me the favor of ignoring me. He's busy shoveling eggs in his face with one hand while he scrolls on his phone with the other. I'll never get used to how this cave has Wi-Fi when Salt Mountain manages with one telephone spliced off a wire that runs to a human's cabin further up the mountain.

"Where's Izzy?" Nia demands.

Rosie groans. "Ever heard of tact, Nia?"

"That's some nob shit. You don't need tact if you've got balls."

Pritchard's wolf is lounging on the bench beside her. He

raises his head, stares meaningfully at her lap, and cocks a bushy, wolfish eyebrow.

"Figure of speech," Nia says.

Pritchard's wolf snorts, steals a piece of ham off her plate, and leaps down before the swat she aims at him can land.

"She's still sleeping," I tell the room at large.

"Sleeping where?" Nia demands.

"My place."

Every female in the vicinity goes "oooooo" at once. Danny, too, the little shit.

My face burns as I head over to the spread to make three plates. Granddad's teeth don't number very many these days, so he gets a bowl of scrambled eggs and crumbled sausage. It's still a balancing act when I'm done since I want to bring them both a mug of coffee.

"Here. I'll help." Flora rescues me as I begin my slow trek back outside.

"Thanks." I hand her a bowl and a plate.

Flora spends most of her time helping with the elders, and since she's related to Granddad, we trade off watching him a lot. She's very easy to be around. Her mate will scowl at you if he thinks you're walking or standing too close to her, and he's always curt when she's not around, but I kind of get it now. My skin hasn't felt right since I left Izzy to get food, and I'm not excited about her being out of my sight and around males again.

Maybe she's not totally committed to the healer thing. She's smart. I could teach her how to fix stuff. Or I could learn how to heal. That's kind of fixing stuff, if you think about it.

Izzy is still sleeping when we get back, but Granddad is up. He's sat up and thrown his legs over the side of his cot, but he hasn't worked up the energy to take it to the next step yet. He's groggily peering at the lump that is Izzy. She's tucked her foot back under the blanket. She must've gotten cold.

"There you are," Granddad booms when he catches sight of us. "There's a female in your bed."

"That's Izzy," I say quietly, hoping he'll follow suit.

"She's got pretty fur," he booms even louder, and then he very obviously notices our company and the bowl of sausage and eggs she's bringing. "Not as pretty as yours, Flora, but nice, all the same."

"Thanks, Granddad. Want to go back to the den with me after you eat?"

"Sure, sure, I can do that. I've got time today."

Izzy is stirring now. Her blanket moves, and I catch a whiff of blood.

I don't panic.

My blood pressure shoots through the roof, and my fangs spike, but I keep my mouth shut and set down the tin plate that I've partially crumpled in my hand. She's not hurt. It's not that kind of blood.

She's drawing herself up, curling herself so her legs are tucked under her butt. Her face has drained white. Flora's eyes flick from Izzy to me. She's scented what's up, too.

Please, let Granddad not notice. His senses aren't what they used to be. And if he does notice, please, by all that's holy, don't let him announce it like he's got a bullhorn. Izzy's eyes dart around the bare shelter, silently panicking.

My mom was always matter-of-fact about her time of the month, but the females at the Academy and those I knew at Salt Mountain treated it as top secret, passing each other supplies like spies, and would never think of talking about it in front of a male.

I don't have supplies. The closest latrine is back in the den. So are Izzy's things.

If I asked Flora for help, she would without hesitation, but I'll be damned if the first time I have to take care of my mate, I foist it off on someone else. Besides, it'd take Flora just as long to run back to the den as it'll take me, and she's got to get Granddad settled for the day.

I climb onto the platform, careful not to spill Izzy's coffee, and kneel in front of her, carefully setting her plate on the plank floor. "Are you okay to eat this while I run back to the den for your things and some water to bathe?" I ask her softly.

Her cheeks blaze pink, and she nods, staring at the plate. She can't look at me. I press my forehead to hers. My wolf rumbles reassuringly.

Her lashes flutter, and she glances up. Our eyes lock. "Thanks," she says.

"I'll be back soon."

"Okay."

I don't want to leave. I have to force myself to take each step. Flora and Granddad are with her. They'll stay until I get back. She's not going to disappear. She's not hurt; she's embarrassed. This isn't an emergency.

My body doesn't believe it. I sprint back to the den, my wolf spurring me to go faster. I ask Rosie to gather Izzy's things, and thankfully, she doesn't question me about it. I fill a bucket, and then it occurs to me—what if Izzy doesn't have supplies?

She should, right? But what if she doesn't. I can't go through her stuff. I blink, look around, and realize I'm standing in the middle of the den, water sloshing over the side of the bucket, huffing like I've run a marathon. I must look moon mad.

I force myself to stop and draw in a long, deep breath. I am capable of caring for my mate. She came to me. I am never going to give her cause to regret it.

I need a mated female. The ones who spend their days around the den tend to congregate in a work area they've set up overlooking the play enclosure they created for the smallest pups. I've fixed their old Singer a few times. It's a beautiful machine, but its drive belt is on its last leg, and a replacement is going to be a bitch to source.

I take a second to collect myself before I go over. I'm still not one hundred percent used to interacting with females. At Salt Mountain, I stayed away from them, and since I was ranked at the bottom of the pack, they took no notice of me. Old Den females don't let you keep to yourself. They're too curious.

I'm still thinking of just how to ask for what I need when I arrive. Instantly, at least a dozen heads rise from their darning and beading and whittling to stare at me, and a half dozen pups trample to their makeshift fence to peer at me over the top. I stop in my tracks. Water sloshes. I drop the bucket before I spill on their territory.

Rae Kemble launches the interrogation. "Trevor Floyd. What are you doing here?"

"Back so soon?"

"Where's Izzy?"

"What's the bucket for?"

"What do you think a bucket is for, Gracie Bedoe? Sheesh."

"I wish I had curls like that. He looks like one of those little naked baby angels."

"Girl, I don't know what you're talking about, that one's all man."

"Ignore them, sweetheart," Drona says to me. "You all need to stop. He's blushing."

At Salt Mountain, a few miles away from town, there is a pond in a dell where the geese stopover in fall. If you come upon them, first they stare, and then they honk. I mean no offense, but the females remind me exactly of those honking geese right before they come for you.

"Thank you," I say to the group at large because it seems like the wisest course of action. I scan the gathering for the friendliest face. They're all grinning like butter wouldn't melt in their mouth. Even the pups.

Drona is closest, and she doesn't seem to be in the middle of anything. She's having a cup of tea.

"Uh, Drona?"

"Yes, sweetheart?" She smiles up at me. I feel like the most awkward male that has ever existed.

I step closer, turn my back to the pack of females—which raises the hairs on the back of my neck—and crouch so I can speak to her privately.

"Uh. Um. I need to borrow—oh, some female goods. If you have any to spare? Pads, I guess? Or tampons? Or something along those lines? Anything. Anything would be good. Thank you." My face is radiating heat.

And then, because Fate has always had it out for me, Seth Rosser appears right next to me, glaring down at Drona and me, reeking of aggression.

"What do you need, Floyd?" he asks, his wolf roughening his voice.

I immediately rise to my feet. I'm in his space, and I don't give way. I throw my shoulders back, and my wolf rumbles a warning. His snarls.

"What the hell are you doing, Seth?" Drona pushes her

chair back and stands, too. She tries to wedge between us, but neither of us let her.

When I first arrived at Salt Mountain, I was fair game, and in a way, it helped me survive. I gladly took a beating from every male in that pack looking to shore up his rank. And then, one day—a particularly bad day—I let Bram Blackburn whale on me to within an inch of my life. Granddad did the best he could to patch me up, and while I was lying on the back porch of the Cameron's ramshackle house, bleeding out, he asked me who was going to take care of him if I managed to get myself killed.

After that, I stopped letting the males win, and eventually, I won more than I lost, and they began to think better of trying me. I'm not a natural fighter, and I never trained like the high-ranked in Moon Lake, but I guess when you're ambivalent about whether or not you make it out alive, it gives you an edge. Anyway, it's been a while since I backed down from anyone. I'm out of the habit.

Seth flashes fang. His wolf growls. I jerk my chin. We can go if he wants.

"Seth, you are acting like a complete jackass." Drona tries to tug him away by the arm, but he's not budging. "Do you think I'm impressed?"

"I'm kind of impressed," Rae says behind us in a stage whisper. "This is not a matchup I would have predicted. The beta versus Mr. Fix-It."

"Five buttons on Seth," someone says.

"Ten on Trevor. I like a dark horse."

"Have you ever seen Trevor fight?"

"No, but I love watching a nob get punched in the face." Mina Scurlock calls over, "I'll go fifty-fifty with you, Trevor, if you wipe that look off his face."

"We're not supposed to call them nobs anymore," someone corrects her.

"Off that arrogant dickhead's smug, superior face," Mina amends.

"No one is punching the dickhead," Drona says, giving Seth another tug. He shakes her off. His wolf growls louder. She heaves a sigh, and then, without warning, pops her fangs and sinks them into the meat of Seth's upper arm, straight through the sleeve of his polo shirt.

Several females hoot.

A pup squeals, "She bit him! No biting! No biting, Drona!"

With her fangs still sunk in his bicep, she backs away. He goes with her grudgingly, his body wired, his wolf snapping in frustration.

My wolf plops his ass back down and proceeds to groom himself, more amused than anything. He's as good-natured as I am. As I was.

Drona pulls Seth a yard or so away, and the females shush each other, trying to eavesdrop on what she's saying to him, making it impossible to overhear. She's giving him an earful. Seth scowls into the middle distance, mouth shut, a flush creeping up his neck.

"Ooo, the beta's getting yelled at," a pup crows.

Poor bastard. Obviously, he feels a claim on Drona, but she's Geralt Powell's mate. My gut twists thinking of the name. He was part of that bullshit around why Izzy's family wouldn't let us mate. Good for Drona that she's left him behind.

She finishes what she has to say and doesn't seem to want to hear his side. He tries a few times, but she cuts him off, and eventually, he jerks a nod and stalks away.

"No TV for him tonight," a pup says and sighs.

"Got to go to bed early," another pup agrees.

Drona returns and smiles at me sheepishly. "Sorry about that."

"It's all right."

"He was out of line."

"You put him right back in."

"I did, didn't I?" Drona grins, and she looks ten years younger. "Let's get you some 'female goods'."

She gives me half a box of tampons and a chunk of soap wrapped in cheesecloth, and ignoring my protests, loads me up with a bunch of sheets and blankets, which she ties in a bundle that I can sling over my back. She says, "If her body's settled enough that she's getting her period, she's going to want a nest."

The words echo in my head, over and over, on the walk back. I want Izzy to feel settled—so much that I can't think about it too deeply—but I never dared even imagine anything like this, so I have no plan. No provisions.

Growing up, Dad taught us to live close to the bone and sock away whatever we could for our future mate. In Moon Lake, I had savings, an apartment, a vehicle. I lost it all when I was exiled, and I never even thought about it. I'd lost Izzy. The stuff was nothing.

But how is she going to feel safe without a bed to nest in? And she's going to want her own space, her own bathroom and kitchen. The scavengers are mostly cool with the communal arrangements, but the ranked wolves who came to Old Den, especially the few females like Lowry Powell, prefer the cabins we're building around the den.

I can build whatever Izzy wants, but it'll take time and materials, which I'll need to trade for or find a way to make.

I walk, the water sloshes in the bucket, and I worry. By

the time I get back to our shelter, I have a list in my head as long as my arm and panic knotted in my chest.

Then I see my mate.

She's still sitting on the bedroll, hiding in the heaped blankets, her eyes brimming with uncertainty as she puts on a brave face and chats with Granddad.

"Here he comes now," Granddad's saying as I set everything down on the edge of the platform. "I told you he'd be right back. No flies on that one." Granddad grins at me. "Do you know how we became pack?" he asks. Both Flora and Izzy murmur that they don't, although Flora's definitely heard the story a hundred times.

"Oh, they don't want to hear about that. Tell them about the time you nearly caught that bog worm," I attempt to divert him as I gather the breakfast dishes. Flora casts me a peeved glance. The bog worm story is twice as long, and she's heard it twice as many times.

Of course, much like the bog worm, Granddad doesn't take the bait. "This one here just showed up one day, you know. Slept on the back porch. Didn't say nothing. Didn't eat. We figured he'd die or wander off soon enough. And then one night, there was a storm, one of those summer storms, right in the middle of August when the sky goes pitch dark in the middle of the day." Granddad stops to cough, and I grab his water from the floor beside his cot and put it in his hand. "No one was home but me and him, and he was dead to the world out on the porch. And then, between cracks of lightning, I heard something."

Granddad imitates a high-pitched whimper. "Like that. Like a scared pup. To this day, I don't know how I heard it. My ears were already shot by then, but Fate wanted me to hear. In my heart, I knew I had to go. The pull—there was something supernatural about it. I shifted because my wolf's knees were better, and like anyone, I was steadier on four feet than two, and I went hunting after that sound."

Izzy is leaning forward, her eyes wide. The scent of her misery lifts, and my embarrassment fades. I guess Granddad can tell whatever stories he wants if it distracts her.

"The rain was coming down in sheets. You couldn't see an inch beyond your face. Couldn't smell nothing. I had a sense, though, so I followed it down to the river that runs down the holler out back of the houses. I don't know how I saw her, either, in all that rain and with no light, but there she was, a young female, trapped on a tiny strip of land in the middle of the raging river, soaked to the bone and shaking like a leaf."

Granddad takes a sip of water, pausing for effect.

"What I never understood was how you heard her whimper with all the rain and the raging flood," Flora takes the opportunity to ask.

The furrows on Granddad's forehead deepen. "I don't understand it, either. By all rights, I shouldn't have been able to hear it, and it was a wolf's whimper, not a female's, and Tandie—her name was Tandie Boyle—she was in her skin. That little island she was sitting on shouldn't have been there either. Some branches had been swept downstream and were diverting the current."

"Fate," Flora says softly.

"Or witchcraft," Granddad suggests, his voice dropping to a whisper. He does have a flare for the dramatic. "Anyway, there was no time. The water was rising. Now my wolf had never been a strong swimmer, but if I spent the time and energy shifting, I would've never been able to get to her. I had no choice but leap in and doggie paddle for it."

Izzy gasps, and Granddad pauses a moment to bask.

He sips his water and continues. "It took every ounce of

strength I possessed to fight that current. I gulped down so many mouthfuls of water that my belly swelled up, dragging me down like an anchor. Many times, I almost gave up, but a voice in my head said, 'Roderick, you can't give up now. That poor little female will surely die.'"

Izzy's lips are parted as she hangs on every word, so invested that she's clutching a sheet. My chest warms. I love to see her like this. Riveted.

"Well, I wasn't as old then as I am now, but I hadn't been a young wolf in many years. Sadly, mid-stream, my energy began to flag. I paddled, and I kicked, but I was taking on water, you could say. Tandie creeped to the edge and reached for me, but I was too far away. I thought for sure it was lights out for the both of us when I heard a shout from the bank. 'Hold on!'"

Granddad cups his hands around his mouth to deliver the line. My face heats, and I can't look at Izzy anymore. I swear, the story used to be shorter.

"This young male of yours strolled into the roaring deluge like it was nothing. It knocked him over, and swept him downstream, and when I thought that we were done for, he popped up, hauling himself up on a fallen tree, and fought his way back to us only to be knocked over again. I managed to get close enough so that Tandie could fish me out, but I was done. I could only lie there and watch this one do battle with the flood coming down the mountain."

"Why didn't you shift?" Izzy asks. I glance over. Her face is etched with worry. For me. I want to wrap her in my arms, and kiss her for it, and lie to her that I was never in danger, and go back in time and whack myself upside the head for being so reckless when she was out in the world alone.

I clear my throat. "I knew I'd have to carry them both to shore. Couldn't do that as my wolf, and I was losing strength. I couldn't rely on being able to shift back to my skin when I got to them."

"And that's what he did. He tucked my wolf under one arm and carried the female on his shoulder, wading through the water up to his chest. He lost his footing a few times on the trek back, but he didn't go under, and he didn't drop either of us until we were safe on dry land." Granddad smiles at me fondly.

Before that day, he hadn't paid me any mind, but afterward, he adopted me as his gopher, calling me at all hours to fetch him things or check out suspicious noises outside. The raccoons at the trashcans behind the garage came to know me so well, they wouldn't run when they saw me. It was a few years before I came to appreciate that he wasn't having me fetch and carry for his convenience. He saw a male drowning and decided not to let him.

"How did Tandie get stuck in the middle of the river?" Izzy asks.

Granddad shakes his head. "She didn't say, and I never got the chance to ask her. She's under the care of the Blackburns, and they keep her on a tight leash." He shrugs. "Maybe she was out fishing."

I don't think that's it. I have no evidence—just a gut feeling—but I've often wondered if she was waiting for the river to carry her away, and we didn't so much rescue her as foil her plans. If so, that's two of us who Granddad saved despite ourselves.

Just then we're interrupted by a whistle from the woods. Izzy tenses. I turn to stand between her and our visitor although I've already caught a whiff of him.

Alec Cameron strides out of the trees, stopping a good ten feet away out of respect. It's clear from the mud spackling his clothes that he's already been working for a while.

He's one of the few who rises at dawn and works 'til dusk. He's always earning his place. I understand that.

"Good morning," he calls over.

I hop down and walk over to greet him so he doesn't come closer. Izzy's pulled a blanket up to her chin. Her uneasiness singes my nose.

"Five more minutes," Flora sings out as she helps Granddad with his boots.

"You said you'd be five minutes an hour ago," Alec grumbles, but not loud enough that she can hear.

He shoves his hands in his pockets, preparing for a wait, and gives me a nod. "How goes the elder cabin?"

"Good. Framing's almost done. Should be starting the rafters today or tomorrow." My gut knots. These are long days, and I don't want to leave Izzy for so long, even nearby in the den. My wolf is sulking at the prospect.

"Rafters, eh?" Alec turns his head to watch Flora fuss over Granddad's shirt buttons and says, "Why don't I take that over for a few days, eh?"

"I couldn't ask you to do that."

"You didn't. I'm offering. I could do with some outside work for a change." He turns back to me and grins. "Maybe I come home not smelling like pipe sludge for a few days, my mate will be tempted into a second heat. Have you seen my pup? She's adorable. I need another one."

Alec isn't much of a talker. Even though we've ended up as de facto family through Granddad, this might be the most he's ever said to me.

My pride stings a little at the prospect of another male finishing my work, but my wolf would kill me if I turned him down, and I'm not about to look a gift horse in the mouth. "Thank you, man. I'll owe you."

He claps me on the shoulder. "Good luck," he says and kind of grimaces. What does that mean?

Finally, Flora gets Granddad sorted enough to move on out, and the three of them leave for the den, leaving Izzy in her bedding pile, staring at me with my bucket and stack of fresh blankets.

Her cheeks flush fresh pink, and she glances at me sideways from downcast eyes.

I stand awkwardly by the edge of the platform.

"I brought water for washing," I state the obvious. Yet again, my voice has dropped an octave on its own accord.

"I'm sorry," she whispers.

"No need for sorry."

"I thought I had another week."

"It's okay."

"It's really bad," she says, almost inaudibly. Now she's staring past my left ear. I'm talking to a spot on the ground in front of her.

I'm not embarrassed. Mom was very forthright about these things, and Dad lectured the squeamishness out of us when he overheard Tarian say "anything that bleeds for five days and doesn't die is unnatural" and ranted for, like, three hours straight about the miracle of female physiology, their proximity to the divine, and the male imperative to not piss them off.

Izzy, though—she's mortified. She hasn't made a move to stand. I want to help her, but I know getting closer is probably the worst thing to do. But I'm her mate. I'm up to bat, and it's go time. She came to me. I get to be the one to take care of her.

My gut knots with the memory of how badly I failed in the past, the shadow of it rising up and cutting me off at the knees, sending my anxiety surging, but I am not a coward, and I am not going to allow this simple thing to be hard.

"Come on." I don't take a step toward her, but I hold out a hand. "I know a good place to wash off. I won't look. I'll keep my eyes right on yours."

"I feel so stupid."

"I'm hungry," I say because it's literally the first feeling that pops into my head.

She's surprised into a short laugh. "You didn't get to eat the food you brought. I'm sorry."

"We'll get cleaned up, and on the way back, I'll show you my favorite berry patch."

"Berries aren't a good breakfast."

"Clearly, you've never talked to a bear."

She laughs again, and it's nervous and polite, but still, I love the sound. "I'm so embarrassed," she says. "I can't believe this happened."

"It'll be okay."

The words hang between us, sharp as glass. I wish I could've said them to her before. I wish I could've made them true. I pray with my whole soul that I can now, that it's not too late, and I know—I can feel under my ribs—that she hears all I mean when I say it, too.

"Ready?" I ask, locking eyes with her.

"Okay." She holds my gaze as she untangles herself from her nest and waddles to me like a penguin, her thighs pressed tight together. The tang of blood fills the air. She's wearing a really long T-shirt as pajamas, and from the quick glance I unintentionally took when she stood, it's a crime scene from the waist down.

Is that a normal amount of blood? Her color's good, she's not shaking, and the pulse in her neck is beating steadily. Going by what happened back at Moon Lake, I'm fairly sure she's been taught to suffer in silence instead of make a nuisance of herself, so I'll have to keep a close eye on her. Get something sweet into her now and some red meat later, for lunch.

She shoves her feet in her sneakers while I tuck a towel, a washcloth, the soap, and a tampon under my arm. Then I pick up the bucket and grab her hand. "Do you like berries?" I ask her.

"Depends. What kind?"

"Juneberries." I help her down from the platform.

"I've never heard of them."

"They look like blueberries." I lead her off into the trees. There's a clearing a few yards away in the opposite direction of the other cabins. I scouted it when I was planning my shelter but decided to build closer to the den so Granddad wouldn't have so far to walk.

"Do they taste like blueberries?" she asks.

"They taste kind of like a cross between a blueberry and an almond."

"Weird."

"Weird and delicious." I smile at her. She makes an effort to smile back, but her forehead's pinched. Even though I'm walking slow, she's struggling to keep up while squeezing her thighs together. She looks miserable.

"You know, when I was like fourteen or fifteen, my dad sat my brothers and me on the sofa and lectured us about females and periods for like an entire afternoon."

That surprises her so much she actually meets my eye. "What?"

"My brother Tarian had said something stupid, and my mom overheard. Thinking back, Dad might've been trying to save Tarian's hide by giving Mom time to cool down. It was very awkward for all of us, though."

"What did he say?"

"I am not repeating what Tarian said." I smile so she doesn't feel like I'm shutting her down. "Dad pretty much did the thing that the Council does when they talk all night long to stop a vote. He just kept going. The thing I remember is that every so often, he'd glare at Tarian and be like 'you're so smart, can *you* birth a pup? You're so big and strong, can *you* birth a pup?' And Tarian would be like 'no, sir,' and Dad would bellow 'no, you *can't!*' To this day, whenever my brothers say no to each other, we shout 'no, you *can't!*' just like he did."

I miss my brothers. They found ways to visit me at Salt Mountain a few times over the years by signing up to fight on the circuit, but it was bittersweet. Mom and Dad couldn't come, and we'd video chat, but Mom would get really upset.

Izzy is smiling, so I shake off the ache in my chest. "It must be nice to have brothers growing up," she says.

"It was."

She's quiet for a few minutes, lost in her thoughts, but she's forgotten to waddle, so that's good.

"When I got my period the first time, Mom basically was like—you're one step closer to finding your mate, no more slacking, you need to get through this Suzuki book, you've been on book four way too long. And I expect you to be careful and prepared. I'm not a drycleaner."

I'm careful not to let the flash of anger show on my face or in my voice. "What is a Suzuki book?"

"It's the book you use when you learn piano."

"Do you like playing piano?" That is going to be a son of a bitch to get for her.

"I hated it."

"Thank goodness." It slips out.

Her lips quirk, and her eyebrow raises.

"It'd be really tight in our cabin with you, me, Granddad, and a piano. One of us would have to sleep on top like those ladies in tight dresses who lie on top and sing in the movies."

She giggles. I am immediately a foot taller.

She also didn't question that I called it *our* cabin.

"Here we are," I say as we step into the glade, an almost perfect circle in the middle of tall trees that is somehow carpeted with dark green grass instead of vines and shrubs. Red mushrooms pop up here and there. My wolf rouses himself and pads to the border between us. He's not uneasy, but there is something about the place that catches his attention.

I set the bucket and supplies down for her. We're back to avoiding each other's gaze.

"Uh, thanks," she says softly.

"I'll just, uh—" I hike my thumb over my shoulder.

She tenses almost imperceptibly. I hesitate.

"Will you, uh, not go too far?" she asks one of the mushrooms by the toe of her sneaker. "It's just, um, I'm pretty sure I know my way back, but uh—"

Even if she didn't, her wolf would, but she doesn't need to give me an excuse for me to stay close. I don't want to leave her, either. Not even to go five feet.

"I'll just go on the other side of that tree." I nod toward a tulip poplar with a thick trunk.

"Okay. Thanks."

"You're okay?" I ask for no good reason.

"I'm okay." She darts a glance at me, forcing the smallest smile.

I nod, and muzzling my wolf who howls in protest, I walk to the other side of the poplar, lean against its trunk, and stare sightlessly into the woods. I am all ears.

I hear the whisper as she pulls her night shirt over her head. The ghost of elastic stretch as she slips off her panties. The dunk and swish of the washcloth in the bucket, and then the whoosh and drip as she wrings it out.

My heartrate picks up. A buzzing tension wakes up every nerve in my body. My cock is instantly hard.

My wolf stands at the ready, motionless, his ears perked straight up in the air.

Izzy drags the washcloth along her arms. Over her breasts. Across her belly. I close my eyes and try to breathe quieter, but it's hopeless. If I can hear terry cloth rub against her skin, she can hear my lungs struggling for air.

She rinses out the cloth and scrubs her neck. Her legs. Her underarms. She's saving her pussy and ass for last.

Dunk, swish, whoosh, drip. My cock throbs. Aches. My ears strain.

The cloth rasps against her bush. The scent of blood mixes with the calendula and shea from the soap. My fingers curl, gripping the rough trunk.

And then, from one second to the next, it's six years ago, and it's not my fingertips pressed into poplar, it's my claws digging into oak bark, gouging through moss, as I fight the horrible thing rising inside me with every fiber of my being while my sweet mate traces the throbbing vein that runs down my neck. The moon shines down, cold and distant, casting shadows on Izzy's gray, sickly face while she stares up at me, hurting, looking to me to make it better.

That night, in the minute before I chased her down like an animal, she smiled at me. She petted my chest to soothe my wolf.

Shame detonates inside me, ripping through me like shrapnel, and I'm instantly soaked in sweat as I gasp for air, for mercy, for rescue from the unbearable, crushing weight of my failure.

"Trevor?" she calls from the clearing. Even with my head ringing and the past skirmishing in my veins and nerves and guts, I still register that she's not calling my name in alarm, like she's sensing my meltdown, but like she needs something.

That's probably the only thing that could allow me to beat back the noise. "Yes," I answer immediately before my brain has even caught up.

"Um. I don't know what to do."

I step from behind the tree and go to her, eyes sweeping the clearing even though I don't scent or hear any threats. She's hiding her breasts with her forearms and smashing her thighs together.

She's trembling.

She's clutching her bloody night shirt in one of the hands pressed to her chest. Her face is crumpled. Over the scent of blood, I can smell her chagrin.

"I forgot to bring a change of clothes," she tells me softly, not like she's confessing a mistake, but like she needs something, so naturally, she's telling me. In an instant, my heart lifts, washing away the wreckage from the flashback as her big eyes steadily hold mine.

I reach behind my back and peel off my T-shirt. "Here," I say, taking the bloody night shirt and tossing it into the bucket. I don't think it's salvageable, but I'll give it a go.

I ease my shirt over her head and tug it down as she works her arms into the sleeves.

"Thanks," she says, blushing.

"Time for berries?" I ask, pretending I don't notice as she sniffs the collar of my shirt and her wolf rumbles happily.

"Okay."

I set the bucket by the poplar to come back for later. The bears who settled here when the Old Den was abandoned by Broderick Moore have learned to give the pack a wide berth, but no need to bait them.

I lead Izzy north, away from the cabins. There are dozens of berry patches in our territory. I don't think it'll hurt to go visit one of the farther ones. The weather's nice, the day is young, and Izzy doesn't smell stressed anymore.

We've been walking for a few minutes when she breaks the silence. "You were freaking out back there."

I nod and look her in the face, so she can see that I mean it when I say, "You don't have anything to worry about. I can handle it."

She wrinkles her nose and rolls her eyes, not dramatically like Nia or Drona, but like it's something she's just learned, and she hasn't got it quite down yet. It's adorable.

"I'll worry about what I want," she says. "And besides, I wasn't worried."

"Okay," I say reflexively while my brain tries to unknot what she said.

"I freak out, too, you know."

My gaze drops to the deer trail I'm guiding her along. "Yeah. It kills me. I'd do anything to take it away."

"Me, too, but I'm not going to pretend everything is fine so that you don't feel guilty or get worried. I don't want to have to do that with you." She takes in a deep, shaky breath. "I don't want you to be the one who suffers in silence while I'm the one who's so broken she can't handle any bad stuff."

"Okay." I don't completely understand what we're arguing about, but I'm never not going to give her a win if I can, so I back up and try again. "I was freaking out back there. Standing by the tree. It made me remember."

"I know," she says. "I felt it." She presses her hand to her chest.

"Yeah?" This is the first time she's said anything about our silent bond.

"I don't want you to pretend, and I won't pretend, either. We'll just say what we feel and deal with it. That's how we're going to do this." She's so fierce, until she catches my gaze, and then she goes pink and stumbles a step. "If you're okay with that."

I grab her hand. "Okay, beautiful girl," I say.

Her pink cheeks blush a deeper red.

"I just say how I feel, and you deal with it," I tease. "That's the plan. Love it. I can one hundred percent get behind that."

"That's not what I said, and you know it," she protests, her lips quirking.

"That's what I feel like I heard. You just have to deal with it."

"Stop playing," she says and playfully smacks me in the chest.

"Oof!" I immediately fold over. "Watch it, killer."

She snorts. "You're ridiculous."

"I am," I agree, grinning, as I grab her hand.

She smiles quietly to herself and squeezes tight. I swing our arms.

"Where is this alleged berry patch?" she asks. "North Border?"

"Not much farther." In my head, I readjust my plan and pick a closer patch. They aren't juneberries, but there are blackberries growing along a stream about a quarter mile due west. "This way."

I lead her off the deer trail and into dense woods. We wade through tangled underbrush, and even though I try to blaze the way as much as possible, it's still slow going. The canopy is thicker here, so the air is dim, cool, and rich with the scent of earth and growing things. It feels like we're alone in the world. I wish we were.

I wish we always had been.

A few minutes later, I hear water babbling and smell the berries at the same time. "Brunch," I say, helping her down an incline to the stream. I kick off my shoes, and she follows suit. The bushes grow right along the bank, so it's easier to pick them standing in the water.

"Hey, these aren't juneberries. They're blackberries," she says, popping one in her mouth.

"False advertising," I say. "I'm sorry."

"No more sorries." She pops a blackberry in my mouth. I'm so surprised I almost don't open up in time. It's the sweetest berry I've ever had. I chew as slowly as I can, stepping away to hunt deeper in the thicket so she can't see me blush and get hard.

Of course, I can't stray far. As soon as I have a handful, I wade back to her side. I select the biggest, ripest berry I've picked and offer it to her. She has to swallow the one in her mouth first before she takes it.

"Thanks," she says. I track her fingers as she slips the berry past her lips. She watches me do it, her tongue darting out to capture a bead of juice. My cock pulses in my jeans. Please don't let her look down because I can't turn away from her now.

She plucks a berry out of my cupped hand and sets it against my lips. "Open up."

I do exactly what she wants, the instant she asks, and every inch of my skin prickles with awareness. The pad of her index finger brushes my lower lip as she pops the berry in. My blood pounds in my veins with want, and also fear.

My wolf stands on alert at the border between us. He knows I won't hurt her. *I* know I won't hurt her. But still, he stands close and watches.

I'm breathing like I've run a race. The burbling water covers the sound, but nothing hides the rapid rise and fall of my bare chest. Izzy isn't looking down, though, she's smiling up at me, waiting. Waiting for what? She glances meaningfully at the berries in my palm.

Oh, yeah. It's my turn. I don't have the brain function left to pick a good one. I just grab and offer.

She wraps her slender fingers around my wrist, holding my hand in place as she takes the berry, her teeth gently scraping my skin. A thousand bolts of lightning zap from nerve to nerve, jolting my muscles, skittering my pulse.

Somehow, the distance between us has shrunk from inches to centimeters. When she inhales, her breasts almost brush my chest. When I exhale, the strands that've come loose from her ponytail flutter.

I want to kiss her, *need* to kiss her, and gather her in my arms, lay her on the far bank, and kiss every inch of her until she hooks her bare legs around my waist, plunging those fingers into my hair and holding me so close that I know she's not afraid, and that she understands in her bones that I will never hurt her again.

Izzy clears her throat. I blink, coming back to the moment, and she's holding a berry for me right in the narrow gap between our faces. I slowly lower my head. She draws the berry back a hairsbreadth closer to her lips.

What is she doing?

I know what she's doing.

She wants me to kiss her.

It should be easy. She's so close. All I have to do is tilt my head forward. That's it. I want this. She wants this.

The berries I collected plunk into the stream as my hands clench in fists, my nails digging into my palms. A thousand memories rise up from the recesses of my mind to beat at my brain with dark wings.

My feet curling over the edge of the High Rise roof, the plaza below gray and cold in the moonlight.

Lying on the Cameron's back porch, wrapped in a moth-eaten quilt, damp with frost, staring at dew dripping down a ripped screen window, every second in my life laid out in front of me like a prison sentence.

That night. Izzy's bare heels flashing in the moonlight. Her desperate sobs as she choked on her own snot.

It all surges up inside me, every horror, every shame, all the ruin, all the pain.

In this moment, the here and now, the happy fuzziness clears from Izzy's eyes, and it's another stab in my chest, another failure. Her brows draw together as she fixes me with a mutinous look and pops the berry in her own mouth. Then she grabs my face in both her hands, rises on her toes, and plants her lips on mine.

I'm a fucking mess, but I'm not stupid. My arms wrap themselves around her waist, and I lift her, squeezing her tight while I lower my mouth to feast. The want is stronger than the horror. Stronger than anything.

Her lips part. My tongue and hers tangle, hungry and uncoordinated and shameless.

She whimpers, in need, not pain. I stagger backward with her, my feet slipping on wet stone, until I land on my butt on the mossy bank. She sits across my lap, almost curled, her breasts flattened against my chest, her knee digging into my rib. She holds my head in place with clutching fingers plunged into my hair. I fold my arms around her, gathering her as close as I can.

I don't ever want to let her go. I want to live here forever, on this muddy bank, with the sun shining and our hearts racing each other, faster and faster.

I kiss her, and she kisses me until we aren't taking turns —we're lost, and time isn't passing anymore, it's waiting patiently for us.

She smells musky and earthy and like my T-shirt. She wants to try everything—nibbling my lower lip, nestling our noses side by side, sucking my tongue into her mouth—and then she wants to try something else and then go back and do it all over again.

She's excited. I smell that, too, along with a hint of blood, and my lower abs tense, and my balls ache.

At some point, our grip on each other loosens a little. The frenzy quiets, naturally, like a breeze that passes. The trickling stream and chirping birds become audible again over the roar of blood in my ears.

She cradles my cheek. I readjust my arms, wrapping them lower so I'm squeezing the top of her ass cheeks. She sighs, arching her back, stretching.

She smiles. I kiss the quirked corner of her mouth.

"You taste like blackberries," she says drowsily, her eyelids drooping like a sleepy cat.

"No way. How is that possible?" I rumble back. I sound husky, like it's first thing in the morning.

She giggles. "It's a mystery." She kisses me again, gently licking my lower lip.

I'm so hard that every time she shifts in my lap, my cock responds like she's stroking it, straining, throbbing with the desire to come. The need is growing. Spiraling.

Gnawing.

My hips need to thrust. I want to take her hand, guide it down between us, and wrap it around my cock. Reach under her shirt. Press my fingers into her heavy breasts, tease her pouting nipples with my thumbs.

Grab her by the scruff of the neck and pin her to the ground.

Slice away her pants with my claws, blood dripping from the gashes I've slashed in her skin.

Plunge my fangs into her soft neck until the tip of my tooth glances off the bone.

A scream ricochets in my mind, and I freeze, every part of me—my muscles, my lungs, the blood in my veins.

These are not my thoughts. They are only shards of memory with no power, but still, I summon my wolf, prepare to seize him from his world and thrust him out of my skin, so I can't hurt her. I'd never hurt her.

But I *did*. Those were my claws. My teeth.

Izzy lifts her head, blinking, her pupils widening. I catch a whiff of her fear, and it cuts me like a knife.

I leap to my feet. She tumbles from my lap and into the stream, crying out in surprise.

I back away, palms in the air, heart racing, stomach heaving.

"Oh, no you don't!" She struggles to her feet. The back of her shirt is soaked and plastered to her body. Her face is bright red, her hands balled at her sides. My nose flares. She doesn't smell afraid. She smells *angry*.

"You stop right there," she shouts and stamps her foot. *Plunk*. Like a frog splash. "Don't you *dare* run away from me." Tears are pooling on her eyes.

The bond stabs me in the chest.

The bond.

It's there. *I* felt it this time.

"*Say* what you feel," she says through ground teeth, her voice breaking. "And we'll deal with it."

I want to hang my head. Seal my mouth shut and never

open it. I'd rather die than tell her the thoughts in my head, than let her know the terror and panic rampaging through my body. I'd never hurt her, but I have memories of the night I did, more vivid and real than any other moment in my life, ghouls that haunt my brain, a horror movie that clicks on with no warning, and it's her screams that echo in my ears.

"*Say it*," she demands, the tears rolling down her cheeks now.

I crash to my knees. "I want you, and it made me remember."

I can't say any more. Please don't let her ask me to because I'll do anything for her, rip myself open and bleed out at her feet if she asks, but I don't want her to know what I see in my head, and I can't bear it that those things live in her head, too.

She gulps down a breath. Then another. Her fingers uncurl. "You dumped me in the water."

"I'm sorry."

"It was good, and then it got ruined."

"I'm so fucking sorry."

She stomps out of the stream and trudges up the bank, peeling the wet shirt away from her back. "I have cramps, you know. I've had them this whole time, and I just didn't say anything because I really liked what we were doing. And I'm really hungry, and the blackberries aren't cutting it." She sinks to her knees right in front of me and sits back, propping her butt on her heels, so we're eye to eye. "I didn't think I'd ever be the more emotionally stable one in a relationship, but I kind of think, between you and me, I am."

The words gut me—kick me in the nuts, really—but there's something in the way she says it, a sliver of pride maybe, like she's pleased that she's not the one losing it, so I can live with it.

"Thank you for being the emotionally stable one," I say.

"You're welcome." She wipes her nose with the back of her hand. "I mean, I would say *more* emotionally stable, but —you're welcome."

"I never thought I'd get this chance, and I am ill-fucking-prepared."

"Me, too," she says. "I have no idea what I'm doing."

"Can I take you home and feed you?"

"Okay."

I stand and reach down for her hands. She slips hers in mine, no hesitation, and my chest cracks open, leaving my heart exposed. Raw.

I help her to her feet. "I'll find you a hot water bottle." Somehow. I might need to rig something up with rice in a sock. I once saw a scavenger female sticking something like that in the microwave.

"I'll have to do the laundry when we get back," she says.

"I'll do it." I keep hold of her hand and lead her back down the mossy bank and across the stream to our shoes.

"I don't want to be left alone somewhere," she says. "I want to go with you."

"We'll do it together. You can measure the detergent. I'll pour." I glance at her out the side of my eyes. Can I tease her? Or is it all still too heavy, too dark, too broken to ever be anything but a disaster waiting to happen?

"Okay, but I want to select the temperature. You can select the cycle."

"You know I'm picking heavy duty every time," I say, squatting to help her on with her shoe.

"As long as you don't pick normal or delicate," she says, balancing herself with a hand on my shoulder as she points her toes and slips her foot into the sneaker. "Normal and delicate is no good for us."

I duck forward to drop a kiss on her moss-stained knee. She looks down and wrinkles her nose.

"I better wash myself again, too," she says. "And frankly, you're a little grubby yourself."

I tug her laces tight and loop them in a bow. "We're grubby together, so it's all right."

She squeezes the hand on my shoulder. I double the knot and then glance up. She's smiling at me with tear tracks streaking down her slightly grubby face.

"I'm happy to be grubby with you," she says. "We're both a mess, so it's okay."

She's telling the truth. Her sweet, tentative, terrified happiness flows into my chest and wraps around my worn heart.

Despite it all, it's a good day.

Maybe the best day ever.

15

IZZY

I never thought I'd be sexually frustrated, but I guess wonders never cease. I don't like being away from Trevor tonight, out in the woods stirring a potion as thick as tar, but on the upside, I get a break from blue lady balls.

All Trevor and I do is kiss—all night long and every second we can get alone. For the past three weeks. It's amazing. I have no basis for comparison, but I can't imagine a male kissing better than Trevor. He kisses like he's in heaven and suffering the torments of hell at the same time, and it's doing wonders for my ego, but it's destroyed my patience. And my focus. And my sense of proportion.

Two nights ago, after we'd been going at it for several hours, he got in his head again and freaked himself out. He bounded out of bed like I'd bit him to go check a mysterious "noise" that was very obviously a raccoon in the trash. I broke down weeping and had a massive tantrum, the kind my parents never would have tolerated when I was growing up.

The only salve to my pride is that I kept it quiet enough

so that Granddad didn't hear through the walls Trevor put up so we have rooms of our own with doors that shut. I kicked every sheet, blanket, and pillow onto the floor, and then I felt like an asshole, so I remade the bed just in time for Trevor to come back to report that Mr. Bandit was dumpster diving for chicken bones in our garbage can. He was so confused when I burst into tears.

So, yesterday, when Rosie came back from a foraging trip with some dragon's tongue, I volunteered to teach a few of the younger females how to cook it down. Abertha taught me how at the beginning of my apprenticeship with her. Rendering the plant into its medicinal form is a pain in the ass, but luckily, a little goes a long way, and this batch will likely last the pack a year at least.

Trevor does *not* like that I'm out in the mushroom clearing without him in the middle of the night, but I told him he can't leave Granddad unattended on my account, and besides, the ritual for making the potion is sacred, and Abertha would be livid if I shared her arcana with a male. He didn't believe me, but he didn't argue, and eventually, after a lot of reassurance that Pritchard's wolf would keep watch, he did leave me here with Nia and Drona's older girls.

And now I miss him.

"I can't believe I got roped into doing this again," Nia groans as she stirs the thickening concoction.

The metronome app ticks on my phone, and several feet away, under a poplar, Avalon and Sara are conked out with their heads resting on the belly of Pritchard's wolf, all of them snoring out-of-time. You have to stir the mixture on a very specific tempo. It'll be a miracle if this batch comes out correctly.

"Want me to take over?" I ask.

"I have two minutes left in my turn."

"I don't mind."

"No way," Nia pants. "Never give up. Never surrender."

"The pups lasted longer than I thought they would." I roll my shoulders out and stretch my biceps, preparing for my turn. My arm muscles ache. They'll be noodles tomorrow. Hand stuff will be completely off the table.

Not like Trevor and I have gotten to hand stuff. We've gotten close. Under the shirt, over the bra. Under the waistband, over the panties, but only the back side. No front action.

It's not like I'm intolerably horny, but making out with Trevor feels good, and beyond that, it's a normal thing that I never thought I'd be able to do, so I don't want to stop right when we're both panting and squirming and tense. I want to see where it goes.

So far, it ends with Trevor wrapping me in his arms in a way that his dick isn't touching any part of me and whispering, "It's getting late. Go to sleep, beautiful. Big day tomorrow."

I blow out a sigh.

"Five, four, three—" Nia counts down. I get into position. "Two, one." I open my hand. She slaps the ladle into my palm. I tune into the metronome and start stirring in time.

"Oh, lord," I groan. The mixture is thick as concrete, and my biceps are nothing like they were when I was playing tennis every day.

"Yeah, each turn gets harder, doesn't it?" Nia slaps me on the back and collapses onto her butt on the grass next to the fire. "Do you really think all the shit really matters? I mean, really? Bury quartz at the four directions on the night of the new moon, hallow the ground with a pint of spirits, and cook over a fire of cherry wood from last light to first light at exactly twenty to fifty beats per minute? I mean, it sounds like bullshit, right?"

"It's called a grave tempo. Twenty to fifty beats per minute."

"See? *Grave* tempo? Doesn't that sound like the witch is messing with us?"

I smile. She's totally capable of it, but in this case, she's not. "I asked her about it when she taught me, and she said when the spell was passed to her, this is how it came. She says that when a spell or potion works, a good healer makes note of everything—from the phase of the moon to time of day to anything out-of-the-ordinary that happens, like you spill your flask of whiskey, whether you think it's consequential or not. Then you just try to replicate it."

"The witch and you are tight, eh?" Nia leans back on her elbows.

"I was her apprentice."

"Rosie was, too, but it turned out that was kind of a ruse. The witch wanted to keep an eye on Rosie since she knew she was the alpha heir's mate. Rosie doesn't have that thing that you have."

"What thing?" I'm so curious, I almost lose my rhythm. No one other than my parents have ever really *noticed* things about me. Before I became the pack's cautionary tale, I was basically a movie extra. I was nice. I did what I was told. Mostly, I was there.

"I don't know. You move really quietly, but not in a scared way. Like you know what you're doing, I guess."

I snort. "I have no idea what I'm doing. I just decide to do it."

Nia grins. "Now you sound like the witch. She's always saying oxymoronic shit like that."

I shrug. "It's true. It's been working for me until—" Until now, with Trevor. I can't decide to take the next step for him.

I flush. Nia's grin widens.

"Oh, now we're getting to the good stuff." She crosses her legs, propping the heel of one combat boot on the toe of the other. "It's been working until...?"

I glance over to Drona's daughters. They're still dead to the world.

I never had female friends like on TV, not the type you could confide in. There was no way I would talk to Brynn or Teagan about anything really private. That would be handing them ammunition.

I'm pretty sure Nia isn't like that. In general, people here aren't like the people in Moon Lake. They aren't competing all the time, trying to one up each other, forming alliances and stabbing backs. I guess when you know you'll get what you need, regardless of rank, other people aren't your enemy.

I already broke down in front of her that first day, and we chat about all kinds of things when she drops by the apothecary to see what I'm doing, and, I suspect, to take a break from busting people's balls, which seems to be her job.

I guess if you can decide to stop being a hermit and become a healer and go on a mission to another pack, you can decide to make a real friend.

"Until Trevor. I want to, you know, *be* mates."

"And he doesn't?" She raises an incredulous, pierced eyebrow.

"He wants it. But he's scared. And traumatized. And I'm scared and traumatized, too, but he's *stuck*. So *we're* stuck. And it's totally possible that we'll finally get to third base or home plate or whatever, and we'll both freak out, and then we'll just have to face facts and give up and be alone forever, even though neither of us want that." We haven't said that to each other in words, but I know. I can feel him now, in my chest. The bond isn't just there. It's getting strong.

"Which is third base?" Nia asks.

"Oh. Uh. Mouth stuff? Or below the waist stuff?"

"Well, if anal is home plate, wouldn't third base be penis in vagina?"

"Home plate is *not* anal."

"What is it then? Like a threesome?" Nia's gold-banded tiger eyes twinkle. She's teasing me.

I roll my eyes. My mother would slap my face if she saw me, but the females here do it all the time, and no one gets offended. I kind of love it.

"Well, that's a real pickle, eh?" Nia flashes a sympathetic smile.

"I don't want him to do something he's not ready for, but like, what if he's *never* ready? And I don't even *know* if *I'm* ready."

Nia glances over at Pritchard's snoring wolf, and her smile fades. "I wasn't ready when Pritchard and I mated. I was sixteen. I did not want to be attached by a mystical umbilical cord to some dumbass slacker for the rest of my natural life." Her eyes soften. "I was so mean to him. It wasn't his fault, but he was happy about it, and that made me so freaking mad. He didn't get it—he was just *incapable* of understanding how I felt—and that made me even madder."

"Are you still mad?"

She seems to really consider my question. "No? It's different here. Moon Lake felt like jail, so Pritchard kind of felt like my cell mate or something, and that just wasn't going to work for me. Now...I do what I want. People listen to me. So it doesn't feel like that anymore."

"So you're together?" If Nia's around, Pritchard is never far away, but they don't seem *together* per se.

"It's complicated." Nia's tough mask slips for a second, and she looks younger. Uncertain. "Once something gets all fucked up, it's hard to fix it, you know?"

"Yeah." I do. I really do.

"I mean, sex isn't the problem, though. That never has been. He doesn't look like it, but Pritchard can lay some pipe." She gazes fondly over at his sleeping wolf.

He's still splayed on his back, his hind legs kind of hovering in the air an inch or two off the ground, his ears folded over his eyes and his tongue lolling out of the side of his mouth. Sara has his tail clutched in her fist, using it as a wubby as she sucks her thumb.

I would literally never have guessed.

"How do you, uh, make it happen, then?" I ask. "If you want to do it, but it's, uh, complicated?" She probably never has that problem. Females complain about males wanting it too much, not about them always going to check on the trashcan raccoons whenever things start to get really good.

"Like how do I let him know I'm in the mood?" she asks.

I nod and stir. I've totally lost track of how much longer I have.

"I mean, usually, I just start to get naked, and he knows the drill."

I'm way ballsier than I've ever been, but I don't think I could do that, and it probably wouldn't work. Trevor would keep his eyes respectfully above my neck and ask me if I hear something behind the cabin.

Nia goes on. "But if he's been pissed, or things have been really weird and he's sulking, I'll tug on his leash. That always works."

"What do you mean?"

"You know. Give the bond a little yank." She reaches out, curls her fingers around an imaginary bond, and jerks. All the way over by the poplar, Pritchard's wolf startles, snuffling awake. He scans the clearing with his eyelids at half-mast and promptly conks back out. Avalon and Sara sleep through the whole thing.

"And then what?"

She grins. "I give him a little of this." She leans so her bare shoulder pops out of her collar and bats her eyelashes. "Or a little of this." She clicks her tongue ring between her teeth. "If all else fails, I keep tugging until he comes close enough that I can grab his dick."

"I don't think I could do that."

Nia's face turns serious. "Yeah. This is a delicate situation. I mean, I hate to suggest it, but have you tried asking for what you want? And being really specific? You know, like 'I'm very horny. Please finger my pussy until I come.'"

I scrunch my eyes closed, my blush almost melting my face that's already sweating from leaning over the fire. "If he said no, I'd spontaneously combust."

"If he said no, I'd eat my hat." Nia jumps to her feet and brushes off her butt. "My turn. Ready?"

"So ready." My stirring arm is one huge knotted muscle. "In five?"

She gets into position beside me. "Five, four, three, two, one."

I let go, and she takes the spoon's handle. I don't have the strength to lift it out of the boiled dragon's tongue. Luckily, the reduction is so thick that the spoon stays stuck straight up.

Nia groans as she takes over. "What I won't do for this pack."

"If people use it judiciously, this batch should last at least a year."

"People will most certainly not use it judiciously. We're going to have to hide it somewhere in Cadoc and Rosie's den."

It's a good plan. "Well, Avalon and Sara should be able to help you next time."

Nia snorts. "Girl, you know that this is your job now." Her brow creases. "Unless you aren't staying. You're staying, right?"

That's the question. On the one hand, I've moved in with Trevor, and after he works all day on pack projects, he spends hours fixing the cabin up for us. I help how I can, mostly by holding things for him while I stand there mesmerized by his flexing back muscles. And biceps. And thighs. He's got rugby player thighs, and when he squats, the seams of his jeans strain.

He doesn't even notice me staring, he's so concerned about whether things are level and plumb and flush and secure. He wants it to be perfect, but to me, it already is. There's never any angry silence or simmering dread. Who cares about electrical and plumbing? My stomach doesn't hurt when I walk in the door. I never want to leave.

But then, we haven't talked it out yet. Our conversations can go to a really dark place, really quickly, so we both avoid any subject that might head in a serious direction. Mostly, we tease each other and make jokes so bad that Granddad shakes his head.

I know Trevor wants me to stay, and I think Rosie and Cadoc would be okay with it, but would Madog Collins?

It's hard to remember most days, but I'm supposedly here on a diplomatic mission. How would Moon Lake react if yet another one of their people jumped ship as soon as they could, especially Howell Owens's niece? No one understands better than me that mate bonds mean nothing when high-ranking males have an agenda.

I can't ask Cadoc to go against his father for my sake. Besides, even if Madog was somehow okay with me staying, he's weaker now that he's back from his mysterious mission to Salt Mountain—physically and politically—and Alban Hughes' followers haven't gone anywhere, and they sure as hell haven't had a change of heart.

Since the scavengers left, Dad is even louder about "the taint of the bog" and "reclaiming the greatness of Moon Lake." For a while, after the Old Den split, Mom would hush him, but as time went on, people got bold again, and Mom started talking like that in public, too. My parents would never just let their only offspring walk away to join a pack of scavengers. Not without one hell of a fight.

And after everything my parents did, can I ask Trevor to stand with me against them? Is that fair?

It's a mess, too much of a mess. I have enough on my plate trying to bond with my mate. I can't figure out how to navigate inter-pack politics on top of it.

I can't say all that, though, so I say, "It's complicated."

"But you want to stay, right?"

"Yes. More than anything."

"Then you'll stay. We're free now, girl. You have self-determination. The rules, what's possible and impossible, all of that is all in your head. They put that shit there, downloaded the program straight to your orbitofrontal cortex. You've got to wipe it from your system." She makes a trippy whoosh sound. Her gold eyes are strangely glowy.

"Have you been sampling the product?"

"Nope. This is one hundred percent punch-drunk exhaustion."

I understand the feeling. My eyes feel like sandpaper, and my arms are dead weight. "We've only got two hours left before dawn."

"Two hours is one million years."

She's absolutely right. I don't remember it being this hard with Abertha, but Abertha has an energy about her that does a weird thing to time. Even if you're just having tea or weeding the garden, it feels like a recital or a do-or-die match, not that kind of pressure, but the hyperawareness and sense that every moment counts. Maybe it's the magic. It follows her around like her own personal atmosphere and raises the hair on your arms.

"You know what—" Nia says, perking up. "The witch didn't say anything about this being a *female* job, did she?"

"She did not." Though I have a feeling she'd object to the very idea.

We both swivel our heads toward Pritchard's sleeping wolf. "Watch this," Nia says.

She reaches out her free hand, wraps her fingers around air again, and yanks. Pritchard's wolf whines, lifts a folded ear, and opens one grumpy eye to glare at Nia balefully.

She draws her arms back like she's reeling him in. He lifts his other ear so he can glower at her with both bleary eyes. The sleeping girls shift.

Pritchard's wolf slowly wriggles away, so their heads are laid gently on the soft grass. They immediately snuggle together. Pritchard's wolf stands, shakes himself off, and with a final disgruntled rumble, trots into the trees.

For a second, I think he's abandoning us, but then he stumbles back to the clearing in human form, wearing a pair of rather undersized gym shorts. He tromps straight over, scratching his bare abs. I see why Nia has so much experience tugging his leash.

"What's up?" he asks, coming to stand next to the fire. He sniffs the dragon's tongue laden air and then leans closer to Nia and breathes in the scent of her hair as a chaser.

"My arm's killing me," she says.

"Okay. Do I just stir?" he asks. No complaint. Not even a hint of patient suffering on his groggy face. The males at Old Den are so different from the males I grew up with, they might as well be a different species.

"Yeah. But you have to do it in time. Like this." Nia grabs his hand, places it over hers, and stirs, counting off the beats. The sleep clears from Pritchard's eyes, and he leans forward so that his chest presses against Nia's back.

"Like this?" he asks, tucking his chin into the crook of her neck so he can whisper in her ear.

I glance away into the trees, my cheeks heating.

"Yeah," Nia says breathily. "You got it?"

"I got it," Pritchard practically purrs.

"How long do you think you can go?" Nia asks, her voice higher than I've ever heard it.

Pritchard's voice drops lower. "How long do you need me to go?"

"Can you go all night?"

"You know I can."

"Bet." Nia ducks away, laughing, her voice back to its normal huskiness. "Izzy and I are just going to take a little nap then. Wake us up if you need a break."

She collapses beside me, and while I'm thinking about how impossible it'll be to fall asleep on the cold, hard ground, and how much it'll suck to get woken up if I manage to drift off, I pass out and don't wake up until Trevor gently shakes my shoulder as the sun is breaking over the hills to the east.

"Good morning, beautiful," he says as he helps me to my feet.

And even though my arms feel like lead, my back is soaking wet from dew, and my bones ache, a little burst of happiness flares in my chest. He came.

Once everyone gets up, Nia and Pritchard take Drona's kids back to the den, and Trevor carries the heavy cauldron to our cabin where we'll let it cool. Right when we leave the clearing, behind a cluster of sugar maples, I can't help but notice the matted undergrowth in the shape of a grown male wolf that smells like my mate.

I smile to myself and grab his free hand.

I guess he never left.

ON HUMAN TV, males are always the one to plan the romantic evenings. They buy flowers, make reservations at a fancy restaurant, sprinkle rose petals on the bed, and light some candles. Shifters, at least ranked Moon Lake shifters, emulate humans in a lot of ways, and our males do the initiating, too, but in a different way. There is a lot more hunting and running in the woods involved. Less perfume and jewelry, more fresh meat.

Regardless, females don't do the courting, so I've got no template. I searched on the internet, and there was stuff about how men never get flowers, and they should. There was also a lot about steak and blow jobs. The steak seemed like the best idea.

Bevan was able to hook me up with two ribeyes—he is the Old Den plug for everything—and since Trevor has built a fire pit in front of our cabin, complete with logs for seating, the plan is to make him dinner, get him all relaxed with a belly full of beef, and then tug his leash. I have no idea what I'm doing after I get him into our bedroom, but I've become a big believer in taking a first step and seeing what happens.

Tonight is the night. After the world's most awkward conversation, held way louder than I was comfortable with, Granddad happily agreed to bunk at the elder cottage tonight. I told Trevor that I'm making a special dinner, and he should be back at the cabin by six. His face was both intrigued and stressed.

Flora and Enid held up a sheet so I could bathe in a corner of the pool. I don't think I'll ever be comfortable enough to skinny dip like the scavengers. Rosie lent me a sundress with tiny yellow and red flowers that look like polka dots from a distance. She has more up top than me, so the scoop neckline sags a little lower than I'm used to, but I feel pretty, and that's what counts.

I also feel terrified. And so far out of my depth I might as well be in the Mariana Trench. What I don't feel is alone. I know that Trevor will be there by six on the dot—probably earlier—and he'll be faking chill and nervous as hell on the inside, too.

If I tuned in, the bond would tell me, but also, I just kind of know. Maybe because I'm good at reading people. I had to be. There was always a lot riding on reading Dad's mood and catching a bad turn before it was too late to make myself scarce.

Reading Trevor isn't like that, though. He's often stoic, especially around the pack, but his face never hardens. His mouth never twists. Reading Trevor is like coming across a patch of ashbalm or a dollar on the ground.

Like, I'll be remaking the bed, casually fluffing a pillow,

and I'll glance up, and he's looking at me while he folds back the top sheet, very nonchalant, but his eyes are zeroed in on my hands, and I know in my gut that he's thinking about me making a nest. That he's *longing* for it. And then Granddad calls out, and the moment's over, but I get to keep it and tuck it away in my good memories with cherry soda and blackberries and our wolves running together in the woods.

I smooth my palms down my dress and check the set up. The steaks are marinating, ready to go on the grill. The potatoes are already in the coals, wrapped in aluminum foil. A chocolate cake is sitting on the stump we use as a table. Drona's oldest helped me make it from a box mix. It was a very close thing getting it out to the cabin without anyone dipping a finger in the icing.

It's five forty-five. The weather is mild and still, and the sky is clear, the blue deepening as the sun sinks. The fire crackles. I started it myself. That's one of the first things Trevor taught me how to do.

He's not pushy about it, and there's no sense that he expects me to earn my keep or carry my weight, but he's always showing me things—how to pull a stripped screw, how to skin a squirrel—kind of like his wolf showed me that bear den. Like he's trying to make sure I'm prepared or capable. It reminds me of how a father is supposed to act.

He'd be a good father.

My cheeks heat at the thought, and at that moment, he whistles from the woods to let me know he's nearby. I busy myself putting the steaks on the grill.

When he emerges from the trees, I can scent his nerves. He bathed, too, and his curls are still a little damp. He's wearing his best pants, the jeans with no tears, and a pale blue polo shirt that I don't recognize. He must've borrowed it. I've seen his entire wardrobe, all five T-shirts, two flannels, and one hoodie.

His hands are shoved in his pockets, his shoulders curved forward. His smile is shy, but his eyes storm.

"You got steaks?"

"Yeah. Come sit. They won't take long." Like all shifters, we like our beef mooing.

He crosses the distance between us and sits on the log, very formally, like this is a job interview. "Where'd you get ribeyes?"

"I traded Bevan."

"What did you trade?" A note has entered his voice. The question is very careful, not accusatory, but not exactly pleased.

"A bag of liberty caps I found foraging."

"Liberty caps?"

"Mushrooms." I flip up the edge of a steak to check the sear. "Magical variety."

He relaxes almost imperceptibly. "You know if you want meat, just ask."

I know. I can't even mention something in passing without him bringing it home in some version or other, sooner or later. My favorite is when we were watching the Friday night movie with the pack, and I whispered that all that was missing was microwave popcorn, and the next Friday, he produced a can of sweet corn and said, "It's the best I could do."

"I wanted it to be a surprise." The sear is perfect. I turn the steaks.

"Is there an occasion?"

"Maybe." I smile at him. I aim for *come hither*, but he flusters me when he watches me like this, with his eyes so stormy, so it ends up less *do me*, and more *get worried*.

His forehead creases. "Did I forget something?" I can see him searching his memory, probably to reassure himself that it's not my birthday.

"No. I just wanted to do something nice."

"It looks great. Is that cake?"

"Chocolate."

He smiles, and the worry's gone. His face lights up with pure delight.

My belly warms. He's so easy to make happy. All he wants is peace and little pleasures.

Like me.

And isn't it strange that I didn't know that's what I was like until I got here, with him? I was so busy getting along, and then getting through, that I didn't know who I was.

I know now, and it feels light. Like bubbles.

"Grab the plates?" I nod at the aluminum pie plates I snagged from the den.

He brings them over and holds them as I serve up the steaks and fish the potatoes out of the coals with a stick, picking them up with a man's leather glove as an oven mitt. Everything is makeshift at Old Den. I love it. There are no "good" dishes or "company" towels that you use afraid that you'll mess them up.

We sit beside each other on the log and eat, our thighs touching and elbows bumping when we take a bite at the same time. The fuller our bellies get, the more our spines relax and our shoulders curve.

"What did you put on this steak?" Trevor groans. "I could eat two more. Right now."

"You can't possibly eat two more. You'd have no room for cake."

"Don't you worry about my dessert stomach. It'll be fine."

"You've got a second stomach? Like a cow?"

"I do. I'm actually cow on my dad's side." His eyes sparkle. "Moo," he says, deadpan. "See?"

"Kind of messed up to be eating steak then, eh? What would your grandparents think?"

"That I had scaled the top of the predator-prey pyramid." He flexes his bicep while chewing his last piece of steak. I scrape half of my remaining bites onto his plate. "Hey," he says. "I share with you. Not the other way."

"We share with each other."

He looks mutinous for a moment, but then he gobbles down the rest of the steak and cuts the cake. It's small, meant for two. When Avalon and I baked it earlier, we separated the mix into two pans so she could have one to share with her family.

Trevor cuts himself a sliver and slides the rest onto my plate.

"Hey," I protest.

"We share," he says, dropping a kiss on my nose. He forks his slice into his mouth in two bites and stares wistfully at mine.

I take a piece and then hold up another on my fork for him. He doesn't hesitate. I feed him the rest—one bite for me, one for him. At the end, he actually ended up with more than half, considering his first slice, but I'm not mad. My happy stomach swirls with anticipation.

I'm excited at the idea of more kissing, and whatever might come after, but I'm also high on the fact that *I'm* doing this. I'm seducing my mate—docile, compliant, broken, tragic Izzy Owens—who turned out to be capable, brave, and resilient. And most of it is because of me, but some of it is because of him. Because he's kind and brave and resilient, too.

After he's had the chance to clean every smudge of icing off the plate with his finger, I put my plan in action, standing to gather our dishes and salvage what I can from the aluminum foil I used for the potatoes. There's nothing left to compost.

Trevor watches me lazily, relaxing on the log, his lips curved. He loves to watch me do basically anything. If he were anyone else, it'd make me uncomfortable, but his eyes on me make me squirm in a good way. Maybe because they're that pale blue-gray, the affection shines in them so clearly.

Per my plan, I finish my tidying on the far side of the fire, close to the shallow stairs he built so Granddad could get in and out of the cabin on his own.

I smile at him. He smiles back, brow hitching in silent question.

I don't reach for the bond like Nia. It's too dramatic a move for me. I just focus on the steady flow that runs quietly between us and imagine that it's a strong vine instead of formless energy. I grab it and coil it around my fist.

Both of his eyebrows rise, and his soft smile breaks wide. He stands.

I tug. He stalks forward, and our eyes lock above the crackling fire. He stops about a foot away and cocks his head. It's a dare.

I back up one step, two, three. I tug again.

He steps up to the first stair.

I back up the last three steps. He follows like we're dancing in slow motion.

I slip off my flats and set them in their place at the far edge of the top stair. He bends over, makes short work of unlacing his boots, and sets them in their place next to mine.

I open the door without turning around.

His big grin fades to a gentle curve of the lips. I reach out a hand. He takes it. I lead him through our common room to the door on the left. The hardwood floor creaks beneath our feet, a newly familiar sound I've grown to love. A few weeks ago, I helped lay the boards. I handed them to him as he tapped them together with a block and mallet and nailed them in place.

I pull him into our bedroom. His breath quickens. He knows what I'm doing. He must. Please God don't let him freak out.

Don't let *me* freak out.

I am not going to think about what is going to happen. I'm just going to think about what I'm doing next.

I reach past him to shut the door and back into the room's small open space until I'm standing a few feet away against the foot of our bed. I grab the hem of my dress. His lungs catch.

I pull it over my head and let it fall to the floor. His wolf rumbles in his chest.

I left the curtains open, so the room is filled with moonlight. My skin glows. The dark doesn't hide anything, but he's felt all the skin he can see. He loves to cup my breasts, stroke my belly, smooth a hand down my arms, trail his fingers down the back of my thighs and over my calves to squeeze my feet in his big palm and play with my toes until I giggle so hard that I snort.

This is safe. I'm safe.

He's not coming any closer. I don't think he'll move until I tug. Or ask. My flushed face heats at the idea. I could never ask.

I reach behind my back and unclasp my bra, letting it fall to the crook of my elbows. He swallows a groan. His gaze darts between my breasts, my nipples puckering in the air, and my face. I can't tell if he's checking my mood or if he just likes looking at my face as much as my bare boobs.

Tension gathers low in my belly. Whatever the reason, I like it. I ditch my bra and hook my thumbs in my panties, dragging them down and kicking them off.

All of a sudden, the game levels up. Trevor hasn't moved, but his stance has changed. His muscles are tensed, and his hands are clenched, but not all the way into fists, like he's being careful not to do anything that I might read as aggressive.

I'm not afraid of him, but my body is nervous as hell, and as always, the past looms in my head, in the background now, but capable of bursting out at any second in a rush of panic, a flash of horror, or the echo of a scream.

It's a live bomb that I carry around. So does Trevor. We're standing here, face-to-face in a field riddled with land mines, and I'm naked.

I tilt my head.

He blinks, kind of shaking himself off, and peels his shirt over his head, quickly following that with shucking his jeans and boxers. I knew he wouldn't make me be alone.

His stomach muscles are tensed into cut ridges. His swollen cock sticks up straight in the air.

"What are you doing?" he asks. It's a weird question with both of us naked and me clearly staring at his dick.

"Seducing you." I dart my glance away from his very thick, very red erection to check his expression.

His lips curve into a painfully sweet, gently sad smile that crinkles the corners of his eyes. "I've already been seduced."

"Seducing you *all the way*." My cheeks flame. The line might work for a female who wears high heels and long nails and those stockings that connect to your underwear with plastic bands, but I sound like I have no idea what I'm doing, and I'm just making stuff up, which is not too far from the truth.

"Are you sure?" he asks.

"Are you?"

"Yes." It's a very determined *yes*. It is not a confident *yes*.

"Same," I say. "I'm nervous."

"I won't hurt you."

"I know."

"I'll stop any time you say. Immediately."

"Okay." We stare at each other, breathing hard, wanting and scared, nothing else in the world except the two of us. "I need you to do it. I—I can't. I don't know what to do next."

"Okay," he says. For a second, he's silent, his jaw working, the pulse in his throat jumping. "Sit on the bed."

I sink down on the edge, my thighs pressed tight together. My pussy throbs. My breasts ache.

"Lie back."

I do. The frame creaks. I stare at the rough rafters and fold my hands over my waist.

There's a soft thud. I crane my neck to see. Trevor has gone to his knees. The butterflies in my belly go bonkers.

"Is this okay?" he asks.

"I'm embarrassed."

"I'm so fucking excited. You smell so good, even from here. I can't wait until you let me closer."

I *eek* like a mouse.

He laughs, low and throaty.

"Okay, but I can't look."

"All right." He rests his calloused palms on the top of my legs and nuzzles my thigh with his rough cheek. He drops a kiss on each of my knees. "Spread these."

I squeak again and do what he says. He chuckles. His breath is warm on my skin. I drop my head back on the bed. My face is on fire, and every inch of my skin prickles with heat. He can see everything. *I've* never seen me from that angle.

My knees clamp together out of reflex, but his hands are already holding me open, smoothing up my thighs as his shoulders brace my legs apart.

The room is quiet except for my shallow pants.

"You're okay," he says. "You're so beautiful." He presses a kiss to my mound, right above my achy clit.

I don't know what to do with my hands. It feels wrong to keep them clasped on my stomach. I stick them straight at my sides and clutch the quilt.

"Trevor," I gasp. I don't know if I'm urging him on or asking for reassurance or what. My brain is a fuzzball. My body is vibrating.

"You're okay," he repeats, lifting my legs and placing my heels on the edge of the bed. "Let your knees fall open."

I can't. I'll look like an obscene frog.

"Show me your pussy," he says, gently nipping the plump bit of my inner thigh. "I'm your mate."

He is. He's in my heart. If I tune in, I can feel him there —happy, excited, and scared—just like me.

"You're my mate," I say and let my knees fall.

His wolf rumbles in the back of his throat as he spreads my folds with his fingers. "This okay?"

"Yeah."

He licks me, all the way back to front with his flat, raspy tongue. I clench my butt cheeks. This is so much. I don't want him back there, don't want to worry about that.

He licks me again, starting farther forward, lapping my lips and then circling my clit, edging, careful not to poke it with his tongue. He does it again and again until my bottom relaxes. He's not going there.

At first, I can't focus on anything but the fact that it's happening, and then it feels nice, and then it feels good. At some point, he scoops up my legs and tugs me closer. I glance down. All I can see is his strong forearms and the top of his curly head.

"Are you getting tired?" I ask softly. I'm not. I think I love this. The good, needy, squirmy feeling is snowballing, and I'm so scared if he stops, I'll burst into tears.

"Never get tired of this." His voice is muffled. He doesn't even stop to answer. He keeps the same pace, the same trail, back and forth, easing off, and then teasing my aching, pulsing clit.

"It feels so good."

I swear, I can feel him smile against my pussy.

"Do you need to come, beautiful?"

"Yes," I whimper.

"I'm going to put my finger inside you, okay?"

I whine.

"Okay?" he repeats, still lapping, gently, with his wonderful, magical raspy tongue. "I need to hear you say okay."

"Yes," I say, my frustrated hands clutching his hair of their own accord. He laughs softly.

"You've got to let go, baby." He gently untangles my grip and then slips a finger inside me as his tongue continues its tormenting circles.

A guttural moan I've never heard before is ripped from my throat. I like this. It feels right. Almost enough.

"More," I pant.

His wolf growls, and the sound makes my pussy vibrate. Everything swirls tighter, pulses harder, and I'm teetering, almost there, frustratingly, agonizingly almost freaking there, and he slides a second finger inside me, and I crash. Pleasure floods me from my belly outward, rushing through my veins to the top of my head and the tips of my toes.

I growl. Not my wolf. Me.

Trevor chuckles, rising from his knees, licking his mouth clean as he crawls up the bed, tugging me higher with him until not even my feet are hanging over the sides.

Part of me is melting, preening with the pleasure, but as the rush ebbs, another part of me is bracing. I can't *not* remember. He's a male. The same male. Not the same *person*, but the body is the same. He props himself above me and gazes down. There's pain in his eyes. He knows what I'm thinking.

Maybe he's trying not to remember, too.

"Hi," he says, brushing a stray hair out of my face.

"Hi," I reply with the same seriousness.

He kisses my lips. Once. Twice. Like he can't *not* with our mouths so close.

"Do you want to stop?" he asks.

"No. But I'm scared. What about you?"

"Same." He leans forward to rest his forehead against mine, but other than that, he doesn't put any of his weight on me. "If this is it, if we don't go any further, you know I'm happy, right? You can feel it in the bond. I'm so fucking happy."

I move my attention from the feel of his breath on my lips to the thumping in my chest, the accompaniment to my heartbeat that flows with happiness, like he said, but also, with something even sweeter and richer.

"You love me," I say.

"Yeah."

"When did you start?"

That crease appears between his eyebrows. He's really considering the question. "I guess when you snuck out to come see me in the stairwell."

"All the way back then?"

He smiles and kisses me again. "Yeah. I've loved you a long time."

"Why?" I don't doubt him, I just need to know. I've figured out that even though my parents didn't have love in them, that doesn't mean I was unlovable, but knowing in your head and knowing in your heart are two very different things. My heart is hungry. Starving. And here is Trevor, my mate, who loves so easily. I want to know the secret.

"You came to me. You were strong and brave, even though you had every reason not to be. I thought to myself that our pups would be safe no matter what. I felt lucky." Pain flashes in his eyes. "I made so many fucking mistakes."

"You don't feel lucky now." I understand, but it hurts. It *wrenches*.

"No, baby. No, no, no," he says between kisses. "I have always been lucky. Fate gave you to me, and after what I did, you came to me again. So strong and brave and beautiful." He draws back so he can look me in the eye. "I failed, but I will make it up to you every day for the rest of our lives."

I'm not sure I see it that way—that he failed—but I think he needs to see it that way. He needs to blame himself because he's a good male, and he wants to suffer for what he's done. I don't want him to suffer.

"I love you, too," I say, tracing his lips with my thumb.

The shadows instantly clear from his eyes, the blue outshining the gray like the water on the lake when the sun is shining high at noon and the sky is bright and cloudless.

"Yeah?" He grins. His next kiss scrambles my brains. "Since when?"

Not since the beginning. I didn't have room inside myself to love back then. I didn't belong to myself enough. "I think when we woke up naked in that ditch, and you made a joke about how you could carry me back to the den, even though I'm the size of a sub-compact car."

His mouth falls open. "I did *not* say that."

"Something like that." I'm teasing. He'd never say anything mean about me. I know that in my bones, and that's the number one reason why I love him. Our pups and I will be safe with him, too.

"See how lucky I am? I call my mate a sub-compact car, and she still loves me."

His happiness makes him so handsome. I lift my head to kiss him, and he kisses me back, and then we're lost in each other again. He slowly lowers himself closer. I arch my back so I can feel my aching breasts crush against his hard chest. His cock presses into my belly.

He cradles my head with one hand and urges my legs apart with the other. We're doing this. The past is there, always there, but it's draped in the background, muted and distant, not nearly as strong as the love warming my heart, not nearly as relentless as the thousands of small steps we made to find our way back to each other.

"Okay?" he asks.

"Yeah."

He slides inside me, gently, slowly, and strokes in and out. I lift my knees to take him deeper. He groans.

His eyes close, his face intensely focused. There's a little stretch, a little ache, but soon enough, it only feels good. He slips his hand between us and finds my sensitive nub again, and it feels even better.

I love the weight of his body on top of me. I love how we

rock back and forth in the same rhythm. We're made perfectly for each other.

He opens his eyes, smiling to see me watching him. "Hey, beautiful," he says, his voice ragged, breathless.

"Hi."

"You ready to come?" He tilts his hips and somehow goes even deeper.

I moan. It's so good. "Right there."

"Right here?" He hits the spot again. A wave ripples through my belly like a stone tossed into a lake.

"Don't stop."

"I won't," he promises, his wolf rumbling in his chest. "Not until you come. Are you ready?"

"Yes," I whine. More ripples are rippling, each a little stronger, but not enough. Not what I need.

He hikes my left leg over his bent arm, opening me wider so he can fill me even more completely. Rising to one knee, he thumbs my clit and slams that amazing spot over and over until my thighs shake.

"You almost there, beautiful?" he asks, his impatience not quite hidden well enough.

I growl, grabbing for him, desperate with need, but I can only reach the hand rubbing my clit. I wrap my fingers around his wrist and squeeze.

"Come for me now," he pants. "Come on my cock. *Now.*"

The submissive wolf in me has never been happier to follow orders. An orgasm crashes through me like a pinball machine. My hips jerk, my toes curl, and I let out a guttural scream that instantly has me burying my face in Trevor's chest. His laughter rumbles against my nose as he slams home one more time, shouts, bucks, and fills me with hot cum.

He lets my hoisted leg go, and I wrap both around his

waist. He nestles his chin into the crook of my neck, brushing reverent kisses along the scar from his bite.

For a few minutes, we breathe together like we're on a seesaw. I inhale as he exhales. Back and forth.

Eventually, the delicious fog in my brain begins to burn off, and despite my fears, there isn't a host of worries and bad memories waiting to rush on stage, just a quiet room that still smells faintly like sawdust and paint and a gentle wind whistling in the eaves.

"Good thing Granddad is sleeping at the elder cottage tonight," I say drowsily.

"Good thing we put up walls," Trevor says. I giggle. He lifts his head to grin at me, pleased with himself for making me laugh.

He tucks a hair behind my ear, and his face grows serious. "You'll stay here, won't you, Izzy? Here in our house. With me. As my mate."

The uncertainty and hopefulness in his voice makes my heart twinge, and my eyes prickle with threatening tears.

I don't answer quickly enough because he rushes to add, "I know what I'm asking. I know your life and your family is at Moon Lake, and if you want to go back, I understand." The blue in his eyes tips in favor of the gray. "I'll be honest —I'll follow you to the border, and wait there for you forever until I grow moss or a beard of ice or whatever, but I will understand." He stops himself to draw in a steadying breath. "Stay with me, Izzy. Please. You'll never want for anything as long as I have breath in my body, and I'll never, ever hurt you again."

I take his head in my hands and press my forehead to his. "Of course, I'll stay. We're in this together. We're a team now."

I've never been on a team, not really, but the idea warms

me deep inside. I don't want him to follow me or wait for me or even provide for me, although that warms me up, too.

I want us to live our lives side by side, like when our wolves run together or when I held up the drywall for this room while he fastened the screws in the studs. I want him to bring me a bucket of water for washing, and I want to snag him a bottle of soda from the communal fridge.

I never learned what love is, living on the nineteenth floor of the Towers at Moon Lake, so I'm making it up here as I go along, and I think it's this—holding on to each other with all our might, as gently as we can.

What Izzy doesn't know is that I talked to Cadoc a month ago. I knew it wasn't a simple request for Izzy to join the pack permanently. The exchange program is supposed to normalize relations with Moon Lake, and losing another pack member to Old Den, especially a female, could have the opposite of the intended effect.

As a male, I was privy to the discussions surrounding the program when it was proposed, even though I had no interest at the time. The exchange was Madog Collins' idea. He showed up one evening alone to talk to his son. That conversation was private, but everyone eagerly added their two cents to the deliberations afterward.

Most of the scavenger males felt strongly that Madog Collins could go fuck himself. Alec Cameron said he'd give his left nut for an experienced pipefitter. Seth and a few of the other ranked males from Moon Lake were focused on the risk of bringing people with unknown loyalties into our territory.

Apparently, even though Alban Hughes is dead and

Gwen Collins is on an indefinite visit to North Border, their followers have changed their tactics, not their mission. Seth, in particular, thinks that if the "rank supremacists" can topple Madog, they'll raid us to get the scavengers back, and as we all saw, Madog is not the male he once was.

I don't think Seth is wrong. Rank is less sweet, after all, if there aren't rankless wolves to exploit. On an even more basic level, wolves won't jockey for rank—and work themselves to death in the process, making money for Moon Lake —if the specter of ranklessness isn't there to scare them into climbing the ladder.

Anyway, I understood the implications when I went to Cadoc about Izzy, and I was also painfully aware I have nothing to trade except my labor. I asked. He said, "Don't you remember? I said you're pack, and Izzy's your mate, so she's pack."

"You did? When was this?"

"When Izzy first showed up. You were fixing the rabbit hutch."

"I don't remember a damn thing anyone said that day. I hardly remember what happened."

"Good thing," Cadoc said, chuckling. "You puked in front of everyone. Very embarrassing, and not the reaction a female is looking for when she shows up."

"It's a damn miracle she agreed to stay."

"I don't know about that." Cadoc slapped me on the back. "Your mate knows what she wants, and she's got a very familiar stubborn streak. I'll pray for you. The only reason I can sleep at night is because my mate has a gargantuan wolf to back her up."

My mate's new stubbornness is on full display today. I told Izzy that Cadoc already agreed that she can stay, but she insists on talking to Cadoc and Rosie herself, and she's nervous. She spent extra time on her hair this morning, rebraiding it until she felt it hung straight, and she didn't touch her breakfast.

She doesn't want me to go with her. I'm compromising by walking her there and sitting with Granddad while she talks to the alpha and his mate. Izzy's jitters rile my wolf, but I recognize that this is important to her, even if I can't quite understand why.

"You sure?" I ask when we get to the den.

"Yes." She smooths her palms down her pants. "You stay here."

Pale but determined, she takes a step toward the small firepit with the rickety wooden dining chairs and over-turned milk crates where Rosie and Cadoc hold court when they're hanging out, and then she stops and glances back over her shoulder at me. "It'll be okay," she says. She's not telling me. She's asking.

My heart cracks open. "Yes. It'll be fine."

She nods firmly and strides off. I make my way to Granddad and sit on the edge of the vacant rocker next to him.

"What are you doing here, pup? Is it raining?"

"No, it's nice out."

"And you're not busting your ass for that female? Finally letting yourself get comfortable, eh?"

Not hardly. I'm happier than I've ever been in my life, but you couldn't tell from my body. Every muscle I've got, as well as my stomach, is a knot. "I'll get back to work in a few. When Izzy's done here."

Granddad squints across the den. "What's she doing talking to the alpha?"

"Asking him if she can stay here when he already said she can."

I'm not really mad—I'm just talking shit—but Granddad bristles, incensed. "Of course she can stay here. She's your mate, and she's a real healer. Those are not easy to come by. Salt Mountain hasn't had its own for decades. They have to make do with the witch, and I don't know if I'd trust her if I were them. She wouldn't piss on half of 'em if they were on fire, as well she shouldn't."

Granddad scowls as Cadoc stands and offers Izzy a seat. She declines. Rosie grabs her hand and tugs her down to sit beside her, and Izzy can't refuse that. She sits all prim and proper, though, which looks especially strange seeing as she's perched on a milk crate.

"Why's she asking anyway, if you said Cadoc already said she could stay?"

"I'm not sure. Maybe she feels like it's something she needs to do for herself."

Granddad nods in understanding. "Headstrong female. Make the best dams, but the pups will test your patience to within an inch of your life."

Izzy's speaking now, her expression deadly serious. Cadoc and Rosie listen intently. I'm sure a lot of males would take offense at their mate wanting to speak to the alpha on their own. For sure, all the males I was raised around, my dad included, wouldn't have tolerated it. Maybe if things hadn't unfolded as they had, my pride would've been injured, too, but I'm nothing but grateful.

Whatever is driving Izzy to speak for herself now, drove her to sneak out of her apartment all those years ago so I could find her in the stairwell. It kept her together after that horrible night, and eventually, it prodded her back out into the world and led her back to me. I would never want Izzy to be weaker just to soothe my pride.

On the other hand, I'm also going to be right there

keeping an eye out, no matter what happens, for the rest of our lives.

Izzy finishes up her spiel. Rosie throws her arm around Izzy's shoulder, squeezing her close. Cadoc begins to speak, his expression kind and earnest. Some of the tension eases from my muscles.

Izzy listens intently, and then she nods, stands, and offers him her hand. He stands and shakes it. Rosie springs to her feet and gathers Izzy into a hug from behind, swaying back and forth with her until Izzy breaks into a grin. I'm able to draw in a full breath again.

"Looks like it all worked out," Granddad observes and pats my knee. "Good thing. Didn't want to have to take things into my own hands." He grins at me.

"You good?" I ask. He's got his water and his quilt. Flora is cleaning up after breakfast. I'm sure she'll be over soon.

"Good as I can get."

I go meet Izzy on her way back over. The sour scent of her nerves has dissipated, but a whiff of Rosie's scent clings to her. It's not a bad smell, but I don't care for it. My wolf butts against the barrier between us. He wants to rub against her until she smells like only us again.

"We're good to go," Izzy says as she grabs my hand. "Let's go find the phone so I can call my parents and tell them."

"We're doing that now? Okay. Let's go." I like this. I want everything settled as soon as possible, too. I've been on edge since she agreed to stay with me. It's everything I never even dared dream of, and something in my bones warns me that Fate has never had a better opening to destroy me completely.

Technically, there is more than one phone at Old Den, and service is bad but not nonexistent, but there is one satellite phone that Cadoc has mandated remains on a specific table near the TV. That's *the* phone.

"You know what you want to say?" I ask.

She shakes her head. "No, but I know what I'll say first." We arrive at the table. "Will you stay for this one?" she asks.

My throat sticks. I nod. If she asks, nothing could make me leave.

I make eye contact with Danny and the other young males playing video games. The other males duck their heads and hop right up, but Danny, of course, waits until my wolf rumbles before he sets down his controller and stalks off, mumbling about a save point.

Izzy takes no notice. She's psyching herself up, taking deep breaths.

I wish with all my heart that I could do this for her, but I'm also so proud of her. I used to think she was mouselike, but she's not. She's all wolf. A small one, but still—all wolf.

"Are you ready?" she asks as if I'm the one about to do the hard thing. I'm on to her. It's easier for her to care for others. It's the healer in her.

"We've got this," I say, and her mouth curves in a wary but fierce little smile.

She dials. Her mother picks up. She's not on speaker, but with shifter hearing, I can hear everything clear as day anyway.

They exchange a few pleasantries. Her mother's tone makes it obvious that even though she says it's a good time to talk, she still considers the call an imposition.

Izzy quickly gets to the point. "I'm calling because I spoke to Cadoc Collins, and I'm staying here at Old Den with Trevor. With my mate."

For a long moment, there is stunned silence, and then her mother barks, "Hold the line."

I hear footsteps. An urgent knock on a door. Raised voices that are far enough away that I can't make them out.

Izzy's gaze locks with mine. At first, there is a paralyzed fear in her eyes, but as I watch, her expression shores up into something more certain. Steelier.

Still, she jerks when her father barks, "Isolde! What is this crap your mother's telling me about you staying at Old Den?"

She swallows hard. She's not looking at me anymore; she's staring blindly into the distance, her free hand curling into a fist. My wolf growls.

Protect her.

I force myself to stand back. It's as hard as reining back my wolf. She needs to do this herself, though. If I've learned nothing else about her during these weeks, it's that the more I do *for* her, the more unsure she gets, but if I work beside her—and ease the way when she doesn't notice—she thrives.

This is different from home improvement or navigating Old Den pack life, though. This is the male who terrorized her to the point she had to sneak away to meet her fated mate.

"I'm going to stay here with Trevor. Cadoc Collins has agreed." Her voice is even, although quieter than usual.

"Bullshit. You will be on that bus on Monday." He laces the words with command.

Izzy's fist curls tighter. My chest constricts.

"Dad, I'm staying here with my mate," she says even quieter.

He snorts. "The mate who raped you in the dirt and left you bleeding out on the sidewalk?"

His words choke my throat like a hanging rope. I can't breathe. I can hardly hear through my wolf's snarling.

Take that thing from her. Smash it.

I couldn't move now if I wanted to. I'm paralyzed, trapped by the guilt flooding my lungs like tar.

Izzy's still staring into the middle distance. If she looked at me, I'd burn to ashes from the shame.

"The mate you kept me from until he went into rut," she says, very calmly. The hand holding the phone trembles, but her voice doesn't.

He dismisses her with a sniff. "No one can *keep* a female in heat from her mate if she wants him. You knew he wasn't worthy of you. The door wasn't locked, was it, Izzy? No one was standing in your way. You could've gone to him at any time if you'd really wanted to, but you hid in your room, gobbling down your mother's little helpers, because you didn't want a greasy mutt from the dregs of the pack, either."

"That's not true," she says, breathily, as if her lungs are filling, too.

"And sure as hell, no one can keep a male from a mate in heat, either, but that mutt wasn't knocking down our door, was he?"

"You threatened his family. You said they'd take his dad and brothers' jobs and throw them out of their apartment, cast them so far down that even the scavengers wouldn't take them in."

Her father scoffs. "A real male wouldn't put *anyone* or *anything* above claiming his mate. He was willing to wait because he wanted to curry favor with his betters, just like every low-ranked ass sniffer. He wanted to move up, and he had no problem making you suffer for it."

It isn't true, but the truth that is in it tears chunks from my skin. I scourged myself with the same words a thousand times. I shouldn't have waited. I chose my family over her. A good male would sacrifice *anything* to protect his mate. I betrayed her.

"A real male wouldn't put anything above his *pup*." Izzy's voice is breaking now. Her distress singes the air. "He'd never ask her to suffer for his benefit."

This has gone on long enough. Every inch of me burns with shame, but the time when I let shame make me weak is over. My mate is *mine* now. I will allow nothing—especially not my own demons—to stop me from keeping her safe.

I step forward and gently take the phone from Izzy's hand. "Mr. Owens, Izzy has said her piece. She's staying here with me."

"So the mutt finally finds the balls to speak for himself," he sneers. "If you know what's good for you, my daughter *will* be on that bus on Monday. Nothing's changed except there's no bog left for your family to take refuge in when we throw them out of the Tower like the trash they are."

The threat hits, but I'm not an eighteen-year-old with no experience of the world anymore. I've started over twice. It would be hard, but I know myself well enough now that I know I wouldn't let my family starve.

"Do what you feel you have to do," I say. "My mate stays with me."

I hit end and set the phone back on the table. Izzy is shaking. My wolf howls. He's pissed that I've let our mate get this upset. He thinks I should've chomped the phone to bits the instant her father spoke to her with that tone.

I wrap her in my arms, gather her as close as I can, and rock. My wolf calms himself enough to switch his howl to a low rumble.

The shame still crawls across my skin, souring my scent, but Izzy is breaking down, and I'm not leaving my brave mate to comfort herself. My chest muffles her wracking sobs, my shirt absorbing her tears.

"I knew it would go just like that," she chokes out. "I don't know why I'm so upset. I knew he'd be just that horrible, and I knew she wouldn't do anything to protect me."

"A punch in the face hurts. It doesn't hurt any less if you see it coming."

She lets out a strangled laugh. "I guess you've got a point there."

"I'm sorry. I wish I could've done that for you."

"I wouldn't have let you."

"I know." I stroke her back. The sobs are turning to hiccups.

"I'm sorry, too," she says, nuzzling my chest to wipe her tears, and a spark of happiness flares to life in the dark mess inside me. Our mating can't be hopelessly tainted, not when she uses my shirt as a handkerchief without thinking.

"You don't have to be sorry about anything, ever," I remind her.

"I just wiped my snot on your one clean shirt," she says. "The others are all in the laundry." Well, I guess it wasn't exactly *without thinking*.

Miraculously, after that horrible fucking conversation, I'm somehow almost smiling. "We'll have to do the laundry tonight."

"I'll measure the detergent," she says.

"I'll pour." I drop a kiss on her forehead and loosen my hold. She wipes away the rest of her tears with her own sleeve.

"We can't let him hurt your family," she says. The wounded look leaves her eyes, replaced with the new steeliness that she's forged all by herself.

My heart swells with pride. "I'll call home later and talk

it through with my father. I'll bring Cadoc in if it comes to it. We'll figure it out. We're not letting the bad guys win again."

"No, we're not." Izzy stands on her toes and smacks a kiss to my lips.

The young males that I ran off from their video games must've been waiting for a cue to return because they slouch back over, but before they plop back down into their seats, they zag over to Izzy and bump her with their shoulders.

"All right, Izzy?"

"You good?"

"Okay now?"

They don't wait for an answer, but their point was made. She's not alone.

17

———

IZZY

I know something bad is going to happen. Trevor did speak to his family and Cadoc, and by Cadoc's invitation, they're coming on the exchange program bus to visit. It'll be the first time Trevor has seen his parents in person since his exile from Moon Lake.

There are no plans for his family to resettle in Old Den, but the invitation to visit is a clear signal to my father that the Floyds are allied with Old Den, and messing with them could endanger Madog's diplomatic mission. I'm grateful, but it's a mistake to think that my father wouldn't love to thwart Madog Collins' plans.

The pack is buzzing with anticipation. The nurses and facilities guys will be leaving, to be replaced by a new cohort of HVAC technicians, math teachers, and to Alec's delight, an experienced pipefitter.

The scavengers who agreed to go back to Moon Lake for the first mission are returning, to be replaced by a different group of unmated males and females. It's not a spoken goal of the program, but living here, I've picked up that basically the only reason Old Den folks have volunteered to partici-

pate is the hope that their mate is one of the remaining members of Moon Lake.

Trevor is vibrating with nerves, which he's trying to deal with by reassuring me.

"I can't wait for you to meet them. You'll love Garan. He's hysterically funny."

"Which one is Garan?" We've hiked out past the felled log barricade that blocks the road into the den, and we're waiting with others waiting for the bus. We're both wearing our nicest outfits. I'm in the blouse and slacks I arrived in, and Trevor's in his good jeans. Our hair is washed, combed, and a total mess—Trevor's from running his hands through it, mine from my stressed-out sweat.

"He's the second youngest."

"And the youngest is Aled?"

"No, Aled is second oldest. Llew is youngest."

"I'm going to get it so mixed up."

"You'll catch on quick. Llew looks like a Llew, and Aled is totally an Aled."

"What does a Llew look like?"

"Annoying."

I giggle. "What's an Aled?"

"A dumbass."

I grin over at him. He's staring anxiously down the road. I grip his damp palm tighter. "I always wished I had annoying, dumbass brothers." Maybe things would've been different with other kids to take some of the heat off me. Or maybe it's messed up to wish my childhood on even hypothetical siblings.

"Well, you do now." He squeezes my hand. "They're going to love you."

I hope so. They have a lot of reasons to resent me. I don't know how I'll handle it if they hate me. I guess the first step is to take them as they come and welcome them to our home. I'm as ready as I can be.

I liberated some lavender, chamomile, and sage from the apothecary and made bouquets to hang from twine strung across our new cabin windows, and I borrowed a motley assortment of chairs from the den with Rosie's blessing so there are places for everyone to sit.

Trevor's wolf caught a few rabbits for stew, and Drona's girls and I made another box cake, this time strawberry. My mother would be aghast that I'd offer guests soup for dinner, but she'd never invite a low-ranked family into her home, either.

Maybe it's time for me to stop thinking about what my mother would do or think. It doesn't apply anymore.

"They were so excited on the phone," Trevor adds.

I summon up a smile. I wish the bus would get here already. I need to check something off my worry list.

I'm sure there's no imminent disaster hovering on the horizon. This is just how my body feels when I'm stressed. I know this. I'm so much better in so many ways, but my nervous system still can't differentiate between an all-out attack and the prospect of a somewhat fraught social situation.

Luckily, we don't have much longer to wait. The bus arrives in a cloud of dust. The scavengers pound down the steps first, running into their loved one's arms. The air fills with squeals of joy and the howls of excited wolves.

The new Moon Lake emissaries file out next with a lot more decorum. They wander forward, clearly looking for direction. Good luck to them. Neither Seth Rosser nor Lowry Powell are here, and they're the only two in the pack who still have Moon Lake-style bossy tendencies.

It's clear which are HVAC technicians and which are math teachers. Alec must know the pipefitter somehow because he greets the male by name as he disembarks. They shake hands and head off together before the others figure that they should get their gear from the storage compartment.

And then, bringing up the rear, Trevor's family climbs out. His brothers bound down first and converge on Trevor as a pack, jostling each other as they pull him into rough hugs, slapping his back, thrusting him toward each other like a game of hot potato. I skip a few feet backward to get out of their way, and for a second, Trevor's eyes track me, but then he's enveloped by another brother.

They tousle his hair and playfully bump him with their shoulders, all the while talking over each other.

"Look at you! They must be feeding you good, eh?"

"Come here. What's with this hair? They don't have scissors at Old Den?"

"Seriously though, you look good, man. Missed you."

A male clears his throat. The brothers settle and turn toward the bus. Trevor's dad descends the steps, leading a female I've never met. Her blue gray eyes are glistening.

"My pup," she says, her voice cracking. The instant her feet touch the ground she opens her arms and staggers toward him.

Trevor strides to her and bends to wrap her in his arms, lifting her gently off her feet before setting her carefully back down. "Hey, Mom."

My eyes prickle.

Tears stream down her face. She can't decide what to do —squeeze him tight, fuss with his hair, hold him at an arm's length so she can drink him in—so she does it all and then starts again.

"You're so tall," she says, the words hitching. "Were you always this tall?"

She doesn't let him answer, squeezing him tight again, rocking side-to-side like she must've done when he was a pup. Her raw sobs crack my heart in two.

It would've been even harder on her than the others. Back in the day, Moon Lake and Salt Mountain would sometimes run together during a full moon, but the runs petered out during Connal Shaw's reign as alpha. Salt Mountain pups still go to Moon Lake Academy, but our wolves are only invited onto Salt Mountain territory for fights, and only the males who are fighting are allowed. That's how his brothers were able to visit Trevor, but his parents weren't.

"Arlais," Trevor's dad says softly, drawing her away to tuck her against his side. "Hello, son."

Since he's comforting his mate, Trevor's dad can only manage to shake Trevor's hand, but he holds on tight, gripping hard, pulling his son close. He murmurs something in Trevor's ear that I can't hear. Whatever his dad says rips another jagged cry from Trevor's mother. Trevor grabs his mother's hand, and the three of them huddle together, foreheads together, for several long somber moments in silence, as if it's enough to be close, to catch their breath together, to touch.

His brothers circle the trio like sentinels. I stand a few feet away, trying not to stare and invade their private moment. The others from Moon Lake filter away, making their way around the barricade, figuring out logistics. Eventually, we're alone—Trevor's family, me, and the bus driver playing on her phone and casting glares at us since I guess she can't leave until all the luggage has been retrieved.

I feel like a sore thumb. Should I get their stuff? I want to be helpful, but I don't want them to think I'm rushing them.

Would they even notice? I don't think any of the Floyds have even noticed me. And why should they? They're here for Trevor. They haven't seen him in years. This is their moment.

Trevor's love—and his grief—rolls through my chest in waves as I hesitate, trying to decide where to look and what to do with my hands. I'm happy for him. I really, really am. I'm a good person. I've grown. I've done hard things. I'm a healer now.

Still, a bitter, corrosive voice deep in my brain whispers—

They hate you. They blame you.

All of these tears—you caused this. No one can keep a female in heat from her mate if she wants him. The door wasn't locked, was it, Izzy? No one was standing in your way.

He's going to blame you, too, when he really gets to know you.

The voice drops lower—

Look at them. They love him so much. They missed him so badly.

You can only imagine what that must be like, surrounded by people who love you like that. And you know why, right?

You just don't inspire that kind of love. You lived in your bedroom for years. Who missed you? Who cared enough to get you to leave?

Your mate didn't even try to get you back. You had to go to him.

I can't stand here anymore. I march over to the storage compartment and muscle the door up.

The Floyds are only here for a week. Trevor made arrangements for Bevan to run them back to Moon Lake in the Old Den van on his way to drop Rosie off at Quarry Pack. She meets with Una every couple months for an "alpha female summit," alternating hosts. Rosie says they do it to swap goodies, gossip, and give their mates the opportunity to miss them so they don't get too comfortable.

There are two suitcases and an assortment of duffel bags and backpacks. I start with unloading the bags, walking them over to the grassy side of the road so they don't sit in the dirt.

I've only dealt with two bags when Trevor appears beside me, lifts a duffel off my shoulder, and slings it over his own. "You don't have to do that," he says. "Come meet the family."

The Floyds have rearranged themselves to face me in a loose semi-circle. Their expressions are polite. Masked. Except for his mother. She averts her gaze as she dabs her cheeks dry. Her jaw is set. I guess she doesn't appreciate me distracting Trevor and interrupting the reunion.

I feel oversized and stupid as Trevor walks me back over to them. "This is Izzy," he says, even though of course they all know who I am.

"Hi." I try my best to smile, and I give a little wave. I should say something else. *Welcome to Old Den. We're so happy you're here. I'm sorry for everything that happened. I'm sorry for the choices I made that caused you to lose your son.*

How do I navigate this? I took the first step, and now I'm standing over a chasm like that cartoon coyote.

"Say what you feel, and we'll deal with it" doesn't work when you're confronting his entire family, and they're staring at you with brutally blank expressions.

Trevor wraps an arm around my waist and tugs me against his side. "Okay, so from left to right, that's Garan, Aled, Tarian, and Llew." Each of them nods or raises a hand in turn. "You know Dad. And this is Mom."

"Macsen and Arlais," his father says. He's not correcting

Trevor. He's just telling me their names. I shouldn't feel like it's a rejection. Still, my stomach twists.

"Pleased to meet you," I say, falling back on the manners my mother taught me. She impressed upon me from the time that I was old enough to be allowed in company that politeness means keeping your mouth shut unless someone asks you a question, so that's what I do.

No one asks me any questions.

Trevor and his brothers grab the luggage, and Trevor falls in step with his mother, leading the group around the barricade toward camp. We decided earlier that it would be easier to walk instead of securing bikes for everyone, and it was a good decision.

Even though I feel awkward and superfluous, I still bask in the pure joy flowing through the bond as Trevor and his family banter all the way back.

"I'm surprised you still wear it short." Tarian musses Trevor's hair.

"Yeah, aren't you a scavenger now?" Llew asks.

"Where's your tail? I thought the whole thing about being a scavenger is you get to let your wolf hang out." Aled tries to snag the back of Trevor's jeans.

Trevor smacks his hand away. "Quit trying to look at my ass."

"Why? Are you ashamed of it? I'd be ashamed of it." Tarian fakes a sympathetic expression.

"Trevor doesn't want you to know that he *is* wearing his tail," Llew suggests. "It's just so small, it gets lost between his butt cheeks."

"I'm so sorry you have an embarrassingly short, stumpy tail," Aled says mournfully. "I'm sure no one's judging."

"I am judging, but I love you anyway," Tarian says.

"Boys," his mother admonishes, laughing. "Be nice to

your brother." She pauses a second then adds, "Your poor stumpy-tailed brother."

Everyone bursts out laughing at that, and the brothers continue to rag on each other for the rest of the walk home. They tease Tarian about his car, which is falling apart, but he won't trade it in because of how much money he's already put into it. They make fun of Aled's hair, Llew's second job as a dishwasher at the High Rise cafeteria—he's apparently the worst for putting his dirty dishes in the clean dishwasher load at home—and Garan for the fact that he's so quiet.

Arlais and Macsen laugh at their antics, alternating between chastising them for going too far and adding their own jabs. I walk along with a smile pasted on my face, forcing myself to laugh when everyone else does. It's not that they're not funny—they are—but the pit in my stomach is growing with every step.

They stroll together like a pack that's been running together for years, which they are. I feel jammed in.

The brothers bump into each other on purpose, throw their arms over each other's shoulders, weave closer and then farther apart, exactly like their wolves. Macsen strides behind his mate like a bodyguard. Everyone is very careful to give me space.

I hate that I feel so left out. Trevor is so happy. Happy in a way I've never felt before.

The pit in my stomach becomes a rock.

When we get to the commons, I'm so relieved to see Rosie and Nia. Cadoc is there, too, along with Seth. The four of them serve as our pack council, and they're assembled to greet the newcomers, along with Enid Wogan and a few of the unmated females who've made wildflower wreaths as a welcome gift. When we arrive, they're crowning the bemused Moon Lake math teachers.

Trevor's family sobers, and they solemnly shake hands with Cadoc as Trevor introduces them one-by-one. When she's introduced, Trevor's mom clutches Cadoc's hand and clasps it to her chest. "Thank you for giving my son a home," she says. "May Fate bless you for it."

"He is a good male," Cadoc answers, his usual stony expression betraying a trace of feeling, a fond sincerity. "He makes our pack stronger."

Arlais bursts into fresh tears and throws her arms around Cadoc. Rosie and Nia exchange a look. Cadoc is not a demonstrative male. He awkwardly pats Arlais' back as Macsen gently urges her to let go. She gives Cadoc a final, fierce hug before she backs away.

Macsen is flushing as he shakes Cadoc's hand. "If there is ever anything me or mine can do for you or Old Den, you've only got to ask," he says.

When Trevor introduces Rosie, there are more tears and thanks and vows, and then the whole group erupts into various clusters of animated conversations. Tarian and Seth are old friends. Aled knows Pritchard, so he asks Nia about him. Llew and Enid know each other, and Arlais has a lot more to say to Cadoc and Rosie. Trevor explains to his dad how the pack is spread between the den and the nearby cabins. His dad has a lot of questions about our infrastructure.

I stand at Trevor's side. When he was making introductions, he was holding my hand. Now that he's talking to his dad, he needs both hands to illustrate what he's saying.

I don't need attention on me. For most of my life, I actively tried *not* to be noticed. I know Trevor loves me, and this is a good day for him that for a long time, he thought he would never see.

So I keep the smile planted on my face and pretend I'm content to listen to conversations that don't include me. My stomach twists and twists. It's a small discomfort, and besides, this moment won't last much longer. At Moon Lake, I spent five years being surreptitiously gawked at in public. Being ignored for a little while isn't so bad.

Eventually, Rosie excuses herself to tend her pup, and soon after, the group disperses, and Trevor leads his family to our cabin. It's a relief to get back to my home territory, and my stomach does unknot. As Trevor shows his family around, I busy myself getting dinner ready.

Granddad is sleeping at the elder cabin during the visit, so Arlais and Macsen get his room. Trevor rigged up a canvas tent between two nearby trees for his brothers. It's not fancy, but if they sleep as their wolves, they should be comfortable.

I borrowed a tripod and cast-iron pot so I could heat our meal and arranged for Flora to drop off the stew I made earlier when she picked up Granddad's change of clothes. While the food warms, I cut the brown bread that Drona gave me as a thank you for keeping her girls busy baking the box cake. Along with the real strawberries I picked to complement dessert, and the carrots and radishes I saved aside for crudité, it's about as good a meal as you can find at Old Den, except for when someone brings down a deer.

No one is going to care that the dishes are mostly repurposed cans and plastic containers, or that none of the utensils match. The Floyds are focused on Trevor, and that's as it should be.

When I finish setting the table I rigged up with a sheet of plywood on top of two sawhorses, they're still talking a mile a minute about Trevor's plans for installing electric and plumbing in the cabin. I guess all his brothers are in facility maintenance. They're very passionate about gravity-fed versus pressurized tank and pump systems.

I wait for a good time to jump in—or for someone to notice that dinner's ready—but when they start talking about taking a walk to see what Alec Cameron has done with his place, I interrupt.

First, I call out, "Dinner's ready." They're already heading toward the path, though, so I jog after them and tug Trevor by his sleeve. He immediately greets me with a smile. Because he loves me. Nothing's wrong. He's just excited to be with his family again, and they're taken with talking to him after so long apart.

"Time to eat," I tell him.

"Oh, great. Thank you." He cradles my cheek and kisses my lips. My unsettled heart warms—until I glance up.

A leaden silence has fallen like a dead weight. His brothers are looking in every direction except at us. His father frowns at the ground. His mother's face is twisted in something resembling horror. My face burns. Is this because he kissed me?

"It's only stew," I babble, backing away from Trevor. "It's getting cold." I don't mean to chastise; I'm just thrown. I don't understand what's going on here, and even my wolf is uneasy now.

"Sounds great. Let's eat." Trevor smiles at me and grabs my hand, trying to smooth the moment over, but I saw their faces. They hate me.

That's okay. I don't need to freak out. It's understandable. I can see it from their point of view. Because of what happened with me, they lost a male they loved. I'm tough enough to handle this. I stiffen my spine and walk with Trevor to lead the way to the table.

I take a seat on the long side, leaving the head and foot for Trevor's parents. His brothers sit with no jockeying or fuss, as if they're taking their accustomed places, except for Llew who looks lost for a second. Guess I'm in his usual seat.

A few more stilted minutes creep by while the butter is passed and drinks are poured from the pitchers of iced tea and lemonade I set out, but as the Floyds begin to eat, something resembling normal conversation returns.

The stew and bread are complimented. Other notable family dinners are recalled—the time Arlais burned the roast, and everyone ate it without comment because Macsen said the first pup to complain would be on bathroom cleaning duty for the rest of his natural life.

They told the story of the time Llew stole a drumstick from Garan's plate, and Garan thought it was Aled, so he bit him, and Aled flailed his arms in surprise, whacking Tarian in the face, and Tarian cursed, and Arlais heard, so Tarian got punished for swearing, and everyone else got away with it.

Soon enough, everyone is laughing, and I'm making myself smile and trying to remember to stop when the laughter dies down.

After the brothers polish off the stew, I serve the cake and strawberries. Macsen retrieves two bottles of sweet wine he brought from Moon Lake and pours everyone a glass before he reseats himself at the head of the table.

He gazes around at his sons, his dark eyes glossy with a sheen of unshed tears. The worn hand holding his cup trembles. His other hand sits fisted on the table.

Everyone grows quiet.

"I never dreamed I would see this day. All my pups

together around a table again with my beautiful mate." He raises his cup to Arlais. She smiles at him softly, tears streaking down her cheeks. "It's a good day. May Fate bless us with many more like it. Cheers."

"Cheers," the others echo, clinking their old soup cans and repurposed peanut butter jars. I tap cups with Trevor, who sits to my right, and Llew at my left.

No one leans across the table to clink my glass. Not like they do each other.

Arlais and Macsen relax in their chairs, surveying their brood with watery smiles. Their gazes slide over me. Trevor squeezes my hand under the table.

I understand. This is hard for them. They don't know how to act with me.

This has nothing to do with the family dinners I sat through for the first twenty-some years of my life, where I was invisible except for when I committed some infraction.

Isolde, elbows off the table.

Isolde, you chew like a cow.

Isolde, eat your food, don't push it around your plate.

I drag a strawberry through the cake's vanilla frosting and listen to the bond. There is muted worry coming through—Trevor isn't unaware of the tension at the table—but his worry, and the ever-present remnants of grief and shame, are overwhelmed by his joy in being with his family again.

I focus on the happiness. His dad is right. This is a good day, and it'll get better. His family and I will get to know each other, and they'll see that I love Trevor, and that we're good together because we *are.*

"So son, tell me about the poor elder who we've kicked out of his own bed," Macsen says, pouring himself a second glass of wine. "How'd you end up with him as a roommate?"

"Granddad?" Trevor answers. "He's a good male. He insisted you take his room while you're here. He's a Cameron from Salt Mountain, but don't hold that against him."

"Your brothers said he took you under his wing back there."

"He did. Izzy and I look out for him now." Trevor shoots me a smile.

"It's good to have an elder so close. You can learn so much," Arlais says. "You didn't get nearly enough time with Grandpa Huw."

No one else was talking, but all of a sudden, the silence around the table is loud.

"I'm sorry I wasn't there when he passed," Trevor says. A fresh tendril of grief flows through the bond. It feels like a nail in my chest.

"Oh, my pup, it wasn't your fault." Arlais grips the edge of the table and leans forward. She's looking at Trevor, pain and love brimming in her eyes.

She's not talking to me. She doesn't mean that it was *my* fault.

No one can keep a female in heat from her mate if she wants him. The door wasn't locked, was it, Izzy? No one was standing in your way.

The silence at the table practically vibrates. Everyone except Trevor and his mom is staring at me from the sides of their eyes.

She's not saying it was my fault, but that's what they all think. It's clear as day. They're too polite—or they love Trevor too much to say it—but they're honest people. Their faces don't lie.

I stand. My chair tips back. I grab it just in time.

"Izzy?" Trevor blinks up at me. I slam the bond shut. I

don't even know how I do it. It's muscle memory. "What's going on?"

The echo of his sadness ricochets, trapped in my chest. He misses his grandfather, and the guilt over not being there for his mother when he passed and regret for the time he lost with him both *eat* at him. And it's my fault. I'm honest, too, and I can't deny it.

"I have to take the stew pot back to the den." I back away from the table like it might explode.

"Right now? Izzy, sit down. It'll wait." His eyes are confused.

No one else is saying anything. They want time alone with their son and brother. Of course, they do. They haven't seen him in years, and here they are, forced to break bread with the female who tore their family apart.

It would be a gift to give them some time and space.

"Yes. They need it. I'll be back soon." I summon up a reassuring smile.

Trevor's brow furrows. "I'll take it later. You sit. Relax. You did all the cooking."

I take another step back. "I'll only be a few minutes."

"Izzy—"

"Trevor." Arlais interrupts him. "She said she'll be right back," she says gently. Fondly. "Let her go."

He doesn't want to. He reaches out to grab my hand, but I'm already striding toward the fire where the pot sits cooling beside it on a trivet I made out of stones.

"I won't be more than twenty minutes." I hoist the pot and hook it over my elbow. "Enjoy your wine." I raise my hand in what I mean to be a friendly wave. It comes across more like I'm cautioning them to stay put.

No one looks like they want to stop me except Trevor. He's tense, his chair pushed back from the table, hands braced on the edges like he can't make up his mind whether to get up or not.

"So is the plan to run water first or water *and* sewage?" his dad asks.

I flash Trevor a smile and nod for him to stay. I see the conflict play out on his face. He doesn't want me to go, at least not on my own, but he also wants to respect my choices. In the end, he watches me go with a slight frown as he allows himself to be distracted by home improvement talk.

I walk away quickly to minimize the chance of him changing his mind. I want a little time and space, too. Not much, just some room to breathe.

I haven't felt so off kilter in a long time, not since before I apprenticed with Abertha. When I finally got the courage to leave my bedroom hibernation, I figured life out. You put one foot in front of the other, and things fall into place. You get farther than you'd ever imagine you could get, and it's so simple. Take one step, and then take another.

The strategy doesn't work with Trevor's family. I take a step—opening the door to our cabin, welcoming them inside—and his mother fails to hide her pain when she sees the empty space and bare walls. Is she thinking about apartment 1248? What she wanted for her son? The basket of blankets she put together for me?

I serve them food, and they all stare at the bowls for a few seconds before they collect themselves enough to dig in. Are they thinking about how wrong it is that this is the first meal they've shared with their brother and his mate? Or are they thanking Fate that they're getting the chance to eat with him again?

Every moment is a raw wound. Every word is fraught. Fault and blame hover over everything.

I arrive at the den in no time, and I've managed to work myself up rather than calm myself down. I hand the pot to Enid, who happens to be heading inside, and keep going. We ate relatively early—and quickly—and the sun is setting later these days, so there's more than enough light left for a short walk.

I don't even think about where I'm going. I just walk. Across the commons. Past the bikes. Down the rutted road. It's the path of least resistance.

Pritchard waves at me from guard duty and calls down from his perch on top of the barricade, "Where you heading, Izzy?"

"Just stretching my legs. I'll be back soon."

He's frowning. "You don't want one of the females to go with you?"

"I just need a few minutes alone. I'm not going far."

He doesn't like it, but he's been dealing with Nia too long to come at me with a show of dominance. "Are you totally, totally sure? I can go get a female for you. It'll be two minutes."

I'm already a yard past him. "I'm good," I call over my shoulder. "I won't leave the territory." I wave and keep trucking. Every step, I feel lighter.

I'm not running away. I'm just taking a break. I'm not the person anymore who hid from her problems.

I'm not that person anymore I repeat to myself because it's a habit now to coach myself forward with affirmations and reassurances, but between one step and the next, I realize that I'm not visualizing a possible future at all.

I'm *really* not that person.

She was broken. She'd been torn apart by her mate and forced to nurse her wounds surrounded by the people who cared so little for her that they'd practically set her up to be attacked. She couldn't handle anything—noise, people, choices.

I fixed her. I *healed* her. Then I came for my mate. I fixed *us*. That's all as true and real as fault and blame and hurt and loss.

I took my first steps, and I kept going, and his family will, too, or they won't. I can feel hurt that they can't or won't welcome me with open arms, but I am not going to feel *at fault*. Or like everything is ruined or hopeless because we had a rocky start. It's not ruined yet. I decide it's not.

My pace picks up. My chest feels lighter.

And then another thing hits me—the key isn't about taking the first step. Or at least, not *just* about taking the first step. The key is knowing that you can keep going. Every step thereafter is just as up to you as the first. I get why I never knew that. Mom and Dad didn't believe I was capable of doing anything right. I was doomed from the start, and all my effort—the practices and studying and extracurriculars —was salt in the wound to them because no matter how hard I tried, I wasn't going to be what they really wanted. A dominant male.

But they're so wrong. I am capable of—

I round a curve in the road. A white van screeches to a halt, kicking up dust and stopping inches away from me. The heat from its engine blasts my face. My heart slams into my ribs. Uncle Howell blinks at me through the window, his hands gripping the wheel. I was so lost in thought, I didn't even hear them coming.

Uncle Howell doesn't drive a white van. He has a Mercedes.

And then the side door slides open, and Dad leaps out, followed by Vaughn Lewis. What's he doing here?

Vaughn is one of Brody Hughes' henchmen. Like Brody, he's been laying low since Madog returned.

Three more males spill out of the van. Two are friends of Dad's from work. The third is Geralt Powell. I thought they were enemies. Even though Dad got the job, he still always talked shit about him. He'd say you can wash the stink of scavenger pussy off your cock, but nothing gets the stink of mating one off.

This is bad. I need to get out of here.

Uncle Howell cranks the emergency brake and gets out, leaving the door open. They all slowly stalk toward me, their hands in the air like they don't mean any harm. Except Dad. His are fisted at his sides. His face is purple, and his wolf is so close to the surface that his jaw recedes as his cheekbones jut forward. He looks like a monster. My skin breaks out in a cold sweat.

When I was little, this is how he looked when he screamed at me. I'd stand in front of him at attention, like he demanded, so scared that I couldn't breathe, all the while fighting off the darkness that edged my vision because surely, if I fainted at his feet, his wolf would eat me.

My body remembers like it was yesterday. I freeze. I need to run or scream, but I'm trapped inside myself by the child who learned too well the only way she could survive a male like him.

"Hello, Isolde," Dad snarls through his fangs. "How considerate of you to come to us. Frankly, I thought it'd be harder."

The males are fanning out. Circling me. I need to run *now*. My pulse thunders, my hands tremble violently, but my legs won't move.

"Not so mouthy now, are you?" he says, stalking closer until I can smell Mom's pot roast on his breath.

Uncle Howell scowls down the road toward the den. "Throw her in the van. Let's thank our good luck and get out of here."

"We said we'd scope the den out ourselves," Geralt Powell argues. "Madog's not going to let us near his little diplomats when they come back."

"Isolde can tell us everything we want to know," Dad says, smirking. "She'll be happy to talk once I'm done with her."

My wolf cowers in a corner. She knows she's outnumbered and overmatched. I need to run, but already it's too late. Vaughn and Geralt have cut off my escape.

Dad exchanges a look with Uncle Howell. They're going to make a move.

Do I fight? Can I even get my arms to swing?

How bad will they hurt me if I fight?

Mom always warned me never to bait my father's wolf. She said he's bigger, meaner, and your father can't control him. Would he kill his own pup?

There's a gleeful gleam in Dad's eyes as he gets ready to do what he's going to do. He hopes I fight. He wants to hurt me—because I dared to speak up for myself and tell him no.

"Last chance to come peacefully," he sneers, bending his knees, getting ready to spring. "You know you don't belong here with *them*."

He says *them* with the same disdain that he says *Isolde*. That he's *always* said Isolde. Because the only difference between me and those he considers worthless is that he thinks I belong to him.

He's wrong. I belong to myself. And Trevor. And Old Den.

And he can take *me*, but he can't take my voice. Not ever again.

"What's wrong with you?" I ask, my voice shaky and thin.

He snorts. "You're about to find out."

I clear my throat and make myself speak louder. "I'm not going back. I belong here now."

"You belong to me. You live where I say you live."

The unspoken part rings in my ears. You live *if* I say you live. That's always been the threat. You'd better make honor roll. You'd better make varsity. The "or else" was always that he'd let out his wolf.

What kind of pathetic grown male has to threaten a submissive female pup with bodily harm to get her to study? He didn't even have to ask. I was doing it anyway.

And here he is now, the dominant, high-ranking wolf, and he needs *six* henchmen?

This time, when I speak, my scorn is clear. "You brought *six* males to kidnap one female. Are you a coward, or are you that weak?"

Dad flashes his fangs and growls, "You better shut your mouth before I shut it for you. I would've thought you'd learned your lesson when that mate of yours showed you that bitches belong on their knees, but I guess some of you need to learn the hard way."

He lowers a shoulder, preparing to rush me. I open my mouth. I don't know what I'm going to say, but I'm not going down silently. The words will come.

I drag down a huge breath. Dad lunges forward. I scream, but as the sound pierces the air, it's immediately drowned out by a terrible, thunderous, bone-rattling baying of wolves.

Dad grabs me, and as my body swings in an arc, my legs flailing, I see the pack stream around the bend. A huge blueish-gray wolf leads the way.

Dad freezes. I drive my heels into his shins and twist in his grasp, but he's strong. He keeps hold of me, but the Old Den wolves are rushing between him and the other males, howling and snarling, herding them away from each other. The Moon Lake males are overrun in seconds. All they can do is sink to their knees and bare their necks.

And that's before Rosie's giant wolf trots into view, bringing up the rear.

Dad doesn't kneel. He wrestles me in front of himself as a shield as I buck and kick. Trevor's wolf strains inches away, his fangs slavering, his eyes flicking between Dad and me, blazing with fear and rage. He lifts his muzzle to howl, and the bond inside me bursts open, flooding my chest with an overwhelming, ferocious love.

Dad stinks of fear, the scent singeing my nostrils despite the throng of wolves crowding around us. We're surrounded by five males the same blueish-gray as Trevor's wolf. The two behind us nip at Dad's heels, causing him to stagger from foot to foot. I've never seen their wolves, but I just know it's Aled and Llew.

The other Moon Lake males are surrounded, too, except Geralt Powell, who's lying flat on his back with Seth Rosser's mottled brown wolf standing squarely on his chest, snapping at Geralt's pasty white face. No other wolf ventures near them.

"Back up!" Dad shouts at the wolves crowding him.

Trevor's wolf inches closer, howling louder, demanding without words that Dad drop me. I squirm, slamming my head back, aiming for Dad's chin. Each time I land a blow, Trevor's wolf lets out a strangled snarl. He wants me to stop hurting myself, but he can't bear snarling at me. He prances from paw to paw, hating this, looking for an opening.

I'm not scared. I'm surrounded by wolves I know. Friends.

A few feet away, Cadoc rises naked from the ring of wolves that have surrounded Uncle Howell. The first thing he does is glance over his shoulder and shout to Rosie's enormous beast, "Stay back there. It's handled."

I'm not sure what's funnier—the note of command in his voice, considering the size of the wolf he's trying to command, or that she casually lowers herself to her belly and rests her head on her paws, making herself comfortable so she can watch the action like we're some kind of flea circus.

Cadoc stalks through his packmates to stand next to Trevor's wolf and consider Dad. I've never appreciated how intimidating Cadoc's stone face and blank eyes can be when he reeks of aggression.

"Release the female," Cadoc says to Dad.

Dad tries to take a step back, but one of Trevor's brothers nips his calf, so Dad ends up stumbling in place.

"As soon as I let her go, he'll be at my throat," Dad says. He's talking about Trevor's wolf.

Trevor's wolf snarls low in his throat as if to confirm that Dad's right.

"You don't have an out," Cadoc says, perfectly cold and calm. "Put her down and beg. Maybe she'll have mercy."

My dad scoffs. He can't help himself. He's beaten and scared, and *still*, he can't admit that a female has the upper hand. That *I* do.

Suddenly, I can't bear this standoff for one single second more. I can't fight him off—he's too strong—but I can make him suffer. I can hurt him worse than he'd dare hurt me.

Cracking my jaw, I summon my wolf. She's wary, but

when she grasps what I'm thinking, she's all in. My fangs descend.

I seize Dad's wrist, holding him in place, and I clamp my teeth on his forearm so hard that bone crunches. He screams and tries to fling me off, but I've got him. I've hooked my canines between his radius and ulna. Blood spurts into my mouth, and it's disgusting, but his roar of pain makes it worth it.

This male terrorized me from as early as I can remember. I didn't dare make a sound when I walked through our apartment. I lived in terror of shutting the door too hard or waking him from his nap on the sofa.

For my entire childhood, I tormented myself over scales and ladder drills and times tables and figuring out how to earn the fifth star on my performance evaluations that in all of pack memory, no intern had ever earned.

I let my mate go into rut because I feared this male—because my mother warned me over and over what his wolf would do to me if I stepped an inch out of line—and I just now realize, with my teeth sunk into his flesh, his wolf never once tasted my blood, but *his* is dripping from *my* mouth.

Ripping my fangs free, I lift my head and howl. He shoves me forward into Trevor's wolf.

Trevor's wolf shifts back into his skin as I pitch into him, so part of my fall is cushioned by fur, and the rest by muscle. He runs his hands down my body and sniffs my neck to assure himself I'm okay, and then thrusts me into a female's arms.

It's Arlais. She was one of the wolves surrounding Dad. The others take their skin, too, as she wraps me in her arms and presses me to her chest. "You're okay," she says. "It's over. We've got you now. Everything is going to be fine."

It's just what a mother is supposed to say.

Then she covers one of my ears with her hand and tucks my head firmly into the crook of her neck to muffle the other. I can still hear her, though, when she screams, "You come near my fated daughter again, I'll kill you! You piece of shit! You have taken enough from my family. No more!"

No, *that* is what a mother is supposed to say.

I burst into tears.

Trevor, who had been looming over Dad, snaps his head around to see what's wrong.

"She's okay," Arlais assures him, rocking me as I stand in her trembling arms. "She's just shaken up."

Trevor nods, and then, without another second's hesitation, he drags Dad to his feet by the collar of his shirt and slams a fist into his face. Dad throws a few punches back—he's righthanded, and I bit his left—and he lands a few, but Trevor's younger and grimly determined. He's set on his purpose, which seems to be making sure Dad never tries anything like this again.

He's got Dad on his back, and he's raining blows down on him when Cadoc and Macsen finally drag him off. Maybe he has lost it a little.

"Easy, son, easy. He's your mate's father." Macsen looks over his shoulder at me. Arlais has me tucked to her side, so we can both watch. Macsen sees our intense interest and arches a brow. "Well, she might not mind now, but she could have a change of heart later. Females are softhearted." Arlais snorts. "Best to let him live," he finishes.

It still takes Tarian and Garan's help to haul Trevor away from Dad.

For a few seconds, Trevor stands stunned, his haunted stare alternating between his clenched fists and Dad cowering in the dirt, cradling his arm. Then he turns to me.

His eyes flare, the gray glinting silver in the last rays of sunlight.

"Trevor," his mother warns.

"It's fine," he answers, his wolf thick in his throat. Then he strides over, seizes me by the waist, and throws me over his shoulder.

I hold on tight.

"Trevor!" his mom protests.

"Leave it be," Macsen says to her, moving to take my place by her side. "We've mucked things up enough. Let them sort it."

Upside down, I watch the pack's wolves stare at me as one while Trevor carries me off into the woods. His distress wafts from him in waves, agitating my wolf. She's whining at me to mark him or groom him or do something to settle him. I'd like to see her try to lick a male while dangling down his back.

I'm not scared. Trevor has momentarily lost it, but he's still Trevor, my mate. He came after me, he fought for me, and he's not leaving me behind. This is not the past. This is a different story.

He doesn't put me down until we're yards away from the others, deep in the woods, in a small glade thick with Virginia creeper.

"Stay right there," he says when he sets me gently back on my feet. I've never heard him so stern. My stomach clenches.

He stalks off a few feet then wheels around. "What were you doing?" He doesn't wait for an answer. "Why would you leave camp alone? If they'd gotten you in that van, I might never have known what happened to you. They could have *hurt* you." His voice is shredded.

"I'm sorry—"

He doesn't let me finish. "Were you leaving me? Without even saying a word?"

No, stern isn't the right word. He's furious and struggling to hold it in, to keep it out of his voice and the bond, but he can't. His bitterness rasps in his throat and claws at my chest.

"I wasn't leaving you. I needed some space. I was just taking a walk."

"Down the road back to Moon Lake?"

I shake my head, but that is what I was doing. I could have headed in any other direction. There are dozens of trails through our territory.

He huffs and paces, raking his fingers through his hair. "I know my family wasn't making things easy, but you have to understand—"

I cut him off. "I *do* understand."

"You don't," he snaps, and then, lowering his voice, he repeats. "You don't. You don't know how hard my father worked to get to the fifth floor of the Tower. And I'm not talking about bragging rights or some bullshit, but the fact that he made enough to feed his family. There are seven of us, and you know when the scavengers go hunt in the woods, sometimes they don't come back." He blows out a breath. "Or maybe you don't know that. I'm not blaming you. I'm just telling you that you don't understand what it was like for them."

He stalks back to stand in front of me, flexing his hands like he wants to touch me, hold me, erase what he's said and undo what he's knocked off balance. He's pissed—gutted— but underneath he loves me, and also, he doesn't get to be mad at me.

He is always gentle, understanding, and protective because I'm the innocent victim, and he's the penitent, forever proving that he's not a monster. I see the struggle on his face now. He wants to erase what he said, but it's out now. It's in the air between us.

"Tell me then. I'm not breakable."

"I don't think you are." He paces again, not far, just back and forth like an agitated wolf.

I fold my arms. "We *can* fight, you know."

"No." He levels me with a glare. "We can't."

"Tell me," I growl.

He simmers for a long moment, his fists balled, staring into the distance, and then he says, "When we mated, Mom was ecstatic. Dad was worried. He knew how it was going to go over in your house." Trevor's mouth twists in an approximation of his usual rueful smile. "When I recognized you that first time at the salad bar, I ran home to tell them. Mom dragged out all her yarn, talking about all the things she was going to do with you. She'd always wanted a female pup. The next day, when I came home from school, she wanted to hear all about you, and I couldn't tell her anything. I couldn't tell her that you wouldn't even look at me. Dad understood. He explained it to her."

My heart is a stone in my throat. I press my hands to my chest like pressure will help the ache.

"She didn't blame you. None of us did. We knew who your dad was. We understood what his likely reaction would be. But still, I was her pup, and she loved me. It hurt her that my mate wouldn't speak to me. And then I hurt you and destroyed all of our lives."

"She does blame me," I say softly. "Of course she does. I do, too." I'm not looking for pity, and I don't want to get out of this—it's just true, and we have to be able to tell each other the truth by now.

"No," he spits, his fisted hands clenching.

"Yes," I answer simply. All of a sudden, I know why I went for a walk toward Moon Lake. I was heading back to my bedroom—to where I didn't have to deal with anyone else's pain and my life was only a tragedy instead of this messy, complicated, unpredictable thing that I have to fight like hell to make my own.

And, if I'm being really honest, I was mad that I made stew and cake and tried so hard and the fucking horrors of the past ruined everything yet again.

And maybe I wanted Trevor to follow me this time. Maybe I wanted *him* to fix something. And it's unfair, I *know* it's unfair, but still, I say, "You never came for me."

The words hit him. They detonate on his face as they rip through the bond. His pain and shame rise up my throat and choke me. Oh, no. I take it back. I step forward and reach out. He freezes, stricken.

I broke it. I broke us.

For a long moment, we stare at each other.

"I couldn't back then," he finally says, holding my gaze. He doesn't say sorry. He's devastated. But he's not broken.

Tears begin to pour down my cheeks. "You came for me today."

"I'll never let you go again," he says, stepping closer although his shoulders are still stiff as hangers.

"We don't say sorry." I sniffle, shuffling forward.

He opens his arms. "Not anymore."

I take one more step, and he gathers me to his chest, squeezing me tight. I dissolve into heaving sobs, and he strokes my back, his wolf rumbling to comfort me. My wolf sits on her butt, utterly confused. Her mate pummeled the bad male who calls himself our sire into the dirt. She doesn't understand why I'm not content.

"Sorry," I mumble into his shoulder. "I was coming back, you know. I'd turned around. I love you so much."

"I love you, too," he murmurs into my ear. "Forever. So much. I'm sorry, too. My beautiful mate."

We cling to each other, rocking, calming, until my lips find the salty skin above his collar. I kiss him. He holds me tighter. My fangs descend. I nuzzle his neck, scraping gently, testing.

"What are you doing, Izzy?" he asks, but he knows. His peppery scent bursts into the air.

It feels right. It feels fated.

I cradle his head and guide his mouth to the crook of my neck, the side that isn't lashed with old scars.

"Are you sure?" he whispers against my skin. He's trembling in my hands.

I answer him by sinking my fangs into his salty skin. He replies by sinking his into mine. My wolf howls in delight. His growls his satisfaction.

Above us, a bird lands on a bough with a flutter of wings and leaves. Even higher still, the very last rays of soft yellow sun peek through the highest branches, but we can't see it—we're lost in each other—but its warmth kisses our cheeks just the same.

EPILOGUE

IZZY

Bevan is selling snow cones from the back of Uncle Howell's white van, which has been painted with psychedelic rainbow swirls. Well, not selling. Bevan is trading, and if you're a pup or a pretty female, he'll take an IOU. I can't imagine where he got an ice shaver, and I don't want to think about the daisy chain of extension cords he must've rigged up to get electricity out here to the commons.

The pack is gathered here on a sunny Tuesday to celebrate a mating.

Aled and Gracie Bedoe.

In the excitement of my rescue, no one noticed that Aled was missing. His wolf had caught Gracie's scent, and figuring that the whole pack plus Rosie's mega-wolf had things covered, he hared off on a side mission. Gracie's wolf apparently led him on a chase, but she let him catch her when she got hungry for dinner.

Since the Floyds now had two sons with ties to Old Den, they decided to stay here when Cadoc sent the Moon Lakers packing—keeping the van and the pipefitter, with his

permission, as restitution for Dad and Uncle Howell's act of aggression.

Cadoc was happy to accept more refugees from Moon Lake with experience in the trades. There's a lot of work to do now that we have the know-how to install water and sewage infrastructure among the cabins. Cadoc was also happy for the chance to flip his dad the finger. I think he really believed his father had good intentions with the exchange program, but there's no way to overlook that Uncle Howell, Madog's second, was part of the plan to not only kidnap me, but also scout the den and get information out of me by whatever means necessary.

That's all a worry for another day, though. Today, the weather's fine. A makeshift band of one guitar, three banjos, and a half-dozen various drummers are rocking out while those with the inclination dance.

I'm sitting on a blanket under a tree with Arlais, watching Trevor spin Gracie around while Aled sulks nearby. The brothers are messing with Aled by passing Gracie between them, and Gracie is happily going along with it.

"She'll keep our Aled on his toes," Arlais observes as she clacks her needles. She's knitting a blanket for Gracie.

If my heart twinges a little thinking about the mating basket I never got, "our Aled" immediately makes it feel better. Something triggered in Arlais during the rescue, and she's become the protective mother I never dreamed I'd have. She's hugged me more times in four weeks than my mother did in my entire life. That makes my heart ache a little, too, but not for too long.

Arlais is also the one who tells me things no one else will. She told me about the hours she spent with Trevor going over paint swatches and appliance reviews to pick the perfect things for apartment 1248, and how his brothers made terrible fun of him for it, but Trevor didn't care in the least.

She told me that when Trevor couldn't sleep or eat anymore, Macsen went to Dad over and over again, and then to Uncle Howell, and finally to Madog himself to beg them not to stand in the way of our mating. It took Macsen a long time to get access to the alpha. Uncle Howell and Madog's mate, Gwen, were very good at making sure Madog only heard what they wanted him to hear. Madog hadn't known what was happening, and he said he'd put a stop to it, but that was the same night that I snuck out and met Trevor in the woods.

And then she told me—gently, carefully, with tears flowing down her face—about that night. How Trevor ran to the High Rise roof, and how she told him to listen to the bond and then dragged him back from the edge with her fangs.

I knew her well enough by then that I knew she wasn't trying to make me feel bad. She told me because she knows I love him as much as she does, and the only way to exorcise a pain like this is to put it into words for someone who truly understands to hear them.

And also, maybe, even though nothing like that will ever happen again, she needs me to know. Just in case. Because now I'm the one who checks to see if he's still breathing in the middle of the night, terrified by the sheer joy of loving him.

I asked her hard questions. She told me hard things to hear. My mother told me hard things all the time, but I understand now that she enjoyed it. It was gratifying to her to have someone in the house to dominate. No matter how

Dad treated her, she wasn't the bottom of the barrel in the house.

During our hard talk, Arlais and I wept together, and then we made a pot of tea, and she dug out a package of Oreos that Macsen had brought her, which she'd been hiding from her sons. I took out the bag of Milano cookies that Trevor brought me.

We're building a new life here. There's room for sadness and grief, but it's not the center of things. We don't let it be.

On the grass in front of us, the music rises to a crescendo, and then the players collapse on their backs, calling for beer. Aled swoops in to claim his mate as the dancers disperse. Trevor makes his way over to me. His bare chest glistens in the sunshine as the breeze tugs his curls. My belly twists. He's the most handsome male I've ever seen, and he's mine.

When he arrives at our blanket, he shrugs back into his shirt and holds out his hand. "Let's go for a walk."

"Not even a hello for your mother?" Arlais teases. He bends to plant a wet kiss on her cheek.

"Sorry, Mom. Hi, Mom." He grins, and Arlais can't even pretend to be miffed.

I take his hand, and he pulls me to my feet.

"Oh, hold on. One second. I keep forgetting—" Arlais rummages in her sewing bag and pulls out a delicately knit blue-gray scrap of fabric. "Help me up." Trevor helps her to her feet, too.

She smooths the fabric into a triangle and lays it gently over my hair, tying its strings behind my neck. It's a head-scarf, and it's lovely.

"Don't think I don't know that I owe you a mating basket," she says to me. "But I'm playing catch up at the moment, so I made you this for now." She squeezes my shoulders. Her eyes are shining. "Thank you for loving my son."

"It's easy," I say, surprised at how true the words feel. It's also been hard as hell, but the one doesn't cancel the other out.

"Come on," Trevor says, tugging me away.

"Thank you!" I call to Arlais as he leads me into the woods.

We dash through the brush until the sound of the crowd fades, and then we slow to a stroll.

"Did Gracie wear you out dancing?" I tease him.

"I've got plenty of energy left, mate," he says, grinning. "Want to race me back to the cabin?"

"Everyone will wonder where we've gone."

"Oh, they'll know."

"What about Granddad?"

"He'll know, too."

His eyes twinkle. I'm about to tell him yes when a shriek rends the air. Gracie barrels through the trees two yards away. Aled chases on her heels.

My heart stops.

Trevor's spine snaps straight.

I run.

I trip on nothing.

He's on me.

My face hits the dirt.

Gracie lets out a peel of laughter.

Aled hollers to her, "I'm letting you win, you know." They disappear in the direction of the cabins.

I drag down air into my starved lungs.

Trevor exhales.

"You're safe," he says to me, his gaze unwavering.

"We're not back there," I remind him, stepping into his open arms. "We're here."

"We're good. We're okay," he murmurs as we cling together as Gracie and Aled's voices disappear in the distance.

My breathing has almost evened out when, out of nowhere, an unmistakable wave of heat crashes over me. My belly tightens, and wet gushes from between my legs, soaking my panties.

I gasp, the tips of my claws springing from my finger unbidden, pricking Trevor's shoulders through his shirt. He hisses, but he doesn't flinch. He's frozen, except for his flaring nostrils.

I can't panic again. I just panicked. I can't breathe or move, either.

"Trevor," I whimper.

The sound spurs him to action. He scoops me up like a bride and storms toward the den.

"Trevor?"

"It's going to be okay," he says, staring wildly ahead. His pupils are huge, but the black doesn't trigger me. I'm already triggered. And besides, his terrified expression is very much Trevor's.

"What are we going to do?" We haven't talked about this. It didn't even occur to me to consider that another heat this soon was a possibility, maybe because my mother only had one, but Arlais went into heat *five times*, and none of Trevor's brothers are more than two years apart.

Shit.

Pups.

Am I ready for pups?

"Pups," I yelp like we're driving, and Trevor doesn't see a car ahead braking.

"Don't worry. We've got the water and electrical done, and I'll have forced heat installed by winter, and if all else fails, we have the wood stove."

I was not worried about heat—my panic hadn't gotten as far as logistics—but oh dear lord, yes, we need another room. A pup can sleep with us for a while, but eventually they need their own space, and what am I even doing, thinking about that?

My skin is drenched. I'm in heat. It's coming on lightning fast, and soon, I'm going to be mindless and begging again like back in the woods at Moon Lake—

"Stop!" I smack Trevor's shoulder. "Stop! I'm going to puke!"

"Shit." He drops me to my feet. I collapse to my knees. He sinks down behind me and snatches my hair back from my face. I fold forward, dry heaving. My wolf yips inside me, excited. Ready. She thinks I'm presenting.

Nothing comes up. After a few long minutes of retching, I gasp, "I'm good."

Trevor sits back on his heels. I plop down on my butt. We're both struggling for air like we ran a race. My wolf whines in confusion. Things are not unfolding like she expected.

We've crushed a little patch in a dense tangle of ferns. Green vines climb the trees around us. I feel very far away from the world, but not alone. My mate is at my back and twined in my heart.

I love him. I want him. This is scary—terrifying—but good. We can do this again, but right. I grasp behind me, and he grabs my hand.

"We're not panicking," I tell him.

"Okay," he agrees, politely not pointing out that maybe I'm talking a little more to myself than to him. He rises to his feet and helps me up. "You ready?"

I nod firmly. I am not. Not even a little. But I trust him. He won't let anything bad happen.

I let him lead me onward and focus on calming myself down. It's impossible. I take deep breaths, but my body instantly undoes the effects with hot flashes and adrenaline spikes. This heat is coming on hard. The world takes on a hazy cast, and my brain buzzes.

It'd be pure misery except Trevor smells *amazing*. Better than ever. I drag his scent into my lungs, and it *unfurls* inside me. He is the most beautiful male I've ever seen. He strides through the underbrush like a pagan forest god, his wheat gold hair tousled by the breeze. There should be music set to his walk, and it should be in slow motion.

My bite mark peeks from the collar of his shirt. I want to bite him again. My mouth waters.

"Trevor," I whine.

"Almost there," he says. We're coming up on a path to the den, heading in the opposite direction as our cabin.

"Trevor, we're going the wrong way."

"Trust me, sweetness." He pulls me closer and wraps an arm around my waist so he's helping me along rather than guiding me. More of his scent bathes me, and my blood pumps a little less furiously.

We get to the den a few minutes later. The commons have cleared except for a few drunk packmates passed out under the trees. It's dinner time, and a feast has been prepared to celebrate Aled and Gracie's mating. The smell of roasting pork turns my stomach.

"I'm not hungry," I tell Trevor, stalling at the den entrance. I also don't want to be around the pack. I need these clothes off. They're sticking to me like wet leaves.

"I know. I just need to get a few things. We'll leave as soon as we can."

As soon as we get inside, I need to get out. There is too much noise, too many people, too much movement. I cling to Trevor. He holds me close, his hand firmly on the small of my back.

His mother must've been watching out for us because she meets us near the entrance. "Have you seen your brother and his—" She cuts herself off when she realizes the state I'm in. "Oh. Oh, dear. Oh, wow." She goes from shock to concern to grandmotherly delight in five words. "This is so wonderful! Aled and Gracie, and now you two—"

"Mom, I need your help," Trevor interrupts. "I need blankets."

"Oh. Oh, yes." Arlais squeezes my forearm. "I'm so sorry, love. I thought I had time. Oh, I'm kicking myself."

I want to tell her not to worry, but my brain is sludge, and nothing moves quickly enough to reach my mouth before Trevor says, "No worries, Mom, but do you have some blankets we can borrow?"

"Of course. Yes! You two stay here. Oh, you must be miserable, poor thing." Arlais pats me a few more times before she hurries off toward the tunnel leading to the den where they've been staying while Trevor and his brothers finish up their new cabin.

Trevor tucks me against his chest. It helps block out the jarring sounds and awful smells. "Not much longer," he murmurs in my ear. "I'll take you home, and you'll make your nest, and then I'll make you feel better, and everything will be fine. I promise." He speaks with complete, unshakeable certainty. I can only feel his fear in the bond.

I'm not sure how much time passes before Arlais returns with two patchwork quilts. Trevor thanks her, and I manage to smile, as he steers me toward the exit, but before we get far, Nia calls from across the den, "Trevor! Izzy! Hold up!"

She jogs the rest of the way. She has a crocheted blanket thrown over her shoulder. She thrusts it at Trevor. "Here you go, you crazy kids."

"Thank you," I manage. My voice is so husky and dry that I sound like a frog.

We aren't even able to turn before our names are called again. "Trevor and Izzy! Wait, wait!"

Drona's girls are racing across the den with Drona in their wake. Drona has a pillow under each arm. She stacks them in Trevor's arms and smacks a kiss on my forehead. "Fate's blessings," she says, fading back as Rosie takes her place.

She adds a blanket to the collection, squeezes my hand, and repeats, "Fate's blessings."

A line forms behind her. Rosie snaps open a sheet and helps Trevor pile the pack females' offering in the middle. Arly, Rae, Mina, Dru, Madwen and a dozen other females share a sheet or scarf or handkerchief—or when Trevor can't possibly carry any more—they give their blessings.

Enid rests a wreath of pink roses, yarrow, and goldenrod on my head. She's woven blue jay feathers into the crown and pinned an origami crane to the front as a diadem.

Flora helps Granddad over. He kisses my forehead, and Trevor's wolf growls. Granddad cracks up, cawing, "Tell your wolf I'm no threat, pup, although sixty years ago it would've been a different story, make no mistake."

Flora reassures us that she'll help Granddad to the elder cabin after dinner, and Pritchard helps Trevor hoist our pack of blankets over his shoulder. He looks like the humans' Santa Claus.

Arlais darts forward to hug us both before we leave. Macsen hangs back, respecting Trevor's wolf's low, persistent rumble, but he raises a hand in farewell, his crinkly eyes smiling.

As we walk out into the crisp evening air, my panic finally ebbs. I'm burning up, but there's also a mellow warmth lingering in my belly. I belong to this pack. To this family. We're surrounded with love and support.

We're blessed by Fate because, in this case, saying makes it so.

Trevor seems calmer, too. Our steps are quicker as we make our way down the path to our cabin. The fireflies are out, floating along beside us on our way. My heart pitter-pats, but it no longer threatens to burst out of my chest.

Somehow, despite the enormous sack he's carrying over his shoulder, Trevor manages to scoop me in his arms when we get to our front steps. I have to turn the doorknob, though, and he kicks it open, carrying me across the threshold like a human bride. He takes me directly to our bedroom and dumps both me and the sack in the middle of the bed.

He grins, pleased with himself. "I'm going to get food and water. I'll just be in the kitchen. I'll be right back."

I'm not even listening. I have work to do. I untie the sack and sort through its contents, sniffing each piece, tossing a few into the corner that smell a little too strongly of other male. Everything is clean, but some males' scents will cling despite a good washing.

Some female scents cling, too, and I'm surprised they don't bother me, but they smell like pack, not like a threat.

I heap the good blankets into the middle of the bed and then work from the inside out, making myself a comfy divot in the middle and arranging the rest from the center. It's hot work. I peel off my clothes and add them to my creation. It's wonderful, fluffy and soft and colorful. Everything is exactly right.

Except that purple scarf. I growl, and from the doorway, Trevor's wolf rumbles anxiously in response. I blink up. He's leaning against the wall, watching me. He's still dressed.

"Shirt." I stick out my arm and open my palm.

He smiles, grabs the back of his collar, and peels it off one-handed, baring his perfectly ripped chest and abs. I grumble as my lower belly twists. He knows what he's doing.

He innocently passes me his shirt. Now I have to worry about this *and* the purple scarf. I growl at him to take the rest of his clothes off. I mean to ask, maybe not nicely but with words, but my wolf is in my throat.

He observes me fuss with these last few items, his muscles taut, his eyes smoldering, and a fond smirk playing at his lips. Part of me knows I must seem unhinged, crawling naked to and fro on the bed, scrunching and piling and fluffing, but mostly I'm concerned that everything is exactly right.

It was so wrong last time. The past hovers, closer than usual these days, and I know Trevor feels it, too. I can scent it on his skin.

He doesn't need to worry. I know what I'm doing.

"Come now," I tell him as I arrange the last pillow just so. I offer my hand.

His smirk melts into the softest, most beautiful smile. "Are you inviting me into your nest?"

I growl at him to get a move on. He takes my hand and climbs in.

My wolf has her rump high in the air with her tail raised. She's fussing at me to present, but Trevor and I always look at each other when we're together. At first, it was so that I could reassure myself by tracking that his blue irises didn't bleed to black, but as time went on, it became more about the connection. It's like a seventh sense when our eyes are locked as we hurtle over the edge, like we're souls shooting into outer space together.

I don't care if it's cheesy. That's how it feels.

"How are we doing this?" he asks, his voice almost smoky, it's so deep.

"I'll show you."

His smile cracks wide into a delighted grin. "You're the boss?"

My wolf yips grumpily—I'm not sure whether at me or him.

I walk to him on my knees. As soon as I'm close enough, I push his chest. He topples onto his back, still grinning like a cat who got into the cream. His fall is cushioned by my well-made nest. Satisfaction swells in my chest as I admire the sight—my beautiful mate, his strong, gorgeous body, his kind, patient, and loving eyes.

I am blessed.

He's more than ready. His cock stands at attention, thick and flushed, twitching in the air as more blood rushes down as I admire him.

"You gonna touch me, Izzy?"

"In a minute." I'm not done looking. His stomach tenses, deepening the muscles that form the V pointing down his hips. I lick my lips. He stifles a moan.

I don't like that. I want to hear him. I want to know that

the gnawing need stoked in my belly has its claws into him, too. I throw a leg over his waist and settle myself on top of his hard thighs. He tracks my every move, his breath quickening.

He wraps his rough hands around my sides, stroking the underside of my breasts with his thumbs. "Whatever you want, baby. However long you need. I could look at you like this forever."

I arch my back, preening. He means it with his entire being.

"I want a knot," I tell him, wriggling forward, grabbing his cock by its swelling base.

He groans out loud, and my pussy spasms. I want this male, every part of him, every bit of his attention. He belongs to me in a way nothing else does, not even my own body. He is my *choice*.

I straddle his cock, notching it against my dripping slit, but before I can sink down, he bucks his hips, driving up inside me while his hands grip my waist so he can hold me in place as he fucks up into me from below. I have no other option than to ride.

His eyes close. His jaw clenches. His head tilts back, revealing the long line of his corded neck. He's lost in it. In *me*. I relax my inner muscles, taking him as deep as I can, whimpering and whining as I get closer and closer, and the greedy yearning in my belly coils tighter and tighter. With each thrust, my teeth clack together, and my knees thump the mattress. If I wasn't being pistoned in place, I'd fall off.

I shove my hands between my legs, searching for my clit, as his eyes fly open.

"Trevor," I cry. I want to keep going and do this forever, but I *have* to come. I need it like air.

"You want my knot?" he gasps.

"Yes," I shriek.

He grabs my hips, digging his fingers into the fleshy globes of my ass, and plunges inside of me one last time, shouting his release the second that I come and my pussy begins to milk his cock like a fist. My orgasm detonates. My body shakes, and my vision blurs.

His knot inflates, locking us together, stretching my channel to the limits. I look down. I can see it curving my lower belly like a little food baby.

"Whoa," I mutter without thinking.

Trevor's eyes clear, and the corners crinkle. He cups the small swell with his palm. "It doesn't hurt, right?" By the calm way he asks, I know he doesn't think it does.

"No. But it feels weird."

"For sure." He grins and then runs his hands down my arms and over my hips, scanning me head to foot, reassuring himself that I'm no worse for wear. He notices my knees digging into the mattress, so he grabs some blankets and stuffs them underneath as a cushion.

I feel boneless, but also oddly awake. The bond sings between us. The flow is mostly happiness and love, but every so often, a shard of fear or an echo of pain passes through like a twig carried along on a current. It's okay. It doesn't have the power to ruin this moment.

The past is part of us. It probably always will be. It made us, after all.

And I am happy, in the end, with the female I've become, and the male that Fate has given me.

"What are you thinking, beautiful?" he asks, massaging the base of my spine with his thumbs. After all the jostling up and down, it feels amazing.

"I'm thinking that I'm blessed," I murmur.

The smile that he gives me back is almost as bright as the love shining in his eyes.

THE FIVE PACK saga began with *The Tyrant Alpha's Rejected Mate.*

It will continue with *The Moon Blessed Wolf's Rejected Mate.*

WANT MORE?

Sign up for the Cate C. Wells newsletter at www.catecwells.com for a bonus epilogue to *Ravaged Wolf* and other exclusive content, updates, and special offers.

If you already subscribe, a link to the bonus epilogue is at the bottom of every newsletter.

ABOUT THE AUTHOR

Cate C. Wells writes everything from motorcycle club to small town to mafia to paranormal romance. Whatever the subgenre, readers can expect character-driven stories that are raw, real, and emotionally satisfying. She's into messy love, flaws, long roads to redemption, grace, and happily ever after, in books and in life.

Along with stories, she's collected a husband, two daughters, and a cat along the way. She lives in Baltimore when she's not exploring the world with the family.

facebook.com/catewells

instagram.com/authorcatecwells

tiktok.com/@authorcatewells

www.ingramcontent.com/pod-product-compliance
Lightning Source LLC
Chambersburg PA
CBHW071241300726
48975CB00002B/516